Jan 6, 2013

Spirits of a Feather

To Daniel

To a really nice guy

Bill

Spirits of a Feather

Charles W. Shirriff

iUniverse.com, Inc.

San Jose   New York   Lincoln   Shanghai

Spirits of a Feather

Published by iUniverse.com, Inc.

For information address:
iUniverse.com, Inc.
5220 S 16th, Ste. 200
Lincoln, NE 68512
www.iuniverse.com

ISBN: 1-58348-547-3

Printed in the United States of America

This being a work of fiction all the characters, places and events are fictitious. Any resemblance to real events, places or people is purely coincidental and unintentional.

However, since the story is fact-based, my friends and acquaintances and even strangers may think that they see facets of themselves within these pages. If you like what you read, then yes, it probably was inspired by you. If what you read does not please you, then it must be based on someone else because I have had nothing negative or unpleasant to say about anyone I have met.

In particular, credit must be given to my young gay amigos who accepted me as an observer of their lives without hesitation or reservation, allowing me to perceive the joy of being gay as well as the agony of being homosexual. Without them this book would never have been written and I would be a much less tolerant person.

My heartfelt appreciation goes to Wilma, Ken, Anita, Henry, and Kitty for their kindness in reading my manuscripts and for providing me with gentle but effective advice (all of which was seriously considered and most of which was implemented).

I'd also like to thank the innumerable people who discussed the novel with me and provided me with excellent ideas and directions. You should be able to recognize your influence as you read these pages.

Special mention must go to Ken whose pertinent short course in structuralist literary theory contributed greatly to the final work, and to Anita whose bantering, incisive comments will forever alter the way I view the world.

Contents

The First Step Is the Hardest 1

At Least It's a Roof 11

Callers In The Night 21

All That Glitters Is Not Silver 29

Life As Usual 43

Guess Who's Coming To Dinner 57

Let the Games Begin 71

Life As Unusual 81

A Hair of the Dog 93

The Passing Parade 107

The Kindness of Strangers 119

Back to Square One 127

If I Had a Hat I'd Be Home 139

You're the Customer 147

So Sue Me 155

The Message Is the Medium 163

Bye Bye Sue 175

Who's Got the Time? 183

I Left My Heart 191

Home Is Where the Hat Is 203

The Illusive Trail 211

Appendix 219

About the Author 253

THE FIRST STEP IS THE HARDEST

Old Grey Goose buses never die in Manitoba. They move north and live out their final days carrying passengers south from the tiny northern communities to join the 90 percent of the Manitoba population that lives within a hundred miles of the United States border.

Jay leaned out into the aisle to ease the pressure on his hurting back. A teenage girl struggled up the steps of the bus, her arms overflowing with a cocoon of blankets. Her diaper bag dangled precariously from her left arm, threatening to spill its contents at any moment. Clenched teeth and her furrowed brow reflected the challenges of premature motherhood. Jay sat back, his eyes squinted in an attempt to feign sleep but only succeeding in looking as if he were suffering from stomach cramps.

Oh please don't let her sit here beside me, Jay prayed under his breath in hopes that some omnipotent supreme being would intercede on his behalf. But the gods do not deign to be kind to suppliants who call only when in need. The girl stopped beside Jay's seat.

"Hold my baby for a minute, eh? I'm going to the washroom."

The girl thrust the tiny bundle of humanity onto Jay's lap, dumped the bag, blanket and paraphernalia onto the empty seat beside him and hurried toward the back of the bus.

"Hey. Where do you think you're…?" Jay started to ask, but the girl didn't wait for him to finish.

At least he's quiet, Jay thought to himself, shifting the baby onto his knee and amusing himself by gently jiggling it up and down. He was rewarded by a twinkle in the baby's dark brown eyes, the hint of a smile, and then by a warm, damp feeling spreading along his left leg. *What a way to start my new life,* Jay thought to himself. *No money, no plans and now my only pair of jeans is wet.*

Jay cuddled the baby safely in his arms until its mother returned, reeking of fresh cigarette smoke. She reached down and scooped up the baby.

"What took you so long?" Jay asked. "I think he needs changing."

Without a word, the mother set the baby on the seat next to Jay and slipped off its diaper. Jay averted his eyes in an automatic concession to the baby's privacy. With two quick flips the used diaper disappeared unceremoniously into the bag and a dry, although not entirely clean, one was pinned in place.

"I hate these cloth diapers. Wish I could afford Pampers, eh." She turned toward Jay. "I'm Serena. Sorry about that, but I had to go. You know how it is, eh?"

"That's OK. I'm Jay."

"From Oakridge?"

"How could you possibly know that?"

"You're the only one around here with that name."

"But you don't really know me, do you?"

"My mom knows everybody. Well, she doesn't know them to see them, but she knows all the gossip about them."

"What's she say about me?" Jay asked, shifting his jacket to cover the damp spot on his knee. *That's all I need is for the whole country to be told that I peed myself on the bus,* he said to himself. *My mother would never let me hear the end of it.*

"Just that I'd be better off with you than with the baby's father. Or with anybody else, as far as she's concerned. I hear a hundred times a day about how much a baby needs its father."

"Are you on your way to see him?"

"Visiting my cousin in Cranberry Portage, a few miles down the road. The guy disappeared as soon as I told him I was pregnant. I don't even know where he lives now. Probably Winnipeg. That's where all the worthless bums go to hang out and party. Being part of the gang makes them feel macho. It's easy to get booze, drugs and women. That's all they care about."

"Every child needs its father."

"You should know. My mom says there's always a man around your place."

"You're right about that. There's always some guy who thinks he owns me because he's shacking up with my mother. But I've never known my real father."

"Is that why you're going to Winnipeg? To find him?"

"Yeah, I guess so," Jay said. He gazed out the window at the blur of evergreens, letting this new idea bounce around his idle brain. "It would be like looking into my future to see him. Sort of like genetic fortune telling."

"You talk funny."

"Sorry. My mom's always getting after me for using big words."

"I hope you don't mean that I'm going to grow up to be like my mother. She can be a real nag."

"You can become any kind of person you want to be. But I'd like to know if I've inherited something I can't change, like a tendency for diabetes or mental illness."

"I guess that makes some sense, but I'm not sure I'd want to know."

"Knowledge is power. If you know things ahead of time, you can maybe do something to head them off." The grinding of brakes broke into their conversation.

"I get off here," Serena said, gathering up her baby and belongings.

Jay's mind drifted back to the events of the past two days. The morning sun was still hidden by the forest when he had started his hike. A short night's sleep in the woods and an early morning walk through the maze of trails brought him to the highway. As he sat waiting to flag down a bus, a sense of relief washed over him. He was finally escaping from the scattering of homes that made up the small northern community unofficially known as Oakridge (population 67 on a good day in July when everyone's relatives were there to visit).

His thoughts drifted back to the perennially makeshift cabin that had been his home for seventeen years. Chickens scratched around the door of a disintegrating lean–to that provided them with meager shelter from the winter weather. A pair of smelly goats ranged freely through the native grass and weeds which partially hid discarded household furnishings that had outlived their usefulness.

A fleeting pang of longing for his earlier life was quickly pushed aside by the dull ache in his right arm. With a conscious effort he relaxed his clenched fists and concentrated on breathing slowly and deeply.

Jay dozed fitfully for several hours, missing the ruggedly majestic hills that pass for mountains in Riding Mountain National Park. He didn't see the herd of bison roaming over the native grasslands. Even if he had, he would not have recognized them as being only a few of the more than 60,000 that live a semi–domesticated life in western Canada.

The bus pulled into the town of Minnedosa, nestling among rolling, tree–covered hills. A lone figure stood in front of the building that served as a bus depot. He was a burly, bulky, teddy bear of a man, dressed in black vinyl pants, jacket and cap. The beak of his cap rode low over his black reflective sunglasses. His long reddish–brown hair poured over his collar, surrounding his face. It hid his ears and mingled with his full, bushy red beard, leaving only his lips and the tip of his nose visible, like a mutant red sheepdog. The task of hoisting his bulk up the narrow steps of the bus required his full concentration. He filled the aisle like a massive plunger, pushing ahead of him the odor of half–eaten lunches and banana peels. A light, fresh fragrance of Old Spice aftershave followed him. Using seatbacks to pull himself down the narrow passage, he lumbered along in search of an empty seat.

Jay could feel the man's presence beside him as he contemplated the semi–vacant seat. To Jay's relief the man flopped into the seat behind him.

The air brakes emitted a reverberating whoosh echoing the man's relaxed sigh and Jay's relief at maintaining a semblance of solitude. With a sputter and a belch of black smoke, the bus reluctantly resumed its journey.

That was close. What's a guy like that doing here on a bus instead of on a motorcycle, anyway? Jay thought to himself. A glance behind showed painfully few empty seats. *We'd better get to Winnipeg soon,* Jay thought. *I can't hold onto this extra seat much longer.*

An unusually hot late–June sun sent heat waves shimmering over the strip of highway that cut a swath through the layer of pine trees blanketing the uncompromising landscape of northern Manitoba. Like a long, black dragon, the road slithered over and around the gentle hills as the bus made a slow but inexorable passage along its spine toward Canada's fourth largest city. Winnipeg sits geographically in the center of Canada as an oasis of mayhem, culture and drugs: murder capital of Canada, home of a world renowned ballet company and site of more than 100 hydroponic marijuana seizures a year. All this and Canada's first openly gay mayor, in the middle of the underpopulated but fertile prairies.

The solid mass of trees gave way to patches of prairie grass interspersed with small clearings nestled among the trees. Jay enjoyed the novelty of being able to see the distant horizon in all directions.

A mother, father and their young son, wandered the gently sloping grass–covered ditch beside the highway, peering intently at the ground.

What on earth could they be doing in the ditch? Jay asked himself. His eyes closed again, letting the monotonous hum of the tires on the highway dull his mind. He briefly pondered possible reasons why a family might be wandering aimlessly in a ditch. It didn't occur to him that they might be collecting empty drink bottles thrown from the windows of cars as they sped down the highway. Jay had never been one to spend a lot of time trying to figure things out. His concern had always been with promoting his own survival and well–being, usually by physically removing himself from unpleasant situations. He tried to be somewhere else when his mother's friends gathered for one of their all–night drinking parties.

"Brandon. Twenty minute rest stop." The disembodied voice of the bus's speaker pushed itself into Jay's consciousness.

Jay found his way to the washroom and looked at the doors. *I'm going either into the room for men or the one for girls in pantsuits.* The tile walls and chrome fixtures dazzled him for a moment, until he discovered the wonders of indoor plumbing and running water. He went from stall to stall enthralled by the rushing swirl of water with each flush until his bladder reminded him of his reason for being there.

He returned to the lunch counter. *I wish I'd thought to bring some food with me. What an idiot I am,* he thought, fingering the few bills and loose change in his pocket. His eyes moved down the list of menu items scrawled on a piece of flaking chalkboard. His tongue flicked over his lips in anticipation of his first food in two days.

"So, kid. Whatcha think looks good?"

Jay had been so engrossed in the menu that he hadn't noticed the big man from the bus enveloping the stool next to him, as well as a good deal of the space between the adjoining seats.

"I'm not hungry," lied Jay.

"I thought skinny guys like you were always hungry."

Jay slid off the stool to escape the man's steady gaze. He felt uncomfortable and more than a little scared by the attention.

"Come on back, fella. I'll buy you a burger if you're short of cash," the man coaxed.

"I said I'm not hungry. Fly off and leave me alone." Jay headed toward the exit.

"Come on. I could use the company. I hate eating alone."

Forget you. I've enough to worry about without having to deal with you, Jay thought. However, an empty stomach usually overrules the head. He returned to the counter. "All right. A burger with fries…and a shake…and a slice of pie…with ice cream." *If it makes him happy to buy me a burger, I might as well make him really, really happy by letting him buy me a bunch of things,* thought Jay. *Besides, anyone that big must have piles of money.* Jay didn't pause in his thoughts long enough to question the logic of his reasoning. He had always found that believing what he said to himself kept his mind empty of conflicting thoughts and made his life a whole lot easier.

"Running away from home, eh?"

The big man's half–question sent a jolt of panic through Jay's mind. *Oh no. Is it that obvious?* Jay wondered.

"Certainly not. That would be stupid. Why would I be doing something stupid like that?" The lie rolled smoothly off Jay's tongue.

"So. Where are you going then? To visit relatives?"

"Yes. My…uh…" Jay remembered his conversation with Serena. "…cousin."

The man pushed his sunglasses up into his hair and looked intently at Jay, trying in vain to look into his downcast eyes. "Where's he live? Winnipeg?"

"That's right." *Great,* thought Jay. *Well I guess it's reasonable that I could have a cousin in Winnipeg. Too bad I don't have one. Or at least someone there to help me out.*

Panic again threatened to take over, but Jay quickly emptied his mind by concentrating on filling his stomach.

"So fella. What's your name?"

"Thomas," Jay shot back with his mouth half–full of burger. *Wow, where did that come from? That's a lousy name. I hate the name Tom. That's what they call turkeys.*

"But people call me Joe." *Oh great. That makes a lot of sense. Why won't you leave me alone?* "Because I was always playing the joker. Get it? Joe, as in joker." *I should stop talking. If I keep on, this guy will never leave me alone. Besides, I seem to have completely lost control of my mouth.*

Jay had the ability to look at himself and what he was doing in a detached and impersonal manner. Not that this perspective ever helped him to behave in a more reasonable or appropriate manner. It was an interesting ability, not one that had ever been of any use to him.

"Well, Joe. Glad to meet you." He grabbed Jay's hand and shook it vigorously.

Jay grimaced at the shot of pain in his sore arm. Disengaging his hand, Jay focused his attention on his plate and wolfed down the last of the pie. He slid off the stool and headed toward the door.

"Bye. Thanks for the lunch. I'll see you around," he tossed over his shoulder.

Back on the bus, Jay firmly closed his eyes, letting the hum of the tires and the warmth of the food in his stomach lull him back to sleep.

"Winnipeg," the intercom intoned, waking Jay with a start as the bus wheeled smoothly into its designated stall.

Jay stood up, stuck his hands in his pockets and headed down the aisle with the other passengers.

"See ya, Joe." The words bounced off the back of Jay's head without eliciting any response.

The depot hummed with more people than Jay had ever seen gathered in one place. People sat or milled around aimlessly. They made Jay think of a herd of cows waiting for their owner to open the gate for their day's grazing.

Jay went to the washroom, more to indulge his fascination with the facilities than for any physical need. Returning to a deserted bench he pondered his fate. *Okay. Now I'm here. So now what?* Jay asked himself, pulling the bills out of his pocket and checking them carefully. *Two fives and a tattered one dollar bill to last me the rest of my life. It is sure going to be a short life at this rate. What a loser I am. Eleven lousy dollars and I don't know a soul from whom to beg, borrow or steal. There's no point in my sitting here waiting for something to happen. As my mom would say, this won't get us any fresh meat for the winter.*

He went over to the exit doors and pulled on one. It didn't budge. He tried the other one without success. A voice behind him suggested, "Push, don't pull."

Dumb way to have doors open, Jay muttered to himself. *One big snow drift and you'd be trapped inside.* He went out into the street.

Evening had come. Street lights lit up the city. The office building walls sported bright rectangles of light. *Wow. This is amazing. There must be thousands of lights.* Jay headed down the street toward the nearest traffic light. Portage Avenue, the street sign beneath it declared. Off to the right a seven-story stone building, dated 1926, squatted on the corner, covering the block like a mother hen protecting its brood of customers scurrying in and out under her wings. Its Manitoba-quarried Tyndall limestone provided background for the yellow-green script proclaiming the building to be 'The Bay'. Across the street a modern twenty-story building, all dark green glass with black metal window frames and pinkish marble, looked down imperiously on The Bay, overseeing the passage of people through its doors.

SPIRITS OF A FEATHER

Waiting for the traffic light to change, Jay began to realize the seriousness of his immediate situation. He had nowhere to go, virtually no money, and no idea which direction he should go. His plan had extended no further than to escape his numbingly tedious days and sporadically abusive nights at Oakridge. He had given no thought to the reality of starting a new life in a big city. *Anything has got to be better than this,* he had thought to himself when he had left the cabin two mornings ago. But now in the darkness of evening, doubts pushed into his mind.

Jay began to feel panic building in his chest. He turned back to the Bus Depot. *At least these people all know whether they are coming or going, which is more than I do,* he thought.

His thumb found its way to his mouth. His restless teeth gnawed at the already short nail. The bank of telephones across the room offered a silent but futile promise of a link to the family he had left behind. But he knew that they couldn't provide him with assistance or advice even if they had a telephone.

"Hey Joe." The voice jolted Jay back to the reality of the waiting room. "What's the matter? Your cousin stand you up?"

Jay looked up. The big man from the bus looked down at him.

"I guess so. He promised he would meet me here but he must have been held up. He'll be here right away." *Go AWAY! I have enough problems without having to talk to you.* Although he kept the words to himself, Jay's face betrayed his annoyance and frustration

Oblivious to Jay's hostile reaction, the man continued, "Maybe I can help you find his place."

Stop being such an idiot, Jay thought to himself. *How are you going to take me to some place that doesn't exist? Go away and leave me alone.*

"You have his address?" the man persisted.

"No."

"Well. You got his phone number? We could call him to see if he's coming."

"His phone won't be connected yet," Jay replied. His face betrayed his increasing irritation.

"You mind if I wait here with you until he comes?"

"It doesn't matter to me." *You've got a long wait ahead of you. What an idiot. You don't have a clue, do you?* A tiny feeling of comfort and safety started to grow deep within Jay and began to push his annoyance aside.

The man, and the boy who thought of himself as a man, sat in silence listening to the announcements as people bustled about.

Jay finally broke the long silence, "Do you know of any cheap hotels near here?"

"Depends on how cheap."

The man looked at Jay quizzically. His eyes were warm but revealed deep–seated pain in his soul. An apprehensive shiver ran down Jay's spine. He had a sudden flashback to his last deer hunting expedition.

It was the day after his fifteenth birthday. Before he left the cabin, Jay took his rifle and carefully chose a single bullet, fondling it in his hand as if it could tell him that it was the one for the task. Ammunition was expensive and scarce in the north. He never took more than one bullet with him but he rarely returned empty–handed. Outside, Jay stood and rotated his head until the breeze blew directly into his face. He turned around and angled downwind through the underbrush toward the tiny lake where deer gathered to drink and rest among the trembling aspens. In a few moments he saw familiar reddish–brown bodies and the white flashes of flicking tails. Jay's heart began to pound from the adrenaline coursing through his veins. Moving closer, he jockeying for position to get a clear view of an eight–point buck feeding on the grass. The buck raised its head high, its ears twitching, and its nose sniffing suspiciously. Jay's muscles tensed with excitement as he thought of his mother's happiness at having a supply of fresh venison for the winter.

He levered the cartridge into the chamber. *Never load your rifle until you are ready to shoot,* he reminded himself of his mother's safety rule. Raising the ancient 44–40 Winchester, he steadied the barrel against a tree trunk. His finger tightened on the trigger. In his mind he could hear the shot and see the deer fall lifeless to the ground. It was often like this when he had a clear shot that he knew would not miss. For that moment, he experienced the future. He could see it. He could feel it. Turning its head, the deer looked directly at Jay. Their eyes locked along the gun barrel for a moment frozen in time. The forest noises stopped as the two psyches met and their energy focused on a resolution of this cosmic conflict. There was no trace of fear in the buck's deep brown eyes. They seemed to say, "Do what you must. My destiny is determined by the laws of nature. If I must die so that you can live, then the cycle of my life will be completed and my soul will go to join with yours."

The strident cry of a circling eagle shattered the silence, breaking Jay's concentration.

The buck reared up, its legs pawing the empty air as if taunting Jay to take his perfect shot. Jay relaxed the pressure on the trigger and lowered the rifle. With a toss of its head to say, "It's your choice," the buck turned and with quiet dignity loped back into the forest giving a disparaging flick of its tail and kick of its heels.

Sometimes, in the silence of the night, when the denizens of the soul liberate memories into the brain of the sleeping, Jay would wake with a start, feeling those soft, sad eyes gazing intently into his own. He would hear the retort of the rifle breaking off the eagle's cry and would see the buck fall. Only as he fought his way into consciousness would he remember that, in fact, he had spared the deer's life. His panic would subside into a feeling of personal power at having altered the path of the deer's destiny through his own strength of will.

Jay recognized a similar resignation to the vagaries of destiny in the big man's eyes. He hastily looked away.

"I have eleven dollars," Jay said, with the memory of the hunting episode unsettling him so much that he inadvertently let the truth slip out.

"That won't get you much of anything in this city. What about your cousin?"

"Forget my cousin. He's an idiot. He never does what he's supposed to do. He's not going to show."

"You know anyone else in the city you could stay with?"

"My cousin was the only one. But I'll make out somehow." Jay said it with a bravado he didn't feel, but having said it, he began to believe it.

"You could stay with me tonight. Then tomorrow I'll help you find your cousin," said the man. "You can sleep on the sofa. It's a hide–a–bed that folds out into the middle of the living room, so it's comfortable enough."

"Sure, why not?" Jay said out loud while thinking, *I have got to go somewhere, and what is the worst that could happen? He might try to keep me awake all night talking to me, but I can choose to ignore him or go to sleep. It's not as if I have any other great plans at the moment.*

AT LEAST IT'S A ROOF

The man and Jay entered an old house that had been converted into four low–rent apartments.

A musty smell of rotting wood permeated the stairwell. The center of the steps had worn down leaving the edges showing their former colors in a rainbow of decrepitation. Like the stump of a tree, their age was revealed by the rings left by layers of paint. The colors were dark or neutral shades, except for one bright orange layer bearing silent testimony to the bold–spirited attempt of some intrepid caretaker to bring life to the otherwise drab hall. The odor of the hallway brought a rush of memories to Jay.

He remembered the root cellar where his family stored meat and vegetables wrested from their tiny garden. A wooden door led to steps down to a crudely excavated space. Jay would descend the steps as salamanders and frogs scurried away from the lantern light. The cool, damp walls of the cellar made ideal conditions for storage, but not an inviting environment for humans. Jay would fill a little pail with vegetables and flee as quickly as possible back to the fresh air and sunshine above. Then there were the times when he was banished to the cellar by his mother or one of her friends. Jay would sit and watch the flickering light, hoping to be released from his underground prison before it burnt out.

Jay always slept near a beam of moonlight to hold at bay the demons from his subconscious memory that might come to haunt him in the dark silence of the night.

The man unlocked the deadbolt and pushed the door open, releasing a rush of stagnant air.

"We'd better let some fresh air in here," the man said as he shoved the key back into the lock from the inside and secured the deadbolt. He crossed the room and hoisted the window open to let in a welcome breeze.

Jay recognized the odor of cigarette smoke which had permeated the fibers of the room as only smoke can do. The fragrance of Old Spice aftershave was overpowered by expensive men's cologne. Another heavy, somewhat sweet, pungent odor with which he was not familiar reminded him vaguely of burning straw. Jay's mouth opened as he gasped for oxygen like a freshly caught fish. In a few seconds the room's stifling closeness grew strangely warm and comforting. His nervousness gave way to a feeling of safety and security.

"Whew. Sorry for the stench, but I didn't have time to air it out after my going away party." He moved around the room spraying Lysol generously in all directions.

"I think the spray is worse than the smell," Jay said.

"Would you give me a hand to clean up this mess a bit?" The man waved his hand around the room indicating the dirty glasses and the sink full of dishes.

"Looks like it was quite a party," Jay said as he filled the sink.

"My friends like to party but sometimes don't know when to go home. You wash and I'll dry."

When the dishes had been put away and the livingroom tidied up, the man gestured toward a threadbare tweed hide–a–bed sitting between the kitchen and the living room. "The sofa's yours for the night, Joe. Believe it or not it folds out into quite a comfortable bed."

"I've slept on the ground lots of nights. This will do me fine."

An opulent white leather recliner chair sat directly in front of the TV set. Its obviously extravagant expensiveness was sadly out of place in a living room otherwise furnished with the leftovers from garage sales.

"Bathroom's there," the man gestured toward one closed door. "And my bedroom's here."

"And what's behind door number three?" asked Jay, pointing to the remaining dark blue door.

The big man ignored the question. "You can use the bathroom, but don't touch any of the things in there. Nobody goes into my bedroom." The big man's voice had taken on an unfriendly edge. Jay did not pursue his question.

"Yes. I get it." Jay felt suddenly subdued. The warm, safe feeling that had started to grow within him shriveled, shrank and disappeared.

I need to get out of here, thought Jay. *This fellow is weird and this place is scary. He probably picks up guys at the Bus Depot, brings them here, kills them, cuts them up and stashes their body parts in that spare room. He's going to wait until I'm asleep. Then he'll kill me, steal my money and stash my mangled body under his bed.*

"Nice place you have here," Jay said out loud. "But maybe I shouldn't stay. I don't have a towel, or soap or anything."

"You didn't bring anything with you?"

"Of course I did. My mother even packed me a lunch. But it got stolen on the way here. While I was asleep."

Jay almost believed himself at that moment although in the deep recesses of his mind he knew his escape from Oakridge was the culmination of a lifetime of frustration and pain. His attempts to save money for several months had amounted to nothing. At his mother's usual end–of–the–month welfare–cheque party Jay's most recent father took out his bad mood on him. After the adults had lapsed into a drunken stupor, Jay rifled their pockets for money and rushed from the cabin in fear that they might rouse and catch him. In his hurry he hadn't thought to bring clothes or personal belongings with him, not that there were a lot of them to bring. It hadn't occurred to him that bus fare would take most of the money.

The man disappeared into the bathroom for a minute. He brought out a bar of soap, a tattered grey towel and a beautifully thick, black washcloth. "Here. Careful with the washcloth. It's one of my good ones," the man fixed Jay with a penetrating look that betrayed his annoyance at having to allow any of his beloved possessions into the unwashed hands of a stranger. "And remember that I don't let anyone touch my personal stuff."

"Is it okay if I use a tiny little bit of the toilet paper?" Jay asked, only half jokingly. He was becoming increasingly frightened by the directives.

"Yeah. But not the cologne, or shampoo, or mousse, or anything like that. And certainly not the razor. Using another man's razor can be dangerous," the man commanded, totally ignoring the feeble attempt at humor on Jay's part.

"It doesn't look like you use it very often yourself," Jay said, looking pointedly at the big man's beard.

"When I decide to get rid of this beard I'll want to use my razor and I don't want to find that someone's been using it. Just don't touch anything of mine."

"But I'll need to shave," Jay stated, realizing that big man was serious.

"Not with my razor, you don't. Keep your hands off my razor and all my other stuff."

"How am I supposed to shave, then? You know I don't have a razor."

The man pretended to scrutinize Jay's face meticulously. "You don't have enough there to need a razor. Soap and water should take that peach fuzz off easy enough. Or grow a beard for all I care. It's your problem, not mine. Besides, you're only here for tonight. Tomorrow you'll be your cousin's problem." The big man's voice began to take on an angry tone again.

"Take it easy. I was joking, honest," responded Jay in an effort to placate the man. "Maybe I don't need to shave. I do appreciate your helping me out like this." *I've got to get out of here, and soon,* Jay thought to himself.

"I've gotta go out for some groceries if we're going to have anything to eat. I expect you're as hungry as I am by now. Anything you want me to get you?" The man still sounded irritated and annoyed.

"No, thank–you. I will manage. Thanks again for helping me out this way. It is surprisingly nice of you," Jay said out loud while thinking, *what have I got myself into? I don't have a clue what this crazy guy is up to. And I don't think I want to know. I had better get out of here while I still can.*

The apartment door closed and a solid thunk signaled that the deadbolt was locked in place. Jay stared at the door, waiting to be sure that the man would be out of the hallway before making his move. He walked over and tried the door. It was locked. He had heard the deadbolt secure it but thought that there must be some way to unlock it. But how? Jay examined the lock carefully. He discovered that it required a key to unlock it. *What kind of a lock is this? It needs a key to unlock it from the inside? That means I am locked in here and cannot get out. What kind of a deal is this, anyway?* The questions ran through Jay's mind as he felt panic start at the bottom of his stomach and move up into his chest. His heart began to beat faster, his breathing started to get short and shallow. *This cannot be happening to me. I'm locked in here until he gets back. But I have got to get out of here,* thought Jay to himself as his eyes darted about the room in search of a way out.

A quick glance at the living room window established that even if he had wanted to attempt the jump from the second floor to the ground, this wasn't a possibility. The iron bars that had been firmly attached across the opening to keep intruders out served as effectively to keep Jay in. An examination of the kitchen and bathroom windows revealed similar protection. *Oh great. What am I supposed to do if there is a fire? Am I supposed to sit here and quietly burn to death?* Jay wondered, although his concern was more with how he would get out before the man returned than with the unlikely possibility of a fire. *The bedroom must have a window,* he thought as he crossed the living room and tried the door. Also locked. *It looks flimsy. I can easily kick it open,* Jay thought to himself as he leaned back to take a kick at it. Thump! Jay's foot hit the door and he could feel it shake. Thump! His second kick missed the door and hit the frame sending a painful shock wave though his foot and up his leg. *Ow! That hurts. The window is probably barred anyway,* he thought.

Jay tried the mysterious blue door, but it was also firmly locked. *This guy certainly does have a mania for locking things up.*

Jay sat in the big leather chair and pushed the POWER button of the TV remote while he tried to plan a new course of action.

Oh wow, Jay said to himself as he pushed the control to get other channels, *he must have hundreds of channels.* The novelty of flipping between the color channels quickly captured Jay's full attention.

The click of a key in the lock startled Jay back to the reality of his present situation. With a guilty start he jumped up, clicked off the TV and stood near the door. A plan began to form in his mind. *When he opens the door, I will knock him to the ground and be out of here before he knows what hit him. It will be easy. They do it all the time on TV.* He tensed himself waiting for the door to swing open.

"Hi. Can I take that bag for you?" Jay asked as the door swung open.

"You been standing there all this time waiting to help me with my bags?" the man asked, handing one of the brown paper bags to Jay.

"What else was I supposed to do? It is not as if I could get the door open to go out for a walk or anything." Jay knew he was pushing, but he had the bravado of one who has reached the bottom of the pit and has nowhere else to go.

"What's the matter, country boy? Don't you know how to open a door?" He was being baited, but Jay was too distressed to realize it, and wouldn't have had any idea how to handle the situation even if he had recognized it.

"You locked it, and you didn't give me a key. What was I supposed to do, kick it open?" Jay didn't know whether to be angry, scared or indignant. His throat tightened while tears of frustration began welling up in his eyes. He wished he were back home. At least there he felt he had some control of his life, even if it wasn't much of a life.

"Hey kid. Lighten up. If I'd given you a key you'd have run out on me," the man countered with a look that Jay interpreted to be menacing.

"How could I run out on you? I have no money and nowhere to go. And now it's night and dark out. I have to stay here tonight, and you know it." Jay suddenly realized he was telling the truth. That could only mean that he was totally losing control of the situation.

The man, realizing that Jay was on the verge of tears, suddenly turned friendly, "Sorry, Joe. I didn't mean to scare you. I'm an all right guy. See, I even bought you a razor." He pulled a cheap disposable razor and a can of shaving cream from one of the bags and set them on the table in front of Jay.

Jay ignored the attempt at friendship. "And stop calling me Joe. My name's Jay. H…I…J. Get it? Jay. Where do you get off with calling me Joe? I never said my name was Joe, so knock it off, okay?" Jay felt he was gaining some semblance of control, so he pushed his advantage.

The man was suddenly confused and on the defensive, "Hey. Sorry. I thought you said it was Joe. Or did you say it was Tom?" He tried to remember their earlier conversation but it wasn't clear in his mind anymore. He thought maybe he was getting confused with a conversation with someone else. "Whatever. Jay it is. I'll try to remember that. Sorry," he concluded.

"Thanks. I appreciate that."

"So whatcha want to eat, Jay?" he asked. "I can cook us a vegetable stir–fry or I've got a frozen pizza, or some tomato soup or a peanut butter sandwich. What do you fancy?"

"I'll have whatever you have. I'm going to turn on the TV." Jay pushed his advantage and stormed into the living room. He plopped himself into the big leather chair. The football game was still on. *Oh, oh. This is probably his special chair. If he catches me in it, I could be in big trouble. I had better ease off while I am still ahead,* Jay thought to himself. He moved over to the sofa.

The sizzling sound of the stir–fry and the fragrant aroma of ginger wafted into the living room. Jay's headed toward the kitchen.

"Turn off the TV, please. We need to save power. My monthly bills are high and I have to be careful with my money. A dollar saved is like a dollar seventy–five, after taxes," the man requested gently.

Jay pressed the button on the remote, silencing the announcer in mid–sentence.

"Pull up a chair," the man offered as he slid a serving of the food onto each of two dark–green plastic plates. The stir–fry looked delicious even though swimming in excess cooking oil.

"Fork?" queried Jay.

"Pardon me."

"Fork. I need a fork with which to eat," responded Jay.

"Chopsticks."

"Excuse me? Chop what?"

"Chop sticks. You eat stir–fry with chopsticks so that it doesn't pick up the metal taste of silverware," the man answered pointing to the pair of wooden sticks.

"I know what they are. I've seen pictures of them, but I didn't think that real people used them. Only those guys in China or Japan and like that." Jay picked up one of the chopsticks and attempted to spear some of the food.

"You have to use both of them together."

Jay took one in each hand and tried to scoop up a mouthful of the food. It didn't scoop well. It slid off the smooth wood and scurried around the plate easily evading his unrelenting thrusts.

"Like this." The man deftly grasped a pinch of food. "Hold them between your first and second fingers and guide them with your thumb," he demonstrated.

Jay tried again, managing to get a few morsels within inches of his mouth before they fell back half onto his plate and half onto the table. With his mouth at the edge of his plate he succeeded in sliding a pinch of food into his mouth.

"This is good," Jay exclaimed. The satisfaction of finally getting some food into his mouth made him forget his initial frustration.

Jay continued flailing his food with the chopsticks, using them more like a shovel than implements for picking up food. With each mouthful, he bent closer to his plate until his chin rested on the table. A chuckle rumbled deep in the man's throat.

"Have you got any more? I'm starved," Jay begged. "And do you have a fork somewhere? Or a spoon? Or anything other than my fingers. These stick things are hopeless."

The man beamed with pleasure at Jay's appreciation of his culinary efforts.

"Where's the meat?" Jay asked. There was always meat on the table in Jay's home. Maybe it would be only rabbit, squirrel or partridge if the hunting was poor, but meat such as deer or moose was easier to get than vegetables in the short summer season of northern Canada.

"I'm a vegetarian."

"What?" Jay tried a joke to stall for time while he thought about the comment. "How does being a veterinarian mean I don't get any meat to eat? You don't like people eating your patients, or what?" Jay asked. "I always have meat."

"Not veterinarian, vegetarian. That's a person who doesn't eat meat. I don't eat meat, ever. If you want meat you'll have to get it yourself and cook it yourself when I'm not around. I won't have anything to do with it," the man proclaimed.

"Never? No meat at all? What about fish?"

"No meat, no fish, no chicken."

"But you bought me a burger. That's meat."

"I was making a special effort to be friendly. I don't do that often."

"Why did you want to be friendly to me?" Jay asked.

"You reminded me of someone I used to know."

"What did you say you call yourself again? A vegetation? Or was it a Unitarian?" Jay asked, making another feeble attempt at humor.

"Don't try to be funny. It doesn't suit you."

"Milk?" Jay continued.

"What?"

"Do you drink milk?"

"Yeah, I need to have something to put on my cereal. I tried using water, but it isn't worth eating that way. I also tried soy milk, but it isn't the same either. Not with cereal. Besides, you don't have to kill anything to get milk or eggs so I don't mind that. I can't bear the thought of having to kill a living creature for food. I'd rather starve."

The image of the buck with its haunting eyes flashed into Jay's mind. He realized that he had never gone hunting since that episode. Suddenly he felt totally exhausted as the tension drained out of his mind and body. He felt the relief that comes from knowing that he was no longer in danger.

So much for my worry about his being an axe murderer. He's nothing but a big, soft, pussy cat who wouldn't hurt a flea, Jay thought to himself as he wiped his plate with a slice of bread. *Anybody who is a vegetarian cannot be all that bad.*

Jay dried the few dishes while the man washed and then put them in the cupboard. "Neatness and cleanliness are two things a guy's got to have. Don't ever put off the cleaning and tidying," the man said.

"I can handle that. Do you have any other gems of wisdom for me?" asked Jay with a grin.

"Sure. Never look a stranger in the eye, don't step on the flowers as you go through life, and if you look after the little things, the big things will look after themselves."

They moved into the living room. The man eased himself into the chair while Jay lay down on his stomach on the sofa, oblivious to the voice of the eleven o'clock news, "...the police are still searching for clues to the identity of the drug dealer's killer..."

The man got a blanket from the closet and draped it over Jay's motionless form. "I guess we'll open up the bed for you tomorrow," he said to the sleeping figure.

CALLERS IN THE NIGHT

It was after three in the morning. Jay was sound asleep on the sofa and the man had gone to bed. The noise in the hallway grew louder and more insistent, rousing him into semi–consciousness even before he heard the knock. He rolled off the sofa and went groggily to the door.

"Who's there?" he demanded, trying to get his brain at least marginally functional.

"Never mind who's out here. Who's that in there?" an impassioned voice challenged back through the door.

"Where be Phil?" another voice from the hallway added.

Phil? Do I know anybody named Phil? thought Jay to himself as he tried to get his sleep–numbed brain into action. *Where am I anyway?* Light from a nearby streetlight filtered through the window curtain. *Oh yes. The bus trip and the big man on the bus. Chopsticks. Oh, I know. I'll bet that the guy on the recliner is Phil.* The thoughts began to get themselves into order but when he looked at the big leather chair it was empty. *The bedroom. That must be where he is,* Jay thought.

He tried the bedroom door, but it was locked. Jay rapped his knuckles against the wood and called quietly but insistently, "Hey Phil. There are people at the door. Should I let them in?" *As if I could let anybody in when the door's locked,* Jay thought, remembering with annoyance his earlier frustration.

There was no reply from the bedroom, but Jay thought he could hear some movement. He went back to the door. "Phil will be here in a minute." *Or an hour, or maybe never for all I know*, he added under his breath.

A disembodied voice demanded through the door. "Well, let us IN, dearie. We can't stand out here ALL NIGHT, you know. The NEIGHBORS will get annoyed." The significant words were emphasized with a short intake of breath before being expressing in an exhaled drawl.

"Okay, Okay. Give us a minute," Jay replied. "Hurry up, Phil, or whoever who you are," Jay muttered to himself.

"Of course I'm Phil. Who did you think I was, Santa Claus? Why don't you unlock the door and let them in?" The voice at his elbow caught Jay by surprise. He jumped out of the way and Phil, for indeed that was his name, turned the key that had been left in the lock and opened the door.

"WELL, it's JUST about time. REALLY. We've been just DYING out here, FOREVER. It's so GOOD to see you again, Phil. You look FABULOUS but maybe a pound or two heavier. You must tell me just EVERYTHING about your MARVELOUS trip. And WHO is this GORGEOUS young MAN? REAL-LY. We didn't know you had gone on a HUNTING trip, but my goodness, what a TROPHY. You MUST introduce us IMMEDIATELY. And so YOUNG, too. But those CLOTHES. A COLORED T–shirt and jeans with a ZIPPER? And those SHOES? Really Phil, I thought you had more taste than that. Could I get a glass of Perrier, or SOMETHING? I'm just DYING of thirst. Do you mind if we smoke? It's just AWFUL that one can't smoke in the cabs any more. And those cabbies are so RUDE. Just one little cigarette and they just simply SHOUT at you as if they OWNED the cab. Be a dear and get me that drink, will you?"

The rush of words preceded the entrance of the visitors and flowed ahead of them like water through a burst dam. The room was suddenly dominated by the heavy aroma of expensive cologne. Steve and Cam swept into the room, flaunting their finely tuned sensuality as they posed like actors taking over centre stage on opening night, luxuriating in the impact on their audience.

Steve took a cigarette from his silver case and flipped the built–in lighter into action. "Care for one?" he asked Jay.

"No. I don't have any bad habits," Jay replied with a scowl. "Besides cigarettes are evil. My mom always got angry when people smoked in the house."

Jay hastily retreated to the kitchen on the pretext of getting another chair while the two visitors monopolized the sofa and Phil slouched into the recliner.

"Jay, these are my friends, Cam and Steve. Would you get Steve a glass of apple juice from the fridge while you're there, please?" Phil requested.

"Apple JUICE. Really Phil. Is that ALL you've got?" queried Steve. "Well, you'll HAVE to bring one for Cam too, JAY." Steve seemed to almost yawn Jay's name, opening his mouth wider than necessary and letting the name slide out slowly and suggestively.

Steve turned back to Phil. "DO tell us ALL about your TRIP. Are the guys in Edmonton still as HOT as ever? I've GOT to get back there or I'll just DIE. And where did you EVER discover this Jay person. He's absolutely ADORABLE," Steve continued prattling on without pausing for answers or comments.

Jay returned from the kitchen with two glasses of juice.

"Hi Phil. Nice to be meeting you, Jay." Cam finally got a few words in.

"Here's your drink," Jay said holding out the glass to Steve. Steve leaned back, stretching his arms out along the back of the sofa. He caught Jay's eyes for a moment before letting his gaze meander leisurely down over Jay's body to his feet and back up until their eyes met again and locked.

So do you want the drink or not? thought Jay. *Maybe you want me to hold it for you while you drink it? What do you expect me to do?* He continued to hold the glass out toward Steve. *Take the glass, dummy, or I will pour it into your lap,* Jay thought to himself.

Languidly Steve took the glass from Jay letting his fingers brush fleetingly against Jay's in the process. With what was obviously intended to be a profoundly suggestive look and the hint of a smile, Steve took the glass. He delicately raised it, took a tiny sip and let his tongue run slowly over his lips, all the time keeping his gaze locked onto Jay's eyes.

Jay handed the other glass to Cam.

"Just be ignoring her. It's one of her fem moods that she's in tonight. She can be such an actress sometimes," Cam advised, nodding toward Steve. Jay was too wrapped up in the situation to even notice the use of the unexpected pronoun.

"DO tell us about your TRIP," pleaded Steve, giving a significant look over the back of the sofa at Jay who had retreated to the relative obscurity of the periphery of the room.

Phil responded: "Knock it off, Steve. He's no chicken for a hawk like you. He's my nephew. I promised his mom I'd look after him for a few days until he gets settled into the city. She was worried that he couldn't look after himself, but I should warn you that he knows Judo, he has a hair–trigger temper and he doesn't take any hassling from anybody. So you'd better back off and leave him alone."

Wow. Way to go Phil. You lie even better than I do, thought Jay. *I guess I owe you one for this.*

The conversation switched to people and places and things of little interest to Jay as the three friends spent the next hour getting caught up on the gossip concerning their mutual friends. Jay used the time to study the two visitors.

Both men appeared to be in their mid–twenties and glowed with the raw feral vitality that comes from dutiful sweaty hours in the gym and a carefully planned tanning salon regime. A thin layer of foundation makeup carefully concealed the ravages of an indeterminate number of years. A hint of eye shadow gave their eyes depth and accented the color (which was the result of contact lenses that neither needed). The judicious use of a dark eyebrow pencil gave their faces the impression of mild surprise.

Steve's bleached–blond hair was cut to a uniform half–inch brush all over. His boyishly round face sported a carefully tailored light brown five–o'clock shadow. He wore a diamond nose stud in a silver setting, three silver rings in his left ear and three silver studs in his right one. His leather vest, held together with eight rows of silver chain, revealed his bare, muscular, smoothly–shaven chest. Supple, slinky black leather pants were tucked into ornate cowboy boots outrageously adorned with masses of shiny silver trim.

Cam's long reddish brown hair was parted in the middle and carefully controlled so that it hung down beneath his ear lobes. His Comanche fringe vest was made of intricately tooled deerskin accented with silver conchos holding the cascading suede laces. It hung open exposing curls of reddish chest hair tapering to a line down his flat, rippled stomach, and disappearing beneath the waistband of his 501 Levi's. They fit snugly, requiring no belt as they hung seductively low on his hips. The bottom button was undone, subtly proclaiming his orientation to anyone who had reason to recognize the sign. His ensemble was completed by knee–hi moccasins, also in supple suede deerskin, with rawhide laces crisscrossing from the foot to the fringed top. An Indian–brave style choker consisting of three rows of bone alternating with black and red and white beads completed the ensemble.

Both men had obviously spent hours of careful preparation to present an impeccably stunning impression, although Jay had no idea what impression was intended.

"It's a bit early for Halloween, isn't it?" Jay asked.

Phil glared at Jay. Steve and Cam ignored the remark.

Jay tried again. "You guys sure have great tans. I wish I had a tan like that."

"Fake and bake is what it is," Cam replied with feigned modesty.

Jay lapsed into thoughtful silence while he tried to make sense out of Cam's comment.

"We dropped by just to say HELLO. And I'm SO glad we did," Steve said, pursing his lips and cocking his head to one side in Jay's general direction. "We'll be off now. DO be a DEAR and phone us a cab, Phil. And be SURE to tell them we are going to smoke in it."

"You'll be inviting me to your next dinner party, I hope, Phil," said Cam. "Maybe I'll get a chance to get a few words in then."

After they had left, Jay picked up the glasses and ash trays and rinsed them off in the sink.

"Must keep things clean and tidy," he said in Phil's general direction.

Phil sat waiting for Jay to come back to the sofa. For a few minutes they sat looking at each other, neither knowing exactly where to start in reconciling the events of the night with their widely dissimilar spheres of experience.

"Interesting friends you have," Jay ventured cautiously.

"Yeah. We go back a long way. We went through school together. Of course, we were younger then. Somehow what with peer pressure and such we seemed to be more alike. Since our school days our paths have diverged a lot, but we've always stayed best friends no matter how much our lifestyles changed."

"So you are saying that you are not like them, is that it?"

"They aren't always like that, you know. It's only when they go to the bars. During the day Steve is a travel agent and Cam is an accountant. They only cut loose like that at night sometimes…and on weekends."

"Yes, but it's more than acting up. Let's face it they're…they're…" Jay faltered.

"They're what?" Phil leaned forward in his chair as if to intimidate Jay.

"They are homos. Fags." Jay peered at Phil's face for some reaction to his use of the terms he had always considered to be contemptuous, but his expression was inscrutable.

"Other than that they look that way, how would you know they are gay?"

"That's easy. Back home we had three tests for fags. One: they can't whistle, at least not by blowing out. Two: they always hold their cigarette between their thumb and first finger instead of between the second and third fingers. Three: when they light a match they strike it toward themselves instead of away from themselves like regular guys do. I spent hours and hours learning how to whistle to make sure nobody would start calling me gay Jay."

"That's as dumb as saying that any man who waves his arms above his shoulders is gay. Did you know that male ice skaters were afraid to have their hands above their shoulders for fear of looking gay until Toller Cranston broke that taboo?"

"I know that when you're in school you don't do anything that looks gay."

"I think you mean effeminate."

"That, too," Jay agreed. *As if there is any difference. Effeminate guys look gay and gay guys are gay. So what's the difference,* Jay said to himself.

"I know what it's like to be teased. At school I got teased quite a bit because I was short and fat. When I got taller and had more weight to throw around, the teasing suddenly stopped. So what if they are gay?" Phil asked.

"I hate gays."

"You're afraid of gays?" Phil asked.

"No. Why would I be afraid of a bunch of fairies? I just don't want them around me. They give me the creeps."

"Maybe you need to get to know them as people."

"You don't expect me to take guys who wear makeup seriously, do you?"

"But they don't scare you?" Phil asked.

"No. I am not scared. I'm uncomfortable. It's like when you walk into a room full of strangers and they are looking at you as if they are expecting something from you, but you don't have a clue what they expect. You don't know what to say or what to do to get them to ignore you. You wish they would go away. Especially Steve. He scares me because I don't know how to react to him. What was he trying to do anyway? Does he think I'm queer?"

"That's just his way. It amuses him to flirt with people, especially straight people. He doesn't mean anything by it. It comes naturally to him. If he were trying to come onto you he wouldn't go about it like that."

"Maybe you're right. Maybe he was only fooling around, but he seemed so, uh, I don't know. Persistent, or intense or something. I hate him."

"He wants people to notice him. He craves attention and you've got to admit that he made an impression on you, didn't he?"

"Oh yes. He made an impression all right. I didn't know if I wanted to run away or to slap him silly to get him to stop looking at me," Jay said, feeling a renewed sense of annoyance at Steve.

"He needs to feel that people notice him...pay attention to him...and like him."

"People certainly notice him all right, but how can they like him when he is hiding behind that phony camouflage? It's like trying to get to know an actor from seeing his movies. The character he is playing is not the real person. Or maybe in Steve's case it is. How would I know? And what were those costumes about, anyway?"

"They like to dress up for the bar scene. If you think that's wild, you should see them when they're ready for a Black and Blue Ball."

"It couldn't be much worse than that," Jay said. "What's a Black and Blue Ball, anyway?"

"It's a fetish thing. People dress up in leather and chains with whips and stuff like that. There is usually a lot of strategically exposed skin, if you know what I mean."

"I'm not sure I know what you mean, but I'd kind of like to see that...from a distance."

"You'd have to pay an extra thirty–dollar voyeur charge if you didn't dress up."

"I'd pay a lot more than that to avoid going around half–naked in leather in public."

"How about in private?" Phil asked, with a grin.

"Maybe with the right girl. But that's a gay thing, isn't it?"

"No. It's gay or straight or both. For something like this, the fetish is more important than the sexual orientation."

The conversation stopped abruptly and the two men sat immersed in their own thoughts, staring into space in the dimly lit room.

After a few minutes Jay broke the awkward silence. "Why did you decide to help me in like this?"

Phil's gaze drifted in the direction of the blue door. "It seemed like the right thing to do at the time."

"Did you mean what you said earlier?" he ventured.

"What did I say?" asked Phil.

"You know. What you said about me."

"You mean about your being my nephew? Of course not. I did that to get Steve off your case," Phil said, deliberately sidestepping Jay's question.

Jay looked down in embarrassment. "No, I meant about your kind of look-ing after me like as if I were your nephew. Did you mean that you would help me out? Kind of like a relative would?"

"There are only three things that a person needs in order to get along in this life: something to do, something to look forward to, and someone to love," Phil said, ignoring the question.

"I'd kind of like someone to love me."

"You'll have to find someone that you can love, first. You don't get love until you give it," Phil said.

"Time to get some sleep," Jay said.

"Let me give you a hand folding down the sofa. It's a heavy brute of a thing."

The click of Phil's bedroom lock sounded peculiarly loud in the eerie silence before dawn. Jay was asleep the instant he hit the sofa.

ALL THAT GLITTERS IS NOT SILVER

Jay awoke to the smell of pancakes and the sizzle of the frying pan. *Bacon*, he thought, *I can't remember when I last had bacon.* He rolled off the sofa and on his way to the bathroom stuck his head into the kitchen.

"Good morning…uncle," he announced, moving quickly into the bathroom before Phil could respond.

Ten minutes later he returned. "See. I look better now, don't I?" he said, rubbing his freshly shaved cheek. A small piece of toilet paper clung to a small nick under his nose.

Phil jumped up out his chair. "You're bleeding. Get out of here and get cleaned up. And get rid of that bloody paper."

Jay retreated hastily to the bathroom. *Wow. I guess he is in a bad mood today,* Jay thought to himself.

"Sorry about that, Phil. Thanks for getting me the razor. I did need a shave. I don't know what I would have done if you hadn't given me a place to stay last night."

Without comment, Phil put a stack of pancakes in front of Jay. *He must be annoyed about the 'Uncle' comment,* Jay thought. *Or maybe he's angry about my being here. Maybe I'm pushing too hard. I'd better back off a bit.*

"Oh good, you mean I get to use a knife and fork for these…no chopsticks?" Jay asked, hoping that his attempt at humor would elicit some reaction from Phil. *I wish he would say something. I can't tell if he is mad or not. How did I get myself into this anyway?* he thought to himself.

Jay lapsed into silence and gave his full attention to eating. He and Phil were almost finished when it suddenly hit Jay, *Phil said he doesn't eat meat and here we are sitting down to a feed of bacon with our pancakes.*

"What is with the bacon, Phil? Didn't you say that you were a vegetarian, or whatever it is called?"

"Tofu," replied Phil

"No, that wasn't it. I am sure you said something more like 'vegetarian'," Jay said in another effort to be funny.

"I mean the bacon. It's not meat. It's tofu. Made from bean curds and fancied up to taste like bacon. What do you think of it?"

Jay looked at the scraps left on his plate with suspicion as if he somehow expected a reaction from them.

"I thought it was good, but now I am not so sure. Is this real coffee or is it made out of something weird, too?"

"No, it's real. But anytime I serve you something that looks like meat, you can bet it'll be tofu…or some kind of bean thing. So, what do you plan to do today, Jay?"

"I guess I should go out and see the big city. To be honest with you, now that I am here, I'm not so sure I know what to do. Do you have any suggestions?"

"What about your cousin?"

"Who?"

"Your cousin. Didn't you say you planned to stay with him?"

"Oh yes. I forgot about him."

"You have his address? I can tell you how to get there," Phil suggested helpfully.

"My mom probably has his new address."

"You're welcome to use the phone."

"We don't go in for telephones much where I come from." *What is it with you and my imaginary cousin?* Jay said to himself. "I'll have to get along on my own for now. Maybe I'll have a look at one of the malls."

"You could do me a favor then, if you don't mind. Did you notice the watch on the arm of the sofa? Or maybe it got folded up inside when you made your bed. Anyway, it belongs to Steve. He phoned this morning to say he left it here, and he'd like to get it back right away. It's not that he needs it, but he's a Cancer and they get uptight about their possessions."

"I know about Cancers," Jay bragged."I'm a Virgo myself, and you know what that means."

"Yeah. You'd have to be a Virgo from the way you talk. Nobody but a Virgo would be so precise in their grammar and speech."

"I've always read every book on which I could get my hands, especially the Bible. Words can be so very powerful. It is important to use the correct words because people are ultimately judged by what they say."

"Were you happy at home?"

"No. I soon learned that physical wounds will heal and the scars that are left make the body stronger. But emotional wounds remain open, and the person is left weaker and more vulnerable. If someone hurts you with words, that hurt becomes part of you until the day you die. You may consciously forgive the person for what they said, but you will never be free of the effect of those words on your life. Particularly if you were a kid when you heard them."

"It sounds as if this has happened to you."

"More times than I like to think about," Jay replied. "I used to get teased all the time for wanting to read. That hurt. But not as much as the feeling of loneliness and isolation that comes from not being understood."

Jay was lost in thought as he wandered into the living room, rubbing his arm. He picked up the watch and casually turned it over in his hand. At first glance it appeared to be three large silver concentric gears with square–ended cogs. On closer examination one cog on each of the inner gears had a tiny diamond chip at the end, one indicating the hour, and one the minutes. *Silver, of course. What else would Steve have?* he thought, remembering the black and silver impression that Steve had made the night before.

"What was it that you asked me to do a minute ago?" Jay asked.

"Taking that watch back to Steve."

"Oh yeah. I don't want to see him again. Why can't he come and get it?"

"He could, but it'd be easy for you to drop it off if you're going to the mall."

"I guess I could so long as I don't have to talk to him. I don't want anything to do with fags like him. Where would I find him?"

"He works at the Trip 'n' Travel Agency. He usually doesn't work weekends, but he'll be there today. It's in the Portage Plaza Mall, about a fifteen minute walk from here. Think you can find it?"

"Back home I used to do a lot of walking and hunting in the woods. I never got lost. One time I kind of did, but I cut through the forest to the river and followed it upstream until I got home," said Jay confidently.

"Well then, go down the street out front until you hit Portage Avenue and pretend it's the river. Turn left and follow it until you hit the mall. It's a bit beyond The Bay."

"Sure, I know where that is." *At least I saw it yesterday so I know it is out there somewhere,* Jay said to himself.

"Trip 'n' Travel is near the east end." Phil unlocked the door and pointed in the general direction.

With the confidence of youth and inexperience, Jay jogged down the stairs and out into the bright early afternoon sunshine. Elm trees sternly separated the black pavement from the deteriorating Victorian houses set back from the street. The neat yards gave silent testimony to the industry of the residents: retired workers who wiled away their spare hours clipping grass and plucking weeds from the neatly trimmed hedges.

Warm sunshine, the sound of the birds and the smell of lilacs reminded Jay of home. He paused to watch two little red squirrels scurry across the street and up an oak tree. They turned to scold him with their continuous chatter. Jay picked up a pebble and threw it at the closest one, missing him by two feet. The sudden movement sent the little rascal scuttling to a higher branch from which he hurled more squirrel profanity at the world.

The blocks went by quickly and suddenly Jay encountered the main thoroughfare with its eight lanes of traffic. *Let's see now. This must be Portage Avenue,* Jay said to himself. *I turn left. Or did he say right? Well, I'll try left, and then I keep going until I find the mall. That should be easy. Malls always have big parking lots. When I find the parking lot, I'll have it made.*

Past several car dealerships (*lots of parked cars, but no mall*), and various separate stores (*a mall needs to have a lot of stores together*), Jay strode down the avenue until he recognized The Bay. Suddenly Jay felt as if he had arrived in a place where he belonged. This was his home now. The lights, the people, the traffic, the buildings no longer scared him. They belonged here and so did he. At this moment he knew that his destiny lay somewhere within the life of this big city.

Jay was so caught up in the euphoria of his togetherness with the city that he almost didn't notice the three–story complex spanning three blocks of the downtown area. People streamed in and out of the building. *There's no parking lot, but there are stores.* Jay looked in vain for some sort of indication that this might be the mall. *Can you have a mall without a parking lot? I don't think so. Well, lots of people seem to be going in so I might as well have a look,* he thought veering into the building.

Jay wandered aimlessly between tables of merchandise set out in the mall for their summer sidewalk sale. He picked up a snakeskin wallet, turned it over in his hands, admired its textured surface, and surreptitiously slipped it into his pocket. He had totally forgotten his mission of delivering Steve's watch until he noticed the sign, Trip 'n' Travel. *Wow, I'm smarter than I thought. There it is, just as if I knew what I was doing.*

Jay was surprised by Steve's appearance. With his tailored black jeans and short-sleeved yellow silk shirt he looked like any of the other clerks in any of the other stores, except maybe for the ear studs.

"Hello, Jay. How are you?" asked Steve rather formally.

"I brought you your watch. You left it at Phil's last night."

"Thanks. I was hoping that it was there. I'd hate to lose it. Sorry, but I've gotta keep working. See you around." Steve turned his attention to a customer and Jay assumed that he had been dismissed.

Well, so much for that. Guess I'll head back to Phil's place, thought Jay. He headed out into the mall in the direction from which he thought he had come. When he arrived the end of the mall he turned around and headed back again, making a few furtive excursions out onto the main street. Jay reached three specific conclusions in rapid succession: he didn't know which direction would lead him back to Phil's, he didn't know the name of Phil's street even if he did get going in the right direction, and he wouldn't recognize Phil's house even if he did get to it.

A pay phone caught Jay's eye and he strode purposefully over to it. Opening the phone book he suddenly realized that he didn't know Phil's last name. He dropped the directory with the realization that the phone wasn't going to help him. *Great. One day in the big city and already I have messed things up completely,* he chastised himself. He bought himself a Pepsi and sat down at a table in the food court to think. Sipping at his drink reminded him of the night before and how Steve had been teasing him. *Yes! Of course. Steve would know how to get to Phil's. I'm not so hopeless after all,* Jay told himself. *Now all I have to do is figure out how to get back to that Travel Trip place, or whatever it's called.*

He wandered through the mall trying to remember the way to the travel agency. It seemed to have moved. Jay tried to think of some way that he could appear to be less incompetent to Steve than he felt at that moment. He ran the possibilities through his mind. *I'm not going to give that fag the satisfaction of knowing how pathetic I am in not being able to find my way home. Let me see. I could say I have a bad leg and he would take pity on me. No. I should have been limping last night if I had a bad leg. It's too late for that. Maybe a sore foot. That could happen suddenly. Yes, that's it. I'll say that I tripped and sprained my ankle. That's good. Then he'll have to give me a ride home. Oh no, what if he walks to work instead of driving? No, Steve wouldn't walk. He's got to be a car person, for sure.*

By the time Jay found his way to the counter in front of Steve he had decided on his story.

"Hi Steve. I tripped on the sidewalk and I think I sprained my ankle. I don't think I can walk back to Phil's. Could you help me out?" Jay asked. Suddenly he remembered, *Oh no. I forgot to limp. I hope he didn't notice.*

"Do you need to see a doctor? I could take you to the hobble-in clinic."

"The what?"

"The walk-in clinic. They have doctors there for emergency things."

"No. It's not serious, but it's too sore to walk on. I'll need a ride home."

"I understand. I'm off in half an hour. Meet me out in the mall and I'll drive you home," Steve promised.

With an obvious limp, Jay left the store and took up temporary residence on a mall bench. From this vantage point he could rest his imaginarily injured ankle while observing the parade of people.

Within the half hour Steve and Jay, favoring his foot obviously, walked to the elevator. *I've got to remember that it is my right foot or I'll give the whole show away*, he said to himself. P2 took the elevator to the second level of parking.

Jay looked at the rows of parked cars stretching out in all directions. *So this is where they hid the parking lot. Very sneaky.* "Wow. How do you expect to find your car in here?" Jay asked.

Without answering, Steve pressed a little box on his key chain. From halfway across the parkade a car obediently blinked its lights and emitted three sharp chirps of recognition.

"That's great," purred Jay. "Could I try it?"

Steve handed him the control. As they walked, Jay made the car call to them as they walked. It gave Jay a rush of power to realize the control he had with one finger. When they got closer, Jay saw that it was a new, black (*of course*) Lexus. When they got into the car Jay tried to figure out the uses of the various indicator lights, switches and buttons on the glistening walnut–trimmed, black leather console, but it was mostly guesswork.

"This is an amazing car," Jay said as the car started soundlessly.

Steve smiled in appreciation. "It's the top of the line. Blackout gauges, side airbags, four hundred horsepower, twenty–four valves and it goes from zero to a hundred clicks in less than six seconds."

As the car zoomed up the ramp and out of the parkade the sound of the CD player at high volume filled the air with Madonna's 'Vogue'. Jay sat back luxuriating in the thought that people would see him riding by in such a magnificent machine. He noticed immediately that the route went at right angles to what he expected, but wasn't concerned until they crossed a bridge over the river.

Hang on there, he thought to himself, *I know I didn't walk over any river. I know that for sure. Where is this guy taking me? I should have known better than to trust a fag.*

As if he could read Jay's mind, Steve said, "Hope you don't mind, but I wanted to stop off at my place before we go to Phil's. I need to get out of these work clothes."

"Would it make any difference if I did mind?" asked Jay.

Steve ignored the question as he pulled into a parking spot in front of a high rise apartment building. "Here we are. Would you bring in that bag of groceries?" he said pointing to a brown paper bag on the back seat.

"If you want to visit somebody here, you buzz them with their code number," Steve said, pointing to the board with names, apartment numbers and push buttons. "If they want to let you in, they unlock the door for you. Otherwise you don't get in unless you have a key. Personal safety is important when you live in a big city. Remember that you can't trust people here the way you did back where you came from."

I sure don't intend to trust fags like you, Jay thought.

The elevator rose to the top floor.

"There wasn't any 13th floor," Jay said.

"Most elevators are numbered so that they don't show a 13th floor, because people are superstitious about that."

"But wouldn't the 14th floor actually be the 13th?"

"Of course. But so long as it isn't called that, nobody cares. It's the words, not the reality that matters to most people."

Steve unlocked the apartment door. The drab grey hallway carpet changed at the doorway to plush, dazzling white inside.

"I had the carpet put in specially," Steve said proudly. "The grey clashed with my furniture. I like things to look right." Steve slipped out of his shoes at the door and looked expectantly at Jay.

I can take a hint, Jay said to himself, taking off his shoes.

The living room was furnished with chintz furniture in a deep blue that seemed to float above the white carpet. A glass–topped dining room table was surrounded with six sculptured chairs in the same blue fabric on black metal frames. Glass coffee and matching sofa tables with two stylized ebony figures exuded an aura of expensive self–indulgence. An elaborate sound–system provided a full surround–sound experience. The walls were tastefully accented with large black-and-white posters interspersed with smaller photographs, also in black and white. Although artistically done, the posters shocked Jay with their unabashed portrayal of nude male figures in relaxed but suggestive poses.

"Holy cow," exclaimed Jay. "The travel agent business must pay well. Or do you have some sort of illegal activity on the side?" As soon as he had said it, Jay wished he hadn't. *What is the matter with me?* he thought. *I don't want to insult this guy by implying he's a crook. On the other hand, if he is a crook he probably doesn't want me to know about it. I've got to learn to keep my mouth shut. That is something I could learn from Phil. Now I know why he sometimes doesn't answer me. At least you don't get in trouble if you keep quiet.* "Just kidding," he added lamely trying to deflect any hostile reaction that Steve might have.

"My job pays the rent and buys the groceries but that's about all," Steve said, apparently quite unconcerned about the personal nature of the question. "The good stuff comes from my old man's money."

"Gee. I wish I had a father like that."

"You might not if you knew him."

"Well at least you have a father. That's more than I ever had. And he must love you a lot to give you that kind of cash," Jay said.

"Let me tell you about him. He's got a successful business in Toronto, and he's been lucky on the stock market, so he's got way more money than he knows what to do with. He sends me a monthly cheque on the condition that I never go home to visit unless I'm invited. I'm still waiting to be invited. He doesn't want me to be around for fear of embarrassing the good family name." Steve turned away, but not before Jay saw a flash of pain in his eyes. "I guess you could say that I'm a modern day remittance man."

"A what kind of man?" queried Jay.

"Back in the 19th century, high–class Englishmen sent the black sheep of their family over to Australia or Canada and paid them a monthly allowance on condition that they stay there to keep from being an embarrassment." Steve explained. "I've been banished from Toronto to Winnipeg."

"This is the balcony," Steve continued as if conducting a guided tour. He slid aside the patio door and stepped out onto the balcony. "Living on the top floor costs more, but it's worth it for the view. Being able to look out across the city relaxes me when I'm uptight."

Jay was spellbound with being able to look down at the river directly below, out across the city, and down onto the rooftops. An all-encompassing sensation of knowledge and power swept over him as he consciously fought back the urge to leap off the balcony and to fly out over the city. He shook his head to bring himself back to reality. *Wow*, he thought, *I wish I were a big bird...maybe like an eagle. I could learn so much by drifting over the world.*

"You have a telescope?" Jay asked, more as an observation than a question. He bent over and peered into the eyepiece. "Hey. This points down at the street instead of up into the sky."

"It's probably still pointed at Phil's house. That's how I knew when he got home yesterday," Steve said. "But don't say anything to Phil about it. He might get mad. He's a bit paranoid sometimes."

"Mind if I look around?"

"Go ahead. Take your time, I'll go in and mix us a drink while you look around. What do you like?"

"Whatever you are having would be great."

Some coins and handful of crumbled bills sat on the coffee table. Jay picked up a five and a ten, slipping them into his pocket. *He'll never miss a couple of bills*, he said to himself.

Steve reappeared with two tall glass filled with a brownish liquid and ice cubes. "Here, try this," he said, handing Jay one glass. "It's Long Island Iced Tea."

"Did you know that there are ducks right down there on the river? And aren't those muskrats swimming around by the shore?" Jay asked.

"Could be. I thought they were miniature beavers. I like the ducks when their babies are little," Steve said. "You should come over and see the view of the city lights at night. It's awesome," Steve said as he went back into the apartment.

"What's with the big, naked, golden guy on top of that building with the lit-up torch?" Jay asked as he swung the telescope over the city.

"That's the Golden Boy. He stands on top of the Legislative Building. His torch is lit when the Legislature is in session."

After a few minutes, Jay left the telescope and rejoined Steve in the living room.

Jay finished his drink. "That tasted good. What did you call it?" he asked.

"Long Island Iced Tea. But don't drink it too fast. It's deceptively potent."

"Potent?"

"It packs a bit of a kick."

"Oh. You mean it is alcoholic? It tastes more like tea than booze. I usually don't drink, but I guess another one more wouldn't hurt."

Through a half–open door, Jay noticed marble flooring in the bathroom. Steve pointed off to a side room.

"This is the spare bedroom," he motioned to the right, "Cam used to stay here with me before he got his own place. I don't use it now."

From the doorway Jay saw a queen–size bed, a black lacquered dresser and a bookcase filled with hardcover books. A computer system sat on a corner desk.

"Have you read all those books?"

"Good heavens, no. I don't have any time for reading. Sometimes I'll pick up a book if I have trouble getting to sleep, but I never finish it."

What a magnificent library. I wish that Phil had some books, thought Jay.

"You could use the computer sometime, if you want. You'd probably enjoy the Internet."

"I think I'd rather browse the library than surf the net," Jay said. "Do you use the system much?"

"Not at all. Cam's the computer nerd. He tried to teach me a lot of stuff but I've forgotten most of it."

"So it just sits there?"

"Sometimes I log onto the Internet so that anyone phoning will get a busy signal and won't bother me. It's better than the answering machine because that way they can't leave a message."

On the side wall, the faces of three portraits looked out from their tradition-ally dark backgrounds and heavy, carved frames. "Are these your grandparents?" he asked.

Steve laughed. "Those are my ancestors, all right. I bought them at an antique store in Montana. My parents don't want anything to do with me so I thought I'd create a family of my own. Cecil there is my favorite. He's such a delightful-ly grouchy looking guy with those mutton–chop whiskers, unkempt hair, and dour expression. Wouldn't it be fun to see his reaction when he found out that his only son was gay?"

"Are you saying that your problems with your father are because you're gay?" Jay asked.

"We were a happy family until four years ago when I 'came out' to them. My old man just totally lost it and threw me out of the house."

"What about your mom?"

"I think she could have accepted it eventually, but she didn't have much of a chance. It was as if I ceased to be their son. After I left, they never phoned or even send a card for my birthday or Christmas. Last year my mom phoned me a week after my birthday but only because someone told her I'd died. She wanted to check it out in case they should be preparing for the funeral. She didn't even remember that I'd had a birthday."

"That's terribly cruel."

"It's not as bad as trying to pass for straight."

"You mean you had to pretend to be straight?"

"When I realized in Grade Four that I was gay and that other kids suspected I was queer, I had to watch myself and do things to appear straight."

"Like what?"

"Like at a dance in junior high when a girl and I spent the whole evening necking up a storm just to throw off any suspicion."

"That wasn't very fair to her. What if she thought you liked her?"

"No problem. She was lesbian. In fact we both rather enjoyed the closeness and the feeling of being in a conspiracy to fool the straights."

"Have you tried to get your father to accept you?"

"I try not to think about it," he said as he guided Jay down the hall.

The bedroom was dominated by a king–sized waterbed and a sound–center large enough for a small theatre. One entire wall consisted of closet space full of expensive clothes and a line of outrageously thick soled shoes and boots along the floor.

"Give me a minute while I change," Steve said, unabashedly slipping off his shirt to reveal the full, muscular torso which had been hidden from view the night before. Jay's impulse was to flee from the room in the interests of modesty, but somehow his feet wouldn't move. He stood there, staring in astonishment at Steve's firm, well–sculptured pecs, and in mild horror at the silver ring adorning his left nipple. Jay gulped down the last of his second drink.

"That must hurt."

"Pain can be pleasurable."

"I try to avoid pain whenever I can."

"It's not real pain. It's more like when you were a kid and had a loose tooth. You couldn't keep from wiggling it, could you? Because you loved the delicious sensation of pain."

"Yeah, but you're not a kid, and that's no tooth."

Steve thrust out his chest toward Jay. Like a moth attracted to a flame, Jay's fingers reached out and touched the ring. It felt warm and smooth. It fit loosely in its sheath and flipped up and down easily. Jay rotated it slowly. The metal moved smoothly through the hole in the flesh sending a strangely sensuous shiver down Jay's spine.

"Doesn't it hurt a lot to get yourself pierced like that?" he asked.

"Not a lot. It only takes a five–second push to shove the needle through, and it's clamped so that you hardly feel anything. Now if you were getting a thick body part done," Steve said with a significant look downwards toward his crotch, "that takes at least a thirty–second push to go through. You have to be mentally prepared for that kind of experience."

Jay refused to allow himself to think about the implications of having various body parts pierced.

Steve went out and returned with another drink for Jay.

He continued. "It feels good and looks good. Part of the attraction is the anticipation of having it done. It's such a great adrenaline rush when they do it."

If the pants come off, I'm out of here, Jay said to himself with conviction. Steve slipped out of his pants but Jay's feet failed to move. He was mesmerized by the strip show taking place barely two feet in front of his eyes. *What am I doing? Here I am in a gay man's bedroom, he is feeding me booze and he is practically naked. I'm glad nobody's here to see this,* Jay thought to himself.

Steve rummaged in his closet, seemingly oblivious to the fact that he was naked except for his socks and pink bikini shorts. Jay found himself admiring Steve's beautifully uniform tan. Steve pulled on a pair of comfortable jeans and a T–shirt that broadcast the message 2QT2BSTR8 across the chest.

"Cute message, eh?" Steve asked, pretending not to notice the stunned look on Jay's face, but well aware of the impact he was making.

"Yes, great," Jay answered without having the foggiest idea what it meant and without the remotest intention of thinking about it. He was struggling valiantly to establish some semblance of composure within himself. He took a long drink from his glass.

"Would you be insulted if I gave you some clothes?" Steve asked Jay. "Those are the same ones you wore yesterday, and I bet they're the only ones you have."

"Yes, sure, whatever you say is fine with me," Jay stammered. "But only if you can spare them."

"Have a look in the closet. Doesn't it look like I could spare a few?" Steve countered. "I've got a lot of things I never wear because they are a bit too tight on me. I've been lifting weights and I'm not as scrawny as I used to be. They might be a bit big on you, but you could turn the cuffs up or whatever and nobody would notice. At least not as much as they'll notice you dressed the way you are. You look like a street urchin." Steve wrinkled his nose as if experiencing a bad smell.

Steve took a gym bag in one hand and started to toss things into it with the other. Jay remained standing there, physically present, but mentally and emotionally his system had shut down from massive overload.

Summoning the remnants of his rapidly failing intelligence Jay managed a feeble, "Thanks."

"Don't get me wrong. Phil and I have been best friends since junior high and we love each dearly, but I should warn you about him. He's had some rough times. At one point he went into a major depression and became dangerously unpredictable. We thought for a while that we'd have to hospitalize him, but he seemed to be able to draw strength from within his soul and came out of it on his own. Having you there might remind him of that earlier tragedy and set him off again. If things ever start looking like trouble, you should get out of there in a hurry."

"Where would I go if I have to leave? He's all I've got."

"You can come here anytime, night or day. The spare room is yours anytime you want it. Let yourself in and make yourself at home."

"That's kind of you. I don't know why people are being so good to me," Jay said.

Steve handed the gym bag to Jay. "Oh, by the way, you should have a set of keys. The square one does the outside door and the round one does the apartment," he added, handing the set to Jay.

"Thanks again."

"By the way, remember not to say anything to Phil about the telescope. He might not like it and I don't need to have him mad at me."

"Okay," responded Jay, filing the information in the back of his brain for possible future reference but without being conscious of what had been said.

They left the apartment and drove to Phil's in silence. Jay was unable to comprehend most of what had happened. He felt as if his head had turned to concrete. A dull throbbing behind his right eye threatened the onset of insanity. He felt slightly dizzy from the unaccustomed intake of alcohol. Steve pulled over to the curb, handed Jay the gym bag and as if it had been a normal routine day, bade him a curt goodbye and waited for him to get out.

Jay had lost all awareness of his surroundings but his natural instincts and habits took over. "Bye, Steve," he said, getting out of the car and heading up the stairs to Phil's apartment.

Phil opened it promptly in response to Jay's knock. "Hi Jay, how's it going?" Phil asked.

"It's not going...it's gone. We have to talk. But later," Jay mumbled. He dropped onto the sofa–bed and fell into a dreamless sleep.

LIFE AS USUAL

Phil and Jay were finishing their breakfast coffee in the kitchen.

"I noticed that your bathroom door opens outwards instead of inwards," Jay commented absent-mindedly. "Isn't that unusual? It tends to block the hallway."

"I had it changed to be that way. It's so that if a person falls while in the bathroom he won't block the door and prevent my getting in to help him."

"That's a clever idea, but why would you go to the trouble and expense to change it like that? Do you have a lot of people passing out in your bathroom?"

Phil ignored the question. "It's strange that in public buildings they modify the washrooms to be wheelchair accessible, but they never think of the obvious things. Like having a shelf to hold equipment and stuff. One thing that most disabled people aren't good at is picking things up off the floor. And they often have extra tubes or bags or some kind of equipment to deal with."

"You seem to have given this a lot of thought. By the way, I was wondering if you are sick or something. Your bathroom cabinet looks like a miniature drug store."

"That's not mine. It's old stuff I haven't got around to throwing out," Phil said. "Did you get the watch back to Steve?"

"Oh sure, no problem. He gave me a bunch of nifty clothes. You want to see them?" Jay began pulling things out of the gym bag and holding them up to show how they would look on him. A T–shirt had the message, 2QT2BSTR8.

"He gave you that?" Phil asked with a grin.

"Yeah. He has one exactly like it. Why, is there something wrong with it?"

"I suggest you don't wear it in public until you figure out what the message means."

Jay held up a black leather jacket covered with decorative silver zippers and brads. ·

"Don't wear that when I'm around," Phil said, turning serious again.

"Why not? It fits nicely and looks really sharp. I don't know why he would give away such a good jacket."

"You know I don't like animals being killed for meat or for leather. I never wear a leather belt or shoes or anything leather and I don't like to see other people wearing things that come from needlessly slaughtered animals," Phil protested.

"Is that right?" Jay asked sarcastically. "So what about that fancy leather chair. You don't seem to care about the cows that died to make it. Or is it all right so long as they are Italian cows?"

Jay immediately regretted the sharpness of his words when he saw the pain on Phil's face.

"No, it's not. But that's another story from the past."

"Hey, look at this other neat stuff Steve gave me," Jay said holding up a sweatshirt in an effort to steer the conversation in a safer direction.

"Give me that stuff. Right now." Phil practically grabbed the shirt out of Jay's hands. "And don't touch any of Steve's stuff until I've washed and disinfected it." Phil was noticeably upset and his voice quivered with restrained emotion.

"Back off, Phil," Jay protested. "He gave them to me. They're mine." But he reluctantly acquiesced to Phil's demand and surrendered the bag of clothes.

"What is the matter with you, anyway, Phil? Are you jealous of Steve or what?" *I'd better be careful,* Jay thought to himself. *It looks as if Phil's beginning to lose it. I'd hate to think what he could do to me if he got violent. Maybe Steve was right when he said there could be trouble.* Jay checked the door and was relieved to see that the key was in the lock.

Phil took a deep breath, exhaled and said in a carefully controlled voice, "You have to be careful in a big city. You never know what kind of things you might get off other people's things, especially their personal belongings."

"You mean like cooties?"

"I mean like things that can make you sick or even kill you. I want you to clean and disinfect all the things you got from Steve."

"Is this only about Steve or do you mean about everybody that's, uh, you know, uh...?"

"It's all right to say the word, 'gay'. Yes it's about all gays. But it is as true about straight guys and girls, too. There are something like twenty diseases that can be transmitted by intimate contact with an affected person. And then there's the HIV virus. You can't be too careful."

"Oh wow. You're right. It never occurred to me until you said it, but I'm not going to wear those clothes. I'm not taking any chances with my health. Get rid of them. Throw them in the garbage. I'm not touching them." Jay pushed the gym bag toward Phil.

There was an awkward silence for a few moments. "Let's be sensible," Phil said. "Those things can't be caught from clothes. But I'll wash the clothes with a bit of Javex just to make me feel better. They'll be perfectly safe to wear." He zipped up the bag and tossed it aside.

"If you're sure they'll be safe," Jay said. "I do need the clothes."

Several days later, Phil said to Jay, "It's kind of inconvenient sleeping on that sofa–bed, I guess."

"For me or for you?" Jay asked.

"For both of us."

"You are saying you want me out of here?" Jay asked. His face took on a worried look.

"No. I only meant what I said. It's a bit inconvenient for both of us to have you sleeping in the middle of the living room."

"If you want me to leave then say so." Jay got up and went to the kitchen. He rinsed his cup and hung it on its designated hook. "I can look after myself, you know."

"Don't be so touchy. I'm trying to have a conversation to help get my own thoughts together. It's confusing for me to have someone staying with me again. It brings back so many memories," Phil said. "Maybe I should have got a dog instead of you."

"I used to have a dog. He was my best buddy for as far back as I can remember."

"What happened?"

"He got old. My mom decided that he couldn't stay outside through the cold of winter. But he wasn't reliable enough about bathroom kind of things to stay indoors. I offered to clean up after him if he stayed inside, but she said he'd be too much trouble."

"I'm sorry."

"She said that since I was the man–of–the–house, it was my job. Besides, I was the only one who knew how to use a gun."

"You were doing him a kindness. Putting him out of his misery."

"I tried to make it easy for him at the end. He was resting in the back yard with his head on his paws looking up at me with trusting eyes. The .22 bullet between his eyes was fast and painless. I cradled him in my arms and took him to a place beside the lake where he used to love chasing the birds, and buried him there at the top of a little hill. My mom said it was a waste of effort to bury him because it would snow soon, but I couldn't leave him lying there exposed to the elements. Giving him a safe resting place was the least I could do after all the years of love he had given me."

"That must have been hard on you."

"I hope he knew that I didn't mean to hurt him."

"You were his friend. He'd understand."

"I hope so. Sometimes I wonder if it was necessary. Maybe he wasn't ready to go. I miss him so much sometimes."

"A person can only do what seems right at the time," Phil said.

Jay changed the subject."If it bothers you to have me here, I'll leave. I don't like to have people doing things for me. It makes me feel guilty because I can't repay them." He took Phil's empty cup to the kitchen. "I paddle my own canoe and I'll take my lumps if necessary."

"You'll have to get over that. Life in the city can be tough. You'll find that you need all the friends you can get."

"I've made a lot of friends here. They invite me to their parties and we hang out together at the mall. It's quite exciting." Jay said.

"Friends or merely convenient buddies?"

"It's all the same to me."

"Some day you'll get into a tough corner and then you'll find out if you have any real friends."

"I'll cross that bridge when I come to it," Jay retorted. "Did I tell you about the social I went to last weekend? I made a lot of new friends, but I never did get to meet the engaged couple it was for."

"A lot of them high on drugs?" Phil asked.

"Not me, if that's what you are getting at. Probably a lot of them were. There was talk about a drug called 'ecstasy' or something."

"If you aren't familiar with drugs, you'd better be careful. There are a lot of things out there that can be bad for you."

"Like what?"

"Well, heroin, for one."

"You don't need to worry about that. I know better than to go sticking needles in my arm."

"Did you know that there's heroin around in capsule form? Quite a few inexperienced kids are overdosing on them without even knowing what they are taking."

"I don't do drugs. Never have and never will. I like being in control of myself."

"And of other people, too?" Phil gave Jay a knowing look.

"I don't like to control other people, if that's what you mean. But I hate to have anything controlling me. There's a difference."

"You need to look out for your girlfriends and make sure that they never leave their drinks unattended. It would be easy for someone to slip a drug into her drink."

"You mean something like an 'ap road eh siac'?" Jay asked.

"A what?" asked Phil.

"You know. Something to make her horny."

"Oh, you mean an aphrodisiac."

"Well yes, I guess so. I know a lot of words from reading that I've never heard anyone say. I had to pronounce them the way they looked. People still make fun of me from the time I pronounced the 'c' in scimitar. Is that what you are talking about?"

"Worse than that. There are drugs like Rohypnol and GHB that can be slipped into a drink to knock a girl out and wipe out her memory of the events after she takes it. They're called date–rape drugs. You can guess why."

"Can't they taste them?"

"Not unless they are looking out for something unusual. It's kind of salty. Tell your girlfriends that if they go to a guy's place and he's serving Goldschalger, then they'd better get out of there. That's one of the favourite liquors to hide the taste."

"If the stuff is so bad, why is it sold?" Jay asked.

"It's not legal in Canada or the US. It finds its way here from Mexico because it's legal for treating anxiety and insomnia. The manufacturers are planning to add blue dye so that it will be more obvious."

Jay continued, "There was talk about some fag that got bashed. He ended up in the hospital with a brain concussion. I think they said he got hit with a telephone book or something."

"It was probably a baseball bat. They put a telephone book up against the guy's head and then hit the book with a bat. That way it doesn't leave outward signs of damage so it's harder to prove assault."

"You'd think that those guys would learn to stay out of other people's faces. They must know that if they keep asking for it they will get it sooner or later."

"I assume you're not talking about my friends, like Steve?" Phil asked through tight lips.

"No. Of course not. They're your friends. I mean those guys that swagger around the Mall making noise and showing off. Sometimes I think I'd like to smash my fist in their grinning faces myself so they'd go away."

"You sound…"

"What, homophobic?" Jay interrupted. "No. I am not afraid of homos. But I don't want them around me, either."

"Check your dictionary, Jay. Homophobic means to have an irrational aversion to gays, and that is exactly what you have."

"Then they should call it 'homoaversive'. I don't fear or hate them or anyone else. But I don't like having to look at them. They should all be rounded up and sent to some far away island so they can be with their own kind. Like England did when they shipped their dangerous convicts to Australia on a one–way ticket."

"Maybe send them to New York City?" Phil asked.

"Or maybe build a great wall around the whole San Francisco area with them on the inside."

"You may not be homophobic but you certainly do sound intolerant."

"It's just that I don't approve of immorality. Check your Bible. Leviticus condemns all that homosexual stuff," Jay said.

"It also condemns lots of heterosexual stuff that most of us do. It also condemns things like rounding off the hair on your temples or trimming the edges of your beard, or wearing clothes made of a linen and woolen mixture, or planting different types of crops together. You don't expect people to follow those instructions do you?"

"Now I know why you have that bushy beard," Jay said. "I try to live a good and moral life. The Bible condemns homosexuality and so do I. So that makes me moral, not intolerant."

"You aren't basing your life on the teachings of the Bible. You're taking the parts of the Bible with which you agree and using them to make yourself feel noble. What if the Bible said that you should be homosexual, would you change?"

"Maybe. You never know."

"Oh sure. That's a bet I'd take."

"I see your point, but I don't want to think about it. Besides, I don't see how that gives you the right to call me intolerant."

"It's fine to live your own life in whatever way you consider to be moral, but when you try to dictate how others should live their lives, then that's being intolerant. Gays don't tell you how to live your life or try to convince you to be like them; they don't want you to condemn them for the way they live theirs."

Jay headed for the door. "I have things to do and places to go. I'll see you later."

As Jay walked past the A & W kiosk in the Portage Plaza Mall, the aroma of hamburgers and French fries enticed him momentarily, but he chose to sit on a bench by the fountain. Letting the gentle rumble of the sixteen little fountain jets soothe his soul, he closed his eyes and imagined himself lying on the bank of the quietly gurgling stream back home with the sun beating down on his bare chest and the plaintive cry of a loon in his ears. Soon, the centre jet gathered its energy and spewed a plume of water fifty feet straight up like a domesticated geyser, bathing the tropical plants in a gentle mist before cascading back into the basin with a thunderous roar.

After a few minutes of reverie, Jay ambled down the mall, wandering into stores to admire the goods and fantasize that he was going to purchase them. *That Gucci watch would look good on me, and it is only $595,* Jay thought. *Maybe I'll win a lottery this week.*

Jay stayed on the lower mall level, avoiding the second level where Steve worked. His thoughts about Steve were a mixture of gratitude for the gift of clothes, distaste for Steve's lifestyle and guilt for avoiding talking to Steve. Jay was not prepared to deal with this combination of feelings.

At the east end of the mall, a courtyard served as an informal meeting place. Small groups of people sat on the marble steps chatting while the huge clock with its intricate gears, chains and hammers chimed away the quarter hours.

Jay paused briefly and then continued on to the food court. *Two o'clock,* he thought to himself. *Perfect timing to meet up with some of my buddies and find out what is happening.*

He bought an order of French fries and chose a table in the smoking section. *I wish my friends didn't all smoke. It's such a disgusting habit, but I guess I have to put up with it if I want to sit with them.*

"What's up, Jay?" asked the pallid-faced youngster wearing a faded Metallica T-shirt, diligently tattered jeans, and sandals. He slung his jean jacket over one chair while his girlfriend took the one across from him.

"Becky, say hi to my buddy, Jay."

"I thought you'd be working, Jimmy," Jay said.

Jimmy's dirty-blonde ponytail attempted to control his hair which was shoulder-length as compensation for his scraggly attempt at a beard. Jimmy fancied himself to be a modern-day Robin Hood, with himself being the poor who needed the wealth of the rich. Unfortunately for Jimmy, he lacked the concentration necessary to be successful at his chosen occupation. There always seemed to be such interesting things to distract him in the houses he entered. One time the owners of a house returned home to find Jimmy engrossed in the television which they had inadvertently left on. When they entered by the front door he roused himself enough to get out the back door before they got a good look at him. Another time he wasn't so lucky because the police found him sorting through a CD collection deciding which ones he wanted to steal. He got six months that time. His skill at springing locks or finding windows that would pry open meant that he never had to break anything to gain entry. He always told his legal-aid lawyers that he wasn't guilty of 'breaking and entering', only entering, but they never seemed to think that would make a good defence.

"Got fired. Again. It was a lousy job," Jimmy replied, letting the words slide out around the cigarette dangling loosely from the corner of his mouth. His left eye squinted to keep out the smoke and his other slate-blue eye stared vacantly into space.

"He didn't deserve to be fired, but it's happening to a lot of people these days. Most companies are only hiring part-time help so they don't have to pay them benefits and can fire them whenever they want," Becky said.

"That's too bad. Maybe you could work with Tony. After all, you were the one who lined me up with him. I appreciate that you did that for me," Jay said.

"I'm still on parole. Tony wouldn't hire me now because I'm a bad risk. Nobody wants to hire an ex–con. That's why I got fired. Somebody must have found out that I have a record."

"Do you have any job ideas for Jimmy or for me?" Jay asked. "I certainly could use some more regular work."

"You'd want a job that would let you party all night and sleep all day," Becky teased.

Becky released her hair from the clip that had been pulling it back so that it fell around her face and shoulders. She adjusted her glasses and applied a careful layer of cherry–flavoured Lypsyl to her thin lips.

"You have to realize that not all hours are created equal," Jay said. "Early morning minutes are much more precious than the ones late at night, so I don't like to waste them by getting up. Who knows? Maybe I'd get to like working regular hours."

"Sure. That's why people who are, you know, like ninety years old, are more impatient with delays and don't like to wait for things to happen. It's because for them a minute is a larger percentage of their remaining life than it is for us," Jimmy said.

Becky turned to Jimmy. "You know, sometimes you almost make sense. Maybe your brain isn't as scrambled as it seems."

"Thanks, I guess. It's something that I was told once and it kind of stuck in my head. By the way, did you know that reality is for people who can't handle drugs?"

Becky continued, "You had any interviews or anything, Jay? I know some people you could..."

"If you know people, then get me a job. I'm your boyfriend," Jimmy interjected.

"I'm trying to be friendly to Jay. You know the same people I do. If you would get off your drugs and go talk to them you might find something," she replied.

"Am I in time for a fight?" a girl's voice asked.

"Hi Tiffany," Becky said. "Come and join us. I think I'm outnumbered by unemployed males and could use some female support."

"It didn't seem that I'd ever get here. I can't seem to get the hang of one–way streets," Tiffany said.

"I never get the hang of Thursdays," Jimmy said.

"You try to go around one block and end up having to go around four of them just to get back where you started."

"Mondays are a total wipeout because I'm usually hungover, which makes Tuesday the first day of the week and cheap movie night. Fridays I can get into because they're a fill–in–time before the weekend."

"Jimmy, what are you babbling about?"

Jimmy continued, "Wednesdays are the middle of the week, and that's cool because then it's all downhill to the weekend. But Thursdays don't fit in anywhere. I never know what to do with Thursdays."

"Are those new shoes, Tiff?" Becky asked, steering the conversation away from Jimmy.

Tiffany looked out of place in the fast–food court. Her flawless grooming was more suited to an expensive restaurant. Her clothes were from Stylite but she made them look like Saks Fifth Avenue.

"Why yes. You like them?"

"They're gorgeous, but they must have cost a fortune. Where do you get money for the stuff you're always buying?" asked Becky.

"I have a system. I get two credit cards and make the minimum monthly payment on one card by getting a cash advance from the other one."

"As if I could ever get even one credit card with my nonexistent credit rating. Besides, aren't you going to eventually max out both cards?"

"That's when I run crying to daddy. He's always a sucker for his poor little girl's tears and her promises to do better next time," Tiffany answered with a self–satisfied grin.

"You're living at home now?" asked Becky.

"I'm usually at home. Cynthia moved out to live with her boyfriend."

"Is Cynthia your sister?" asked Jimmy.

"No, she's my mother."

"You call your mother by her first name?"

"She prefers to be called that ever since she started out on this infernal quest to find herself. I stay at home with Mr. Mudge."

Jimmy looked confused. "You call your dad, 'mister'?"

"No, silly. Mr. Mudge is our dog," Tiffany said. "I'll probably be staying with Richard tonight."

"Richard is your dad, then?" asked Jimmy, his brow furrowed from his concentration in following the story.

"No, he's my boyfriend. Maybe I should draw you a diagram."

"Jimmy, either focus on the conversation or get out of it," Becky said.

Jimmy shifted his attention to Jay. "You got any spare cash? I need some for food."

"Sure. I owe you for setting me up with Tony. What do you need?" Jay replied.

"Whatever you can spare."

Jay slipped a couple of folded bills into Jimmy's hand under the table.

"Did any of you catch that talk show where they had a lady who remembered a previous existence under hypnosis?" Becky asked.

"She must have been on acid. You remember lots of things when you're high on acid," Jimmy said.

"It was so weird," Becky continued. "The girl knew all about a place in Ireland a hundred years ago, and she'd never even been to Ireland. I wonder if people can be reincarnated like that."

"Maybe it's something like a child prodigy. You know, like a five–year–old kid who seems to be born knowing how to play the piano and compose music," Tiffany said.

"Yeah. Like Mozart," Becky said.

"Maybe they're a reincarnation of some previous person and they somehow have all the knowledge from that person's life available to them right from when they are born," Tiffany continued.

"Maybe we are all reincarnations but most of us can't tap into our previous lives," Jay suggested.

"Any of you want to go to a psychic reading?" asked Tiffany.

"Has that got anything to do with getting a job?" asked Jimmy.

"Maybe nothing, maybe something. I know this intense girl who does psychic stuff like Tarot cards. She even contacts the spirit world sometimes."

"You mean like with the Ouija Board? I used to play with one sometimes." Jimmy said.

"Not with that. She says that's an instrument of the devil. It's controlled by evil spirits that were never alive, so they will misguide you. It's not a safe toy."

"Can she predict the future?" asked Jimmy. "I'd like to know when I'm going to find a job."

"Are you sure you'd want to know?" asked Tiffany. "What if she said that you would never get a job and that you were going to slowly starve to death? Would you want to know that?"

"Or what if you were going to be hit by a bus next week? I wouldn't want to know something like that," added Jay.

"I don't believe in that sort of thing," Becky said. "It's nothing but smoke and mirrors and made up stuff."

"Maybe it is, but she's an interesting person, and I try to keep my mind open about things I don't understand," countered Tiffany. "She showed me how to make a crystal ball out of a plain, round–bottomed glass tumbler. You fill it with water and put it on a soft piece of black cloth. If you practice looking into it, you'll soon see images."

"That's all there is to it?"

"Some quiet background music helps you to concentrate."

"So I am seeing things in the ball. How am I to know what they mean?" Jay asked.

"That's why we need to have a session with a medium. She can teach us how to interpret these things if we are willing to learn. Six or eight people make a good psychic circle. Who wants in on the seance?"

"I'll try anything if it might help me get a job. Count me in," Jimmy said. "I need all the help I can get if I'm ever going to have my life together. Or even have a life, for that matter. If I don't get some money coming in soon, I'll have to go back to living with my parents," said Jimmy. "They'll take me back but I'd have to give up my freedom and promise to follow their rules."

"Is that a crack at those of us who live with our parents?" Tiffany asked. "Except for you, most of my friends live with their parents."

"And Jay. But then he might as well be with his parents. Phil looks after him like a mother hen."

"More like an uncle," Jay said with a serious look.

"Not much difference…"

"A lot of difference. He doesn't boss me around."

"…as far as I can see," said Becky, completing her sentence.

"How about you for the seance, Jay?" asked Tiffany

"Sure, I'll be there if I can work it into my busy social calendar," Jay replied with a grin. He suddenly stood up and excused himself, "There's someone I have to see."

He went across the room and sat opposite a well–dressed, slightly overweight, middle–age gentleman sitting by himself with his back to the wall. After a brief discussion Jay received a small package and left the mall with a wave to his friends.

GUESS WHO'S COMING TO DINNER

"Morning, Jay," Phil said, going into the kitchen. "You have plans for supper tonight?"

"You know I never make plans. I take life as it comes. Did you have something in mind?"

"I've invited a few friends over to help celebrate the July 1st holiday. It would be nice if you could be here." Phil said setting out a plate of crepes and tofu bacon.

"Would that include Steve and his fag friends? You know that guy gives me the creeps. I don't want to be here if he's coming. I don't want anything to do with him."

"Steve did ask specifically about you, and I said you'd be here. You do owe him for the clothes he gave you."

"You have no business saying what I will do, or where I will be, or what I should do. And I never asked him for his stupid clothes. I don't owe him anything," Jay barked. "Didn't we agree that you weren't going to mother me to death?"

"Maybe so, but you're living here and eating my food and I haven't seen any money for rent or groceries or anything so far. It wouldn't hurt you to be nice to my friends. And I do wish you'd stop calling them fags. I hate that term."

"He makes me feel uncomfortable. I hate being around him."

"Oh come on now, Jay. You've seen him only twice. I don't ask much of you. I'd consider it a favour to me if you'd be here. And try to be civil to him," Phil requested.

"No, I'm not doing it. I'm out of here. Why don't you make like the birds?"

"Like the birds?"

"Yes. Flock off and leave me alone." Jay stormed out the door, down the stairs and onto the sidewalk. He took several long deep breaths of the fresh summer air and thought to himself, *That wasn't smart of me. If I don't go back to Phil's I have nowhere to go…except, of course, Steve's. But he's the one I'm trying to avoid so that wouldn't make much sense. Talk about the frying pan into the fire. I guess I'll have to go back and face Phil.*

The stairs back to the apartment seemed steeper and longer than before. *I hope he's not mad at me, but I deserve it if he is. He's been good to me and here I am acting like a spoiled teenager.* Halfway up the stairs his resolve gave out. He stopped, turned, and started back down. After three steps down, he turned again and continued back up to the apartment.

"I'll be here for dinner if it's that important to you," Jay acquiesced. "And you're right about the clothes. I should thank him for them even if I can't stand the guy. They are great clothes. I even get compliments about them from the girls, although I expect they are more impressed by what they see in them than with the clothes themselves," Jay said with the exaggerated confidence of youth.

"It's up to you. Do what you like. But remember that you're free to move out of here anytime you want. I don't need you and your grouchy attitude around here to make my life miserable," Phil said.

"I'm sorry. I do like staying here. Would you like me to stick around and help you get the food ready for tonight?"

"As if you had any clues about cooking," Phil said in a friendlier tone. "I could use some help if you don't mind. We haven't had much time together since you moved in. This would be a good chance for us to get to know each other better."

"Good. But I have to go out for about an hour this afternoon to do some business. I have people that depend on me, you know. But I'll be back by three o'clock to give you a hand. So long as you tell me what to do, because you're right, I've never done any cooking."

"That should be fun then. But I thought you didn't like people telling you what to do," Phil teased.

"Just this once," Jay responded. *And you had better not be thinking of making a habit of it,* he thought to himself.

"Before you go would you give me a hand to fold up the sofa and hide your bedding and stuff away in the closet? We'll need as much room as we can get for our guests."

"What about your spare room?" Jay asked.

"What spare room?"

"There must be a room behind that blue door, isn't there?"

Phil scowled. "That door is locked and it stays that way. There is nothing there that concerns you. Please don't mention it again."

Jay let himself back into the apartment at half–past three thinking, *I never did thank Phil for getting me a key to the door. I should do that.*

"Hey, Phil. I'm back, and I brought you a present. Hope you like them. I thought they might look nice on our dinner table." Jay talked a bit too fast and a bit too loudly because of his embarrassment at being late. He handed Phil an arrangement of silk flowers in bright, spring colours.

"They're a little thank–you for giving me my own key. That meant a lot to me because it makes me feel like I belong here." He thought, *I might as well get as much mileage out of them as I can.*

"Thanks, Jay. They're beautiful, but you didn't need to do that. You can't afford that sort of thing. Where did you get them anyway?"

"I bought them. What do you think, that I stole them?" *They wouldn't fit under my jacket,* Jay said to himself, *or I wouldn't have had to pay for them.* "There are lots of ways of getting money," Jay said in his most indignant tone.

"Don't be so touchy. I don't mean to pry into your personal life, but if you are short of cash I can always lend you a few bucks."

"I'm doing adequately well for myself. You don't need to worry about me," Jay said confidently.

The white linen table cloth was set for six with long thin stainless steel cutlery and tall, thin elegant wine glasses. Jay put the flowers on the table as a centre piece. *Not bad, if I do say so myself,* he said to himself. "What do you think, Phil? They look elegant, don't you think?"

"Great. Nice, Jay. Thanks," Phil replied. He set a pair of black candles in silver holders on the table at either side of the flowers.

"I thought about getting you real flowers, but I was afraid that it might upset you that they would have to die," Jay said. He braced himself for Phil's reaction.

"Fresh flowers are always nice, but these will last forever. I'll think of you and your ugly face whenever I look at them."

Jay smiled. "What's the menu for tonight? Beans, vegetables and tofu?"

"Not exactly, but I'm always careful to arrange a good combination of foods."

"I don't get it. What's the big deal about combining foods? So long as they taste good, who cares?" Jay asked.

"Vegetable sources provide different partial proteins that your body can combine together to make a complete protein like you get from eggs or meat. If there isn't a complementary partial protein available then some of the value is lost. For example, my Lima Bean Peanut Loaf combines beans and nuts which complement each other to provide a complete protein. It would be even better to use a cereal like millet or barley with beans but it's hard to work them into a tasty recipe. I always try to have nuts, seeds or a cereal together with the beans."

"You mean seeds like in birdseed?" Jay asked half–facetiously.

"I guess you could if you wanted to, but I expect most people would prefer something like sunflower seeds or sesame seeds. If I weren't using peanuts in my bean loaf, I'd use nuts in the appetizers or desert or somewhere in my next meal. You want to try your hand at making the appetizers? Follow the recipe and ask if you need help." Phil mixed the mashed lima bean with the other ingredients before pouring the mixture into a cake pan which would serve as a mold for baking.

Jay and Phil were soon engrossed in the preparation of the meal. Phil explained the importance of providing alternate sources of iron, zinc and vitamin B12 that are low in most vegetables, and the importance of folic acid in the diet. "A good rule of thumb is to make sure you select lots of dark green, bright orange or yellow produce. You do that, you'll have everything that you need."

"I think I'd rather reach for a good chunk of steak or a few fried eggs."

"Suit yourself. It's your life. But don't expect me to be an accomplice to your heart attack."

"What made you decide to become a vegetarian?" asked Jay.

"A couple of years ago, I became aware of the importance of life...not only for people and animals but for our planet itself. People are destroying the planet, you know."

Oh great, here we go again, thought Jay. *Why is it that I don't seem to know anything when I talk to this guy? He makes me feel as if I'm from the backwoods.* "Yes, I know. It sure is terrible." Jay hoped that his confidence would fool Phil, but of course it didn't.

While they prepared the meal Phil carried on a monologue about the environment, sustainable development, the ozone layer and other things about which Jay had been completely unaware. *Is this for real?* Jay wondered. *The world looks all right to me. Maybe Phil is going off the deep end again.*

"This is nice to have someone working alongside me again. It makes me realize how lonely I've been lately," Phil said.

"You used to have a roommate?"

Phil ignored the question and carried on with his discussion of life and the environment while they finished preparations for the meal.

"Phil, so nice to see you again," said Steve. He threw his arms around Phil for a big hug. Then Steve held him at arms length and scrutinized his face carefully. "You're looking good," he asserted. "And Jay, how are you?" he asked looking over Phil's shoulder toward Jay.

Oh no, he is going to hug me, too, Jay thought as Steve headed toward him. There was no escape and Jay braced himself mentally and physically for the unavoidable hug. Steve put his arms around Jay and pulled him close, their chests pressing firmly together. Jay concentrated on making sure that his face and crotch area were well out of range of any possible contact with Steve. *What do I do with my arms?* he wondered. *It feels so stupid to have them hanging by my side.* Jay put his arms around Steve and gave him a tentative little pat on the back. *Good grief, I feel like I'm burping a baby,* he thought to himself. *How long is this supposed to last anyway, I wonder?*

After what seemed an eternity to Jay, Steve held him at arm's length. "Nice to see you again, Jay. How's life treating you?"

"Fine. Good to see you, too," Jay mumbled, escaping to the relative safety of a chair.

Steve moved off to look at the table.

Cam bypassed the welcoming preliminaries except for a nod in the general direction of Phil and Jay.

A bottle of wine, with Jay serving, and the plate of appetizers assisted the idle conversation of the three friends while they awaited the arrival of the other guests. Jay took an active role in the discussions, and in the wine drinking, without letting the fact that he didn't have experiences in common with the others, or much new information on anything for that matter, restrict him. Jay was surprised to notice that the affectations of voice, gesture and clothing which had been so evident with Steve and Cam when he first met them were totally absent now.

"Feel free to have some soda water, Jay," Phil said.

"Is that a subtle hint that I'm drinking too much?" Jay asked.

"Take it as you will."

Steve changed the topic. "You'd never guess. I won two tickets to San Francisco for being the company's top salesperson last year. I'm taking some vacation time as soon as the weather turns cold and heading for sunny California."

"What a wild idea. I'd give anything to go to San Francisco," Jay said.

"You'd have to get some new clothes. Those look like they were hand–me–downs from an older brother," Steve retorted with a grin.

"If that's all it takes, I'll buy some tomorrow. I have money, you know," said Jay.

"Yeah sure. Wasn't that you I saw sitting on the sidewalk outside Portage Plaza with a tin cup yesterday?" taunted Steve.

Jay made a sour face in Steve's general direction.

"Seriously, Jay, what is it that you're doing for money," asked Cam.

"I'm doing well. I make deliveries for a fellow I met through a friend of mine. He gives me packages that I deliver to people and bring the money back to him. He pays well to get fast service and to make sure that the packages don't get lost. I make a few deliveries every day at twenty bucks a shot. And it only takes me a few hours. No hassles and no questions."

Steve, Cam and Phil exchanged speculative looks with each other.

"A bit unusual isn't that?" Cam suggested.

"You think that's unusual? The other day in a washroom downtown some old guy asked me if I wanted to make twenty bucks. I said, 'I have to see the money first'. When he held up the twenty–dollar bill to show me I grabbed it and ran out of the washroom without even finding out what he wanted. I figured there was nothing he could do to me even if he caught me, except maybe try to take the money back. Besides I was sure I could outrun him easily. I guess you could say I ripped him off."

"He was going to rip you off anyway, Jay," Steve said. "A prime quality young guy like you would be worth at least fifty bucks for whatever he had in mind."

"If anybody wants to give me money, I'll take it," Jay said.

The doorbell interrupted any further discussion. Phil opened the door and a statuesque girl floated into the room on stiletto–heeled shoes. A toss of her head caused a tidal–wave of silky blonde hair to engulf her shoulders. Her face and nails looked as if she had spent the whole afternoon in a beauty parlour. She carried her twenty–two years with the poise and assurance of a person accustomed to always getting exactly what she wanted, and to getting it when she wanted it. The modest neckline of her blue dress struggled to hide the fact that she would look stunning in an evening gown. "Good evening, everyone," she purred to the room in general.

"Hi, Tiffany," Cam, Steve and Phil said in unison.

Jay's mouth dropped open in surprise. "Tiffany. Is that you? I certainly wasn't expecting you. How do you know these guys?" he said.

"Tiffany went to school with me. We've been friends for years. But how do you two know each other?" Phil asked looking at Tiffany and Jay.

"We hang out at the mall," Jay said, giving her a big hug. "You look absolutely ravishing," he added with sincere appreciation.

Close behind Tiffany, a younger girl with short brunette hair sported an impish grin. She wore no makeup and dressed for comfort in flat–soled shoes and a casual sweater and skirt.

"Sue. I'd like you to meet Jay. He has been staying with me for the past while," said Phil.

"Hello, Jay. What's a nice guy like you doing hanging out with these reprobates?" Sue asked with a smile that lit up her whole face and made her eyes twinkle.

"And whom might you be calling reprobates?" asked Cam. "I doubt that there be any of us here who even know what that means."

"I know. It means a person with low morals, like a villain," Jay said, eager to show off. "And I don't think that is a nice word to use for my friends," he added with mock indignation. "At worst they might be scoundrels," he added.

"Sorry, guys. I didn't mean anything by it. It's my new word for today. I thought it would be kind of nifty that nobody would know what it meant. I guess I'll have to be careful around Jay."

"Wherever did you learn words like that, Jay?" asked Steve.

"I may be a hayseed from the sticks, but I am not stupid. I happen to be a very erudite and literate person. I usually don't like to show off." He paused for a moment and then added, "I must confess, it comes from studying the Reader's Digest Word Power. We had a whole pile of old copies at home that someone had left. I memorized them frontwards and backwards. That, the Bible and the first volume of the World Book, were my main reading materials."

They sat down to the meal. Phil bowed his head. "Good Mother Earth, we thank you for this food that you have provided for our enjoyment and sustenance. Help us to learn how to maintain the health of this planet so that our descendants may also share in your bounty. Heavenly Father, we thank you for the good friends gathered here and for our friends who are not here with us today. Teach us to live in peace and harmony with all of your people and to accept them as they are, and help them to accept us. Amen."

"Jay, would you fill the wine glasses, please? And I'll have another soda water, if you don't mind," Phil asked.

The meal progressed through a lentil soup, the peanut lima bean loaf in the shape of a star, and assorted vegetable dishes, washed down with copious quantities of dry white French wine.

"The bean loaf is delicious. Would it be peanuts that are in it?" asked Cam.

"That's to complete the protein of the lima beans," said Jay, showing off his newfound knowledge. "You can get as good protein from beans and grains as from meat, but you have to combine them with nuts to get the most protein with the smallest number of calories."

"Well, and aren't you getting to be the vegetarian expert," Cam responded to Jay.

"How long have you been here, Jay?" Sue asked.

"I flew in two weeks ago Tuesday," Jay said with a smile.

"You flew?" asked Steve.

"You bet. On a Grey Goose," Jay said with a laugh.

"So you're a comedian as well," Sue said. "What brings you to the big city?"

"I'm here to find my father."

"He lives in Winnipeg?" Cam asked.

"I don't know. I've never met him. At least not that I remember."

"Have you tried looking on the Internet?"

"Would that work?" Jay asked.

"It might."

Tiffany looked over to Phil. "Did you call this 'mincemeat' pie?" she asked. "It's good, but I thought you didn't eat meat."

"Well, it's made from green tomatoes and apples instead of meat and suet, but you'd never know the difference would you? Except that this is a lot better for you than the real thing."

"A great meal it was, Phil. Have you the recipes for these things somewhere? I'd like to try them again sometime," said Cam.

"I thought somebody might ask, so I put all the recipes in the back of this book, for people like you."

After the meal the guests moved back to the sofa and chairs for more wine and conversation. Phil and Jay set about to clear the table.

"Keep the angels separate from the rest," Phil said.

"Sure thing," Jay replied scooping up a handful of silverware.

"Hang on, Jay. What did I say?" asked Phil.

"I don't know. I wasn't listening."

"I said to keep the angels separate."

"I thought you were joking. What do you mean?"

"I mean keep the unused dishes and cutlery separate from the used ones. That way we don't have to waste effort washing things that are clean."

"Why didn't you say so, instead of babbling about angels?"

"That's what the grandmother of one of my friends used to call them."

"Oh. That is kind of a cute expression, although I think I'd call them 'orphans' because their relatives get to go into the dishwasher and they're left out."

"And I suppose if you found a dirty knife when you were setting the table you'd call it a 'devil'?" Phil asked.

"Makes sense to me."

Jay and Phil joined the others. Phil offered brandy but it was declined by everyone except Jay.

"Sorry we have to leave so soon, but we have a big day tomorrow. Mom and I are going shopping," said Sue. She and Tiffany waved their informal goodbye and thanks for the dinner while they collected themselves to leave.

"It was nice meeting you, Sue. Maybe we could get together again sometime," suggested Jay, his words slightly slurred from the wine and brandy.

"I'd like that. Give me a call. Phil has my number. In your condition I doubt that you'd be able to remember it," Sue replied, tossing Jay a big smile from the hallway.

After the door had closed behind the girls, Steve folded one leg under himself on the chair, rested his chin on the back of his hand and leaned forward with the intent look of a person about to divulge the secrets of the universe. "Well, now that the fish have gone, we can get down to some serious gossip."

"Fish?" Jay asked. "Do you mean that they are gay?"

"Gracious, no. Those fish are straight swimmers. But they get their kicks from hanging around with gays at the clubs. We call them 'fag hags'," Steve said.

"Gays call all females 'fish'. Maybe because of their lips, but I wouldn't be knowing about that," added Cam.

Phil, Steve and Cam launched into gossip about their mutual friends.

"Did you hear what Chris was saying about Bev at the bar last night? She's got a male friend. Maybe she's not a lesbian after all."

"Oh, she's a lesbo all right. She's only going with the guy because he takes her to expensive clubs."

"Besides, he's probably gay, too."

"And Cole is going out with Chris. As if that will ever last! They are both so vain they hardly even notice when they are with someone else."

"They're the veritable S and M queens of the bar."

Jay tried to get into the conversation, "You mean they do sado–masochistic stuff?"

"No, silly. When they are in the bar they 'stand and model'. It's so ridiculous that it's funny."

Jay poured himself another brandy.

"You and Cam used to live together, didn't you?" Jay suddenly asked Steve. "I guess that means that you were lovers? Do you still have sex with each other sometimes?" The unaccustomed intake of wine and brandy had not only loosened Jay's tongue, it had also turned off what limited common sense and caution he normally exhibited.

Steve and Cam both looked at Jay and then at each other before they broke out laughing.

"You really are crazy. We have no interest in each other that way," said Cam.

"We aren't attracted to each other sexually," declared Steve.

"Never have been," confirmed Cam.

"And, never will be," added Steve, determined to get in the last word.

"You guys are putting me on. You were both living together. So you must have been having sex with each other. That's what gay guys do. They have sex with each other." Jay struggled to gain some understanding of the situation through a dense alcohol–induced fog in his brain.

"Gays make a distinction between love and sex. I can love someone, male or female, without it having anything to do with sex. And I can have sex without it having anything to do with love," Steve said.

"But that's because you're a gay," Jay said.

"Not really. Prostitution is quite popular with happily married men, you know. There is something rather appealing about anonymous sex for a lot of people. There are no expectations for commitment, or even conversation as far as that goes."

"Some people use the terms 'gay' and 'homosexual' as meaning different things. Gay is the romantic, emotional feeling of being in love; homosexual is, well, you know, the sexual part," Steve said. "Gay ministers in particular have to make this distinction to accommodate the prejudices of their congregation."

"The sexual part is what I don't know anything about," Jay said. "I can't imagine how that would work. And I certainly don't want to even think about it."

"The terms 'straight' and 'heterosexual' don't mean the same thing either. You can love a girl without being sexually involved with her," said Cam.

"Oh sure, if she were my mother or my sister. Otherwise, forget that. I know you guys are lying to me, and trying to confuse me, but I'm not buying it. Every gay guy is out to seduce every other male he can find. Gays can't have children of their own so they have to recruit young straight guys by seducing them. Everybody knows that."

"People are born gay, not recruited. Do you think that you could be seduced into being gay?"

"Not me. But then, I'm enthusiastically heterosexual. There must be a lot of guys who are kind of on the fence, so as to speak. They could be seduced."

"And so all we have to do is convince them to switch sides?"

"That's the way I see it, and I know I'm right. Don't try to kid me. I may be a country boy, but I know what you people are like."

"You do realize that it's insulting when you refer to gays as, 'you people' don't you," Phil said.

"It would be insulting to me if someone called me a gay," Jay retorted.

"No. I mean that when you refer to 'those people' or to a person who is gay as, 'a gay' you are forcing a stereotype on them and making them a part of a depersonalized group. Steve isn't 'a gay' he's a person who happens to be gay. There's a difference."

Jay lapsed into what would have been a thoughtful silence if any two of his brain cells could have managed to get into focus together at the same time on the same topic.

Cam and Steve awaited the arrival of the cab.

"We should get together sometime, Jay. We'll play Scrabble or something. You like words, so you'd be good at it," Cam suggested.

"Sure. Why not? I don't know the game, but if it has to do with words I can probably figure it out."

Steve asked Jay, "Why don't you come with us now? You could stay at my place tonight and maybe pick out some more clothes, and then we'd go to Cam's tomorrow."

"Oh no. You are not getting me alone. You think that because I've had a bit to drink I would be an easy target for you. Well you had better forget about that idea. I'm staying here with my Uncle Phil. He and I are buddies." Jay went over and put his arm around Phil's neck. "We are like the two musketeers. We look after each other, right Phil?"

Phil gently disengaged himself from Jay's arm and went to see his guests out. When he returned, Jay had taken off his shirt and opened out the bed.

"That's a nasty bruise on your arm," Phil said.

"It's nothing. It was an accident."

"I've seen a lot of bruises in my day. A big fist did that. Or maybe a stout piece of two–by–four."

"It was an accident. Ray was just fooling around. He didn't mean to hit me."

Phil went over for a closer look. "Are those welts on your back?" he asked.

"Leave me alone. It's none of your business."

Phil took Jay by the shoulders and turned him around for a better look. "You'd better have something on that before it gets infected. I have some salve that's good for that sort of thing."

Phil gently rubbed the salve on Jay's back. His face was blank but his eyes flashed with anger. "Who's this Ray guy who did this to you?"

"Please don't be mad, Phil. I deserved it."

"Nobody deserves to be beaten."

"I shouldn't have made him angry."

"There's no excuse for what he did."

"I argued with him when he was drunk. My mom told me never to do that, but I wouldn't listen."

"This wasn't the only time, was it? You've got scars here, too."

"I'm stupid. I never learn. Please don't be mad at me. I'll try not to be bad."

"You have to realize that it wasn't your fault, Jay."

"Of course it was. He didn't want to hurt me. I made him do it. If it hadn't been for me it would never have happened."

"We'll talk in the morning."

Phil helped fold down the sofa and got blankets out of the closet.

Jay lay down and said to himself, *Now if this room would only settle down and stop spinning I would like to get to sleep before I get seasick. I wonder what's in that spare room, anyway?*

LET THE GAMES BEGIN

"How's the back this morning?" Phil asked.

"It's fine. You make too big a deal out of things. I don't want to talk about it," Jay replied.

"You've never told me about your family."

"There's not much to tell. I have a brother fourteen and a sister twelve. I'm going to move them and my mom here when I get established and can afford an apartment like this great place you have."

"Does Ray beat them, too?"

"Hang on there, Phil. Ray's a nice guy. He doesn't beat anybody. Sometimes when he's drunk I try to get away with stuff that I shouldn't and he has to keep me in line. It says in Proverbs 23 not to withhold discipline from a child. If you beat him with a rod, he will not die; you will save him from hell. Ray just does what the Bible requires."

"You can quote chapter and verse?"

"He always quoted the Bible so that I would understand why he had to discipline me. The rest of the family knows how to behave, but I don't. He loves me enough to take the time to teach me how to behave. I appreciate that."

"Has he always done this to you?"

Jay ignored the question. "He's only been with us for a couple of years, but they've been good years. He loves us and helps us out all the time. The guy before him always shouted at us and took our food away. I didn't like him."

"You've had a lot of men in the house?"

"Five that I can remember. Joe was the best. I was only a little tyke and don't remember much about him except that he was always affectionate with me. I'd wake up at night sometimes and find him there, lying beside me. He'd be gone by morning. I don't remember anything else."

"What about your real dad?"

"My mom never mentions him. I've asked, but she says I'm better off not knowing. All I know is that they called him Nobby McNabb. That, and 609561826."

"A number?"

"It was scratched on the wall, like what someone would do to make sure he didn't forget it. I memorized it for something to do. My mom got angry when I asked about it and she scraped it off the wall. I think it had something to do with my father. Maybe he was a criminal, and that was his prison number."

"Not likely. But it could be a clue."

During the weeks following the dinner party Sue and Jay were inseparable. Sue was quickly accepted by Becky and Jimmy as one of the mall gang. When they weren't together, they were chatting on the telephone.

"Why don't you come with me to Cam's place tonight?" Jay asked Sue, shifting the receiver to his other ear. "He said we'd play Scrabble or something. That would be more fun with more people."

"If he wanted me there then he would have invited me. It's obvious you are the one he wants to be with," Sue replied.

"That's what I'm afraid of. I'd feel uncomfortable being alone there with him."

"And why would that be?"

"Oh you know. I'm not like that."

"Like what?" Sue teased.

"Never mind. Just say that you'll come with me. Otherwise, I'm not going."

"Don't be like that. I expect that he'll have some other friends over. And besides, Jamie will be there," Sue said.

Oh sure. And Jamie would be another gay faggot, no doubt, Jay thought. "That settles it. You've got to come with me."

"If you're going to be such a baby about it, I guess I'll come to hold your hand. You go ahead and I'll meet you there."

Jay checked the apartment number and rang the buzzer. The door opened and Jay found himself looking into a boyish face with clear blue eyes, short, straight brown hair and firmly defined features. The loose blouse, worn over slacks, didn't manage to conceal several months of pregnancy.

"Oh. Excuse me," Jay stammered. "I must have the wrong apartment."

"I don't think so. You're Jay, aren't you? We're expecting you."

"You know who I am?" Jay asked.

"Cam said you were cute. I'm Jamie."

"Oh. I was expecting a…" Jay faltered mid-sentence. "…Cam," he ended lamely.

"He'll be back soon. He got held up at the office."

"Some sort of accounting emergency?" Jay asked.

"In a way, yes. He had to work overtime to finish financial statements for a client's presentation tomorrow morning. For an accountant that's about as close as you get to a real emergency. Their emergencies are mostly in their own minds, but they're real enough to them. Come on in."

"Sue should be here soon," Jay said standing awkwardly in the entrance way.

"Oh good. I was hoping you might invite her. Now we'll have a foursome. Do you play bridge?"

"About as well as I play any other games. I'm more a man of action than a player."

"Cam said you're good with words. Have you ever played Boggle?"

"The only game I've ever played is poker. Even that's been mostly as a spectator sport while my mother and her friends played. I'd play the odd hand to fill in when someone had to go outside to the bathroom."

"Sit and tell me about yourself. How do you like Winnipeg?"

"It's exciting. People have been so good to me. I feel like I've lived here all my life."

"Phil's a real sweetie–pie."

"He's been kind to me, but I don't feel that I understand him. He scares me sometimes."

"He's always been a bit of a puzzle to me, too."

"Have you known him long?"

"Since I met Cam a few years ago."

"You and Cam have been living together long, then?"

"A couple of years."

"That must mean that you and Cam are…" Jay said.

"We're POSSLQ's."

"You are what?"

"Persons of the opposite sex sharing living quarters."

"So you are sharing the apartment and not actually living together?"

"I'm not sure what you're asking."

"How does it work that you're pregnant and Cam is…"

The door opened and Cam finished the sentence for Jay, "Cam is home, and here be Sue that I found skulking about outside. Let the games begin."

"Let's play something that doesn't take too much thought," Jamie said. "That way we can talk and get to know each other better."

"I'm having a beer. Who will be having a drink?" Cam asked.

"I'd like a tall cool something," Sue said.

"Me too," added Jay.

"How about a Long Island Iced Tea?"

Jay frowned. "What's Steve been telling you about me?"

"Nothing. You wouldn't be having a guilty conscience about something, would you?" Cam asked with a grin.

"Get the drinks, Cam, and leave Jay alone," Jamie said.

The foursome settled down to a game of Monopoly.

Jay summoned his nerve to ask, "I don't mean to be rude, but could someone explain to me how this POSSLQ thing fits together? I thought that Cam and Steve used to live together. Would that make them PSSSLQ?"

"Don't be silly. You can't pronounce that," Jamie laughed.

"Seriously, Jay," Cam said, "I lived with Steve for several years when he was in the closet."

"By in the closet you mean…"

"Not telling the world that he is gay. When Steve came out, I thought it best to live somewhere else so people wouldn't assume that I was gay."

"Why didn't you admit that you were gay?" Jay asked.

"Even if I were, I wouldn't risk getting thrown out by my family the way Steve was. That's not something I'd be willing to risk. He lost a lot of his friends, too. It's a big decision to come out because you stand to lose those who are most important to you."

"So then you moved here?" Jay asked.

"Jamie was living here and she kindly took me in."

"It wasn't kindness. I needed help with the rent," Jamie said.

"A year later when Jamie got pregnant, we decided to keep the baby. We both love kids."

"So wouldn't the father help look after the baby?" Jay asked.

Cam replied, "Of course I will."

"You mean that you are the father?"

"I thought that's what we said. Maybe you didn't hear us because you don't think a gay guy can be a father?"

"OK. Now you've got me confused. Cam, are you gay or straight?"

"Maybe I'm both."

"You mean you're unisexual?"

"I think you are meaning bisexual," Cam said. "I guess there's only one way you could be finding that out for sure." Cam grinned at Jay.

"Let's get back to the game," Jay said. He looked at the board for a moment. Then a look of horror swept over his face as he realized the implication of Cam's remark.

"Relax, Jay," Cam said. "I'm heterosexual, although I can't imagine how that would ever make any difference to you."

"But you looked so gay the other night at Phil's."

"I love the gay lifestyle. It's so full of frivolous, outrageous clothes and parties. And the people are so friendly and sensitive to each other. Except, of course, when they are cutting each other down or bitching about something."

"So you're pretending to be gay?" Jay asked.

"It's more than that. I consider myself to be gay, but I'm not homosexual. For some people the two don't go together."

"You'll have to explain that one for me," Jay said.

"You know how the graphic equalizers on a stereo mix different amounts of bass and treble frequencies to produce the quality of the final sound. In every person there are three components: the body, the spirit and the soul. The body and spirit each can be tuned separately to anywhere on a continuum between highly male and highly female, determining the sexual quality of the person's soul."

"How's that again?"

"A person's physical appearance, sexual actions and mannerisms can vary anywhere between macho and effeminate. That's his body."

"And his spirit is?"

"His spirit is what he does for recreation, work, and of course, love. What is male or female is determined by society's perception."

"That leaves his soul."

"Which is the inner, eternal essence of the person. It is what he feels himself to be. It's the combination of body and spirit."

"Give me an example," Jay said.

"In my case, my body is heterosexual but my spirit is gay."

"And your soul?"

"That would be at the mid–mark, I guess. Except when I'm out with Steve, of course. What about you?"

"All switches set to full male. And firmly locked in position," Jay proclaimed. "Why do you hang out in gay bars, anyway?"

"Think of the gay community as my tribe. It gives me a sense of security and of belonging and feeds my soul."

"Sort of like belonging to a gang or club?"

"Except that membership isn't restricted and there are no rules. Before I joined the gay community, I felt isolated. A person never feels so alone as when he is surrounded by a crowd of people who don't understand him. The gay community provides me with a ready–made supply of friends. I travel a lot, but anywhere I am I have instant friends just by going to a gay bar."

"To change the topic, Steve says you're a computer expert," Jay said.

"Compared to him, I guess I am," Cam replied. "You want me to show you a few things?"

"Sure. It'll give the girls a chance to talk about us."

Cam sat Jay in front of the computer. "Click the left button on that icon and it'll connect you to the Internet. It's a great source of information."

"Can it find my father?"

"We could check the telephone directories. What's his name?"

"Nobby McNabb."

"We should start with a search of a geographical area. I don't suppose you know where he lives."

"Try Minnedosa. The bus to the north goes through there."

The screen displayed the names and addresses of fourteen McNabbs.

"How about Manitoba?"

After a couple of minutes they discovered that there were seventy–seven people named McNabb living in Manitoba.

"It doesn't show any called Nobby," Jay said.

"I don't suppose Nobby is his real name. Probably a nickname. You know nothing else about him?" Cam asked.

"The number 609561826. But I don't have any idea what it means."

"I don't suppose you'd want to try to contact all seventy–seven people. Besides you don't even know if he's one of the ones in Manitoba."

"Maybe I should forget about it. But I would like to know what he's like. It would be kind looking through a window into my future. I'd see what I'll be like when I get older."

It was after midnight when Sue and Jay parked in front of Phil's place. An hour slid by unnoticed while they enjoyed each others company discussing the evening and their hopes for a future together. Their lingering goodnight kiss promised more than the circumstances of the moment allowed.

Jay had been asleep for a couple of hours when he was roused by the same heavy, sweetish, pungent odor that he had noticed when he first arrived at Phil's apartment. He still couldn't identify it, but it felt comforting and friendly and somehow reassuring. Opening his eyes slightly, he noticed Phil sitting in the recliner. It had been turned from its usual position facing the TV to face Jay on the folded–down sofa. The room was dark and the TV silent. Jay couldn't see clearly in the dim light, but he had the spooky feeling of being closely observed.

"What are you looking at?" he asked softly so as not to wake Phil if he were indeed asleep.

There was no response.

"Are you awake?" he asked loudly.

Still no response.

Jay rolled off the sofa and walked noiselessly over to stand directly in front of the chair. Phil's open eyes stared blankly into space.

"Hello?" ventured Jay waving his hand in front of Phil's face.

"Yeah, I'm here. I was thinking." Phil's voice was more mellow than usual and somehow seemed far away.

"Have you been sitting there looking at me?" Jay said more as an accusation than a question.

"I guess so, yeah."

"So what is the big idea? Why doesn't anybody around here leave me alone? Is that so difficult? I don't ask much, just that people stay out of my life."

Phil was silent as if he had not heard Jay. Then he answered as if from a great distance, "Sorry. Sometimes you remind me of my nephew who used to live with me. I was thinking about him, not about you."

"So you do have a nephew that you looked after. Does that mean that the story you made up for Steve was partly true, then?"

Phil was quiet again for long time before he got up. "Let me show you something. Maybe that will help you to understand."

He went to the dark blue door and unlocked it. He flipped on the light and stood back so that Jay could look in.

The room was fully furnished. A waterbed was made–up ready for use. The top of the dresser was neatly arranged with a comb, hair brush and a bottle of men's cologne. Photos, cards and newspaper clippings were haphazardly stuck between the glass and the frame of the mirror. Hockey, baseball and football heros caught in frozen action looked out from blown–up photos and posters on the walls.

The closet was full of clothes, the hangers uniformly spaced. Shoes, mostly sports wear, were lined up as if for inspection along the floor of the closet.

Against the wall a small table draped with a plain white cloth was bathed in a soft blue light. On the table three photographs formed a backdrop for the items lying on the table in front of them: a wallet, a gold school ring, a sheet of loose–leaf paper with a hand–printed poem, and an incense burner. A wisp of smoke rose listlessly from the incense burner.

"Somebody lives here?" Jay asked.

"No. Not anymore."

"May I go in?" Jay asked, feeling shy and subdued.

Phil nodded his permission.

Jay walked slowly into the room and stood humbly in front of the table feeling as if he were in church in front of the altar. In one photo he recognized Phil, his arm around a handsome blond lad a few years older than Jay as they displayed their fishing trophies. A second photo showed the same boy in a formal high school graduation portrait.

The third photo showed people standing around a patchwork quilt composed of eight individual three–foot by six–foot panels of cloth sewn together. It focused on one panel showing sporting scene with a fishing rod forming an arched rainbow over the words of a poem and the word, 'Scotty' underneath. Jay tried to read the writing but the photo was too small. In the background thousands more quilts were spread out with walkways between them.

He leaned over and read the shaky, hand–printed words on the paper:

DEATH BY DIVISION

Like a cuckoo's egg
in a robin's nest,
The invader hid as one among millions,
Stealing shelter and nourishment, unnoticed.
Biding its time
Waiting to strike.

A receptive disciple
and a swift conversion,
Now there were two, then four, then eight—
Increasing in galloping geometric progression.
A covert army collecting its power.

One by one
but thousands at a time,
Each converted cell saps my remaining strength,
Until there is none left and my body dies.
But it is only my body
Not my Soul.

As if on a cue from some unseen director, he and Phil backed out of the room. Phil closed the door and locked it. Silently they returned to their earlier positions in the livingroom.

Finally Phil said quietly, "I've never shown that to anyone before."

"Not even Steve?"

"Nobody"

"I don't understand. What's it about, anyway?" Jay asked.

"It's my way of remembering someone that meant a lot to me."

"Scotty?"

"Yes. My nephew. We were always friends, but during the time he lived with me we became close."

"You mean like best buddies?"

"More than that. We were soul mates. It was with Scotty that I first understood the meaning of the Shoshone nation's word, 'shundahai'."

"Which is?"

"There's no word in English for it. It's the feeling you get when you are hugged by someone who loves you unconditionally. It opens your soul to join with the other person's soul. A child may get that feeling when hugged by its father. For most people it will be experienced only rarely because adult relationships are usually conditional on behavior."

"I never knew my father, so I guess I've never experienced it. I've never been hugged much."

"Let me tell you a little story about Scotty that might help you to understand. We were having an argument one day and I was beginning to lose my temper with him. He said, 'I don't want you to be mad at me' and he put his arms around me and he hugged me. The frustration and anger completely drained out of me as if a tap had been opened. He's the only person I've ever known who could do that to me."

"You and Scotty were in love then?"

"Yes, we loved each other. But in a totally non–sexual way. It's strange that the English language handles the concept of love so poorly. In English when people have sex we sometimes say that they are making love or that they are sleeping together. So we have three ways to say, 'having sex', and one of those ways uses our only word for love. The Greeks did better than that. At least they recognized that there needed to be three separate words to describe different kinds of love."

"So you loved each other, but you weren't in love with each other?"

"See what the English language does? It makes a person sound like a babbling idiot. The wealth of vocabulary that a language assigns to something reflects the importance that the society puts on it. The Inuit have thirty–one words to describe various kinds of snow because it is such an integral part of their life and survival. I guess our society doesn't care much about love."

"Tell me more about Scotty," Jay said.

"Maybe another day. It's time for sleep now."

LIFE AS UNUSUAL

In the morning neither Jay nor Phil mentioned the events of the previous night. They were finishing their noon–hour breakfast when the telephone rang.

"Why do you get me into these things?" Jay asked Sue over the telephone.

"I've never been to a rave but I think it would be fun," Sue said, shifting the receiver to her other ear. "I told Becky that we'd go with them on Saturday. You know I don't go anywhere without you."

"You know that I don't like parties. They make me feel uncomfortable because I never know what to say to people and I never know what to wear."

"A rave isn't like a party. I promise. I'm not supposed to say anything, but they want to surprise us with a little anniversary celebration before we go."

"Anniversary of what?"

"It's the first month anniversary of our officially going steady. And they said it wouldn't last."

Jay looked confused. "Was I supposed to get you something?"

"Of course not. Besides, it doesn't count as a gift if you have to ask about it first."

"What if I say I'm not going to get you anything and then I do. Does that count? It would be a surprise then."

"Not if I know that's why you said you weren't getting one."

"So, you plan that we'll drop in on them and then go to the rave later?" Jay asked, escaping from the discussion.

"Sure. I don't have any other plans."

"What is a rave, anyway? I've never been to one, Sue."

"All my girlfriends go to them. I'd like to see what they are all raving about, if you'll pardon the pun."

"Why not go to a night club?" Jay asked.

"Night clubs only play only the top–40 music. The best place for something like Trance or House or Techno, is to go to a rave. They do all the great underground music. I'm looking forward to hearing some great hip–hop."

"And what sort of weird stuff would hip–hop be?" Jay asked.

"It's kind of an inner–city electronic rap."

"That sounds harmless enough, although I haven't any idea what it means."

"You have to get fixed up in something unusual."

"Like a costume party?"

"Not exactly. You don't dress up like someone or something else. It's more like you go as your alter ego," Sue explained.

"I barely have any ego of my own let alone an alter one. Give me a hint, what would I wear?"

"Oh, I don't know. Change your hair color, or spike it, or wear makeup or glitter. You know, something unusual. Let it all hang out."

"Hello. This is me. Jay. I don't do hair color or glitter or makeup. I don't have a clue what you are talking about."

"The whole idea of a rave is that you try to look unique and maybe make a statement. Wear something unusual. You know, torn clothes, shiny pants, platform shoes, something like that."

"How about if I go like a normal human being. Wouldn't that make me stand out from that crowd as being unusual?"

"I don't think that's the idea. You must know somebody that can help you out with an outlandish image."

"Oh sure. I guess I'll have to call on my good old buddy, Steve. He always seems to have solutions for problems I didn't know I had. Boy, I hate that guy."

"Great. We should be at Becky's around seven so we can have a bite to eat and a few drinks before we go to the rave."

"You want me to pick you up?"

"With what? The Winnipeg transit? Or do you mean, will I pick you up?"

"Don't be like that. It's not funny. I meant that I could come to your place and then we'd drive over together in your car. It would be easier for me to meet you at Becky's place, but I'll come to pick you up if you want me to."

"I'm sorry. I didn't mean to put you down for not having a car."

"That's all right. So which will it be?"

"My parents are dying to meet you. They always want to meet my friends. I think that they're afraid somebody's going to try to marry me for my money."

"Now that you mention it, that's not a bad idea," Jay said.

"You mean to meet my parents or to marry me for my money?"

"To meet your parents, of course. Money doesn't mean anything to me."

"That's because you don't have any," Sue teased.

"I've got more than enough. And soon I'll have a lot more. I'm getting a lot more work lately and I'm being given a lot more responsibility."

"You never did tell me where you work. You seem to be making a lot for a glorified delivery boy. I never know what I should tell Dad."

"I'm not a delivery boy. I'm an independent entrepreneur in retail sales."

"Whatever that means. I gotta go. Are you meeting me here or at Becky's?"

"Better we meet at Becky's. I can always meet your parents another time."

"See you there then. Around seven. Don't eat before you go," Sue suggested.

"When you get there will you wait for me in the car, please? I've never been to their place and I hate embarrassing myself. I don't want a rerun of the Cam and Jamie fiasco."

"You're such a wimp sometimes."

Sue pulled her Mustang over to the curb. The dashboard clock showed 6:58. She turned on the radio and settled in to wait for Jay. Almost immediately a black Lexus pulled up directly behind her and an apparition cloaked in a shiny black, skin–tight jumpsuit got out the passenger side and slid into Sue's car.

"Good grief," Sue exclaimed. "Is that you, Jay?" She tried to discern the features that were partially obscured by huge triangles of white makeup around his eyes. The eyes were rimmed with bright–blue eye shadow.

"Do I look all right?" Jay asked. "Steve said this would be great, but he wouldn't let me look in a mirror. If he's made me look like an idiot, I'll kill him. What I know for sure is that this latex body–suit is way too hot."

"You mean sexy hot or temperature hot?"

"Very funny. I mean that I feel like I'm wearing a rubber glove."

"But it is so form fitting. You'll have the girls wild over you. I'm insanely jealous already."

"Is that what you are wearing?" Jay asked. "You make me look more than a bit overdressed."

"I didn't realize that you were going to be that excessive. Come on, let's go in and see what the others are wearing."

"Wait a minute. I have something for you." Jay handed Sue a small green box, professionally store–wrapped with a silver ribbon and bow.

"You shouldn't have, but I do love presents." Sue took the heart–shaped gold locket out of the box. "What's inside?" she asked, examining it carefully before opening it.

Jay looked at it in surprise. "I didn't know it opened," he blurted out. "I bought it as a pretty pendant."

"It's adorable, and I love it. I'll love it even more when you give me a picture to put in it."

"You mean a picture of me? I don't have a picture."

"Well, we'll have to get one so that I can have you around my neck always." Sue leaned over and gave Jay a lingering kiss.

"Why don't we skip the rave and go somewhere private?" Jay asked.

"Don't be silly. They're expecting us. Come on, let's go in."

Jay went around the car and opened the door for Sue. "Here, take my arm."

"My, aren't you being the real little gentleman tonight?"

"Gentleman nothing. I don't want to fall over. I'm not used to walking in shoes with two inch thick soles. How do I get myself into these situations, anyway?"

Jimmy, Becky and Sue sat looking at Jay.

"Why are you staring at me? Steve said that this is what I should wear to a rave," Jay said.

"It's probably what he would have worn a few years ago when he was into the rave scene, but I'm not sure that it's the real you," Sue suggested. "Or anyone else either, for that matter."

"I kind of like it," Becky said. "It makes a perfect outfit. Running shoes with two inch soles and sequins, blue glitter sprinkled in your hair to match the eye shadow, and that latex jumpsuit which must have cost at least four hundred bucks."

"Don't listen to Sue. She's never been to a rave. You'll be a smash," said Jimmy.

"Oh great. That's what I've always wanted to be. A smash," replied Jay sarcastically. "What about the rest of you. You're not going looking like you are now, are you?"

"We were going to," Becky replied, "but now you've shamed us into a bit more effort. We can do some face makeup and maybe switch to some tattered jeans or something. Jimmy, you look fine the way you are with your tattered jeans and torn T–shirt that shows off all those muscles you wish you had. Sue, you come with me. Let's have a look in Jimmy's closet. He must have something that would look weird on you."

"Excuse me. Should I take that as an insult?" asked Sue. She and Becky headed toward the bedroom.

Jimmy handed Jay another beer and sat on the sofa. He sank into the soft cushions that were no longer getting much support from the tired springs. "I hate to ask this, Jay, but can you let me have a hundred bucks for the rave tickets? Becky thinks I have the cash, but I'm a bit short."

"You're already into me for more than twice that much now. When will I get it back?" Jay asked.

"As soon as I get a job. I promise."

Jay reached into his jumpsuit, fumbled around inside and pulled out his wallet. "Why don't you let me pay?"

"I don't want Becky to know. We're supposed to be treating you guys. The tickets are twenty bucks each, so if you could spare a hundred that would cover the tickets and still leave me a few bucks for the week until I get my welfare cheque."

The rave was noisily underway when they arrived at the warehouse a little after midnight. The penetrating electronic music, revolving colored spotlights, strobe lights and the gyrating dancers near the makeshift stage generated a wild energy and abandon reminiscent of an Indian war dance. The only thing missing was a bonfire.

"Stick close to me," Sue said to Jay hanging onto his arm. "If we get separated, I'll never find you again."

"At least you have the keys to the car, so you don't have to worry about getting stranded in this madhouse."

Sue and Jay worked their way through the crowd around the doorway and moved off toward one wall. Oversized pillows and foam pads provided comfort for small groups who were totally engrossed in massaging themselves and each other.

"What's that all about?" Sue asked.

"I assume that's a rhetorical question," Jay responded. "I'm new here, remember?"

"That's the E–toy section," a white–faced phantom dressed in a black, tattered dress volunteered as she made her way past them and toward the dance area.

Thanks. That helps a lot, Jay thought to himself sarcastically. *And is that supposed to explain why they are using Vicks inhalers? Maybe it's the area for people with colds and stuffed–up noses.*

Jay looked around the room. Several people shared bottles of water to offset the dehydrating effects of the heat and the frenzied dancing.

"Come on, let's dance," Sue said, dragging Jay toward the center of the floor.

"There's something you don't know about me."

"There are probably a lot of things I don't know about you."

"I mean, that I don't know how to dance. I've never been to a dance before."

"This isn't a dance. It's more like an experience."

"Everybody seems to know what they are doing but how do I know what to do?" Jay asked.

"Can you feel the throbbing beat of the music? Just close your eyes and let it carry you along."

Jay let his body sway. His arms began to move in synch with the electronic rhythms.

"Don't think, just do. Let yourself go," Sue urged.

"So it's like a sort of Zen experience thing."

"Sometimes you scare me, Jay."

"If you expect me to do gymnastic things like those guys over there, forget it."

"They're break–dancing. You don't have to be fancy like that, just enjoy yourself."

Sue and Jay alternately danced and luxuriated in the uninhibited intimacy of the crowd. Jay had unzipped his jumpsuit to below the navel in the hope that some air circulation would give respite from the heat.

"Good grief. You're looking more like Steve all the time. We'd better go home soon or you'll be stripped down to your shorts," Sue said.

"Good idea."

"I hope you mean leaving and not stripping."

"I'll see if I can find the others," Jay said.

Sue and her three friends left as dawn was breaking. "Let's stop for a cup of coffee," she suggested, pulling into a Robin's Donut parking lot.

"Go ahead, I'll stay here," Jimmy mumbled, slouching in the corner of the back seat.

"Can we get you anything?" Becky asked, but received no response.

"Is Jimmy all right?" Sue asked as they sipped their coffee.

"I guess he's tired from his trip," Becky said.

"What trip?" Jay asked.

"He's been dropping acid again. Didn't you see him sucking on that little square of paper? It's no wonder that he never has any money and no ambition to get a job."

"I didn't see anybody using drugs," Jay said. "Was it only Jimmy?"

"Most of the drug use isn't obvious, but you can always recognize the people on 'ecstasy'. They go around enjoying physical sensations. If you see somebody caressing a piece of wood or rubbing a piece of cloth as if it were the most sensuous thing in the world, then you can bet that they are on ecstasy. There's usually an area set aside for their toys - the things that stimulate their physical sensations. They also get off on massage."

"I saw that area. But what about the Vicks inhalers?" Jay asked. "That isn't a drug, is it?"

"It enhances the effects of ecstasy. If I had money I'd buy shares in the Vicks company." Becky mused.

"Were the three of us the only ones not using drugs?" Sue asked.

"The kids don't. You know, the ones between twelve and sixteen. They usually don't do drugs. With the older crowd the drugs, music and excitement kind of go together to make a total experience. I've been hoping that Jimmy was getting away from the drugs. I guess it's tough to keep away from drugs when Winnipeg grows more marijuana than anywhere else in North America, with the possible exception of Vancouver. It's one of our major exports to the U.S., and it isn't even covered under the Free Trade agreement."

"In this climate?" asked Jay.

"They grow it indoors hydroponically. The cops find millions of dollars worth every year, but there's tons they never find," Becky explained. "I had hoped he'd stay clean tonight because I knew he was out of cash and I thought he had run out of people stupid enough to give him money."

Jay looked downcast. "That would be me. I thought I was being helpful."

"It's not your fault that you acted as an enabler," Becky said.

"What's an enabler?"

"Somebody that makes it possible for a person to continue a bad habit. They don't mean to encourage the behavior, but they make it possible for the addict to continue. A lot of wives unconsciously act as enablers for their alcoholic or abusive spouse by providing justification for the actions."

"If I hadn't given Jimmy money, he wouldn't have been able to buy drugs. That makes it my fault. I'm sorry."

"You meant well. Besides, Jimmy's the one that took the drugs. He's the one who's responsibility for his actions, not you."

"So why don't you dump him?" Sue asked. "You don't need that kind of nonsense."

"Of course I don't, but he needs me. How can I leave him when he's down and out like this? It could destroy him, and I don't want that on my conscience. He needs all the support he can get. Besides, he's such a sweet guy when things are going right for him."

"What's it like to be on acid? I hear that you get weird hallucinations," Jay asked.

"Some people do. Jimmy says that it makes him feel good and enhances the mood of something like the rave. He doesn't even believe people when they tell him about their 'trips'. Myself, I think it's a cheap, dirty high," Becky explained.

"Dirty?" asked Jay.

"Yes. He says it gives him gut rot. It leaves his whole body feeling dirty and disgusting. He's usually sick and depressed for days after a trip. He says that it isn't the acid that makes him feel lousy. It's the strychnine from the rat poison in it."

"Why would they put rat poison in with the drug if it is going to make people sick?" Sue asked.

"They probably don't. It's likely an urban myth," Becky said.

"We'd better go and get Jimmy into bed to sleep off whatever he put into his system," Jay suggested.

Back at the car Becky tried to rouse Jimmy. "Wake up. Are you all right?"

Jimmy's eyes opened and he muttered though motionless lips, "I can't move. I think I'm dead."

"What's the matter?" Jay asked.

"He's having some kind of reaction to the drugs. We'd better get him home, Sue."

"Shouldn't we get him to the hospital?" Sue asked.

"They wouldn't be able to help him. This isn't the first time this has happened. He just needs time for that junk to work its way out of his system," Becky said. "I'll look after him."

"If you're sure," Sue said. "I still think we should get him to a doctor. This scares me."

"So long as he's conscious he's all right. If he passes out then we'll get him to a doctor."

They carried Jimmy to his bed. Jay said, "He's got to get better. I'd never forgive myself if something happened to him because of me. He's one of my best friends."

"He'll be better in a day or two," Becky said.

"I want to stay here and be with him," Jay said.

"There's nothing you can do. You might as well go home," Becky said.

"I can be here for him. He'll know that I'm here and that I care about him. I won't let him die."

"Would you like me to stay, too?" Sue asked.

"Please. That would mean a lot to me," Jay said. "I always feel better having you around."

By mid–afternoon the next day Jimmy was talking better and able to move his fingers. Sue dropped Jay off at home on her way home. Phil was sitting in front of the TV.

"Big night?" Phil asked.

"Yeah. Raves go on forever, you know. Even for two or three days sometimes. You didn't wait up for me, did you?"

"In a way I did, but it's no big deal. I have a surprise for you. You remember before you left we were talking about…" Phil started to ask.

"Sure. Fags. That's all we ever seem to talk about."

"No. I meant about it being inconvenient having you sleep on the sofa."

Jay furrowed his brow. "You're going to ask me to leave, aren't you. I knew it. You're angry about what I said about your gay friends."

"Come here. I'll show you." Phil opened the blue door.

Jay looked in. The table which had held mementos of Scott was gone. All evidence that this had once been Scott's room was gone. Even the pictures and posters had been removed from the walls.

"This is your room now, Jay."

"You mean I get to use the whole room? Just for me?" Jay asked in surprise. Phil nodded. Jay went over and stood beside the bed. He looked over at Phil. "I don't know how to say this, but did Scott...?" Jay said hesitantly.

"Yes, he slept here. Is that a problem?"

"I know that. But did he...uh... you know."

"He didn't die here, if that's what's bothering you. When he knew his time had run out he asked one last favor of me. A few of his closest friends and I took him to a hotel room. He died peacefully there of a drug overdose."

"You could have been charged with murder, couldn't you?"

"We didn't think about that at the time. As it turned out I used to work with some of the guys on the police force who dealt with the case. They treated it as an accidental overdose."

"That must have been hard on you."

"It was, but it was what he wanted. Friends do what they have to do for each other."

"It's so hard to know what's the right thing sometimes," Jay said.

"He died as he had lived. Surrounded by his friends, and without pain."

They sat for a moment of silent thought.

"I've never known anybody who died. I couldn't stay in the same room where someone died. Not even in the same house. Death scares me," Jay said.

"You should realize that it is only the person's body that dies. The soul doesn't die, and that's the real person. The body is nothing but a convenient place for the soul to spend this lifetime. Scott's soul lives on with me and with all the people he met."

Jay went over and lay down on the bed. With a contented little gurgle the water in the bed moved over to make room for him. Jay rocked from side to side and front to back, enjoying the floating sensation.

"This is the greatest, Phil," Jay said.

"It didn't make sense for me to keep the room empty, particularly with you taking up so much space in the living room. But it's still only a temporary arrangement until you get your own life."

"This is the nicest thing anyone has ever done for me," Jay said wiping his eyes. "I wish there were some way that I could repay you."

"Don't try to repay me. Do something nice for someone else some day. That's what would make me happy, because it produces good karma," Phil said.

Jay retired to the privacy of his own room early that night. His ever present demons did not bring a nightmare this night.

A HAIR OF THE DOG

As the days passed, Phil and Jay developed a relaxed relationship. "Coffee?" Phil's voice slowly worked its way into the leaden mass that was Jay's brain. "It's half past two in the afternoon."

Jay's eyes tried to focus on Phil, standing over him with a mug of coffee. He tried to sit up, but a sharp pain that went from the left side of his head to the other and back again convinced him to lie back.

"Set it down. I don't feel well," Jay said.

"You're hungover. You must have tied one on last night."

"We were celebrating something, and everyone was drinking Wild Turkey Bourbon. I should have stuck with beer."

"Maybe the coffee will help."

Phil set down the mug of coffee and went to the kitchen to finish making some whole wheat toast for breakfast. "I'll make you some toast, too. A bit of food might help settle your stomach."

Bracing himself for the head pain and nausea he had come to expect from movement, Jay sat upright and sipped a bit of coffee. He gently eased himself to his feet and made his way to the kitchen.

"You don't have a drink around here, do you?" Jay asked.

"Didn't you have enough last night?"

"My mother always said that having another drink would cure a hangover. You know, a hair of the dog that bit you."

"In your case wouldn't that be a feather of the turkey that pecked you?"

"Don't be funny."

"Either way it sounds more like a sure way to becoming a drunkard," Phil said. "Let me make you something."

Phil separated the slimy, yellow egg yolk into a glass, added a shot of Worcestershire Sauce, a dash Tabasco Sauce and sprinkled it with salt and pepper.

He handed the glass to Jay and said, "Here. Don't look at it, just toss it down."

Jay tossed the egg down his throat. "Ugh. That's awful. What was it?"

"A Prairie Oyster."

"You don't mean the ...you know...the things of a male cow?"

"That would be a bull, I think."

"Whatever. Nuts are nuts. You're vegetarian. You wouldn't feed me that. Would you?"

"No. This was the other kind of Prairie Oyster. It's an egg thing that cures hangovers."

"Thank goodness for that. It tasted awful, but my head's beginning to feel a bit better."

"I have to go out today. I'm picking up my motorcycle in Minnedosa," Phil said.

"You didn't tell me you had a bike. What's it doing there?"

"It broke down on my way back from Edmonton. That's why I had to take a bus here, remember? The guy phoned to say he finally got the parts for it. It's a great old bike but sometimes takes forever to get it fixed."

"So you'll be riding it back? I've never ridden a motorcycle."

"You're welcome to come, if you think that you are up to it."

"Why would I want to do that?"

"For fun. Besides the guy who's fixing my bike is named McNabb. Maybe he could help you find your dad."

"Not likely."

"It's a long shot, but you have to start somewhere. Your dad probably took the bus through there to go north."

"Give me time for a hot shower and a change of clothes and I'll be right with you," Jay said.

"Wear long pants and a long–sleeved shirt. The wind can be hard on bare skin if you're not used to it. I've got an extra helmet. We'll have to catch the 3:30 bus so we need to be out of here in half an hour."

They arrived at the bus depot with five minutes to spare. Jay was surprised to see how much smaller the depot looked now, compared to what it had seemed a few weeks earlier.

When the boarding call for Edmonton was announced, Phil started toward the bus area.

"We're not going to Edmonton, are we?" Jay asked.

"No, but they only announce the main cities at the end of the line. You're expected to know which route goes through the town you want. If you were going home, you'd get on the bus headed to Thompson or maybe Flin Flon to make sure you would be headed in the right general direction."

Jay and Phil found a pair of seats near the back of the bus and settled in for the two and a half hour ride. Jay wedged his head between the seat back and the window and dozed off.

"Wake up," Phil said, nudging Jay awake. "This is where we get off." The two travellers stumbled off the bus and made their way to the garage.

"It's after six," Jay said. "They'll be closed."

"I phoned and he said he'd stay open for me at least until six–thirty."

As promised, Phil got his motorcycle. He paid his bill and climbed onto the seat. "Hop on behind," he said to Jay. "You can put your arms around me to hang on if it makes you feel safer, but it rides best if you let your arms hang down and relax. Don't try to balance the machine by leaning. I'll do that. Don't you try to do anything except relax and hang loose back there."

With a roar the Harley took off. Jay's arms firmly hugged Phil from behind.

Oh my goodness. What have I got myself into this time? Jay wondered. He couldn't keep from leaning in reaction to the bike's movement, causing an erratic, weaving path down the street.

"Stop trying to balance. Trust me. We won't tip over," Phil shouted over his shoulder.

After about four blocks of travel Phil wheeled into a parking spot in front of the Paradise Restaurant. "We need to eat. Then we'll give it another try," Phil said.

"Great. I need a few minutes to get myself together. Are we going to travel like that all the way back to Winnipeg in the dark?" Jay asked. His head sent him strong negative messages about the wisdom of being vertical, let alone being mobile on two roaring wheels.

"It's up to you, but maybe we should spend the night here and head out in the morning," Phil suggested.

"I'd prefer to travel in the morning when we can enjoy the scenery." *And maybe by then my head will have stopped throbbing and I won't feel so much like throwing up,* Jay said to himself.

"Suits me. Let's get a room first and then eat." They wheeled back down the street to the Minnedosa Hotel.

After registering, they made their way to the hotel dining room that also served as a general purpose bar. Phil scanned the menu with a frown.

A waitress in a plain blue dress, soiled apron, and hairnet, stood in bored silence, her pad and pencil poised for action.

"A burger and fries would suit me fine," Jay said. "And a beer," he added.

"There's nothing vegetarian on this menu," complained Phil. "Could I get a grilled cheese sandwich, some French fries and maybe some coleslaw?" he asked the waitress.

"I'll check. Anything to drink?"

"Coffee, please," Phil responded.

They had started in on their meal when Jay suddenly looked up. "Oh no. I had three deliveries to make this afternoon. I totally forgot. Tony will kill me."

"We could be back by noon tomorrow if we leave early in the morning. Maybe you could phone Tony?" Phil suggested.

"That'll be too late. It's too late already. Those guys need their delivery on time and I am already six hours late. I'm in big trouble."

"It's drugs, isn't it? You're either a mule or a runner for Tony."

"Of course not. That would be illegal." Jay finished his second beer and ordered another. His face furrowed in thought. After a few minutes he said, "Yes. I might as well admit it. I'm a mule. Maybe more like a stupid donkey for getting into this mess. Why did I ever let myself get sucked into this? You have any suggestions, Phil?"

"We might as well get a good night's sleep and head out early tomorrow. It might help to phone Tony and tell him the situation."

"No, forget that. I've been thinking that I should get out of this business anyway. If I don't show up, he'll get someone else, or deliver them himself. But he'll be steamed at me. It's better if I never see him again. Besides, I don't know his phone number. I doubt that it's listed in the Yellow Pages under drug dealers."

"Won't he come looking for you?"

"I was clever enough not to give him my real name or tell him where I live. So he's out of luck. There is no way he can find me. And if he did find me there is nothing he could do about it. I don't owe him anything."

Jay ordered another beer.

"You can't escape that easily, Jay. People are responsible for what they do. Their actions always have consequences," Phil said.

"Not for me they don't. What is he going to do, sue me? I have nothing of value," Jay said. "Anyway, he couldn't find me even if he tried."

"It's your life. Do what you want with it. But I think you should quit with the beer. I don't want you throwing up on my shoulder."

"Darn. I promised to take Sue to go to the movies tonight. She's going to be mad at me, too."

"She's a nice girl. She'll forgive you. You two have become a real item."

"Oh yeah. I'm desperately in love. I think she loves me, too."

"She's a great girl. You'd be good for each other."

"I'm going to call her and apologize. I'll tell her it's your fault. You kidnapped me."

Jay went to the pay phone.

Phil went up the squeaky stairs to their room. The hallway exuded a smell of stale cigarette smoke and spilt beer. Inside the room a double bed, a sink and a dresser with a tiny TV sitting on it awaited their temporary new owners. A water–stained landscape picture hung crookedly on the wall surrounded by peeling wallpaper. The window looked out into the back lane. A toilet and shower were down the hall.

"Oh my," said Jay. "This is antiquated."

"Isn't it? This room must be at least a hundred years old. It's funny, though. Hotel rooms don't have any history. They have a present while people are in them but when the people leave there is nothing left behind to make up a past."

They went in and Jay looked around. "Where is your bed, Phil?"

"We'll have to share," replied Phil.

"We cannot do that. We need another bed."

"That's fine with me," said Phil, "but I'm not paying for two rooms. You got the money for another room?"

"I'll sleep on the floor, then. I don't sleep with other men."

Jay thought for a minute. "I'm going to the bar for a nightcap. You coming, Phil?"

"No, and I think you've had more than enough to drink already. I'm going to watch a bit of TV and then go to bed."

Jay returned to the room a couple of hours and half a dozen beers later. Phil was well over to one side of the bed, sound asleep. Jay lay down on the bare hardwood floor but found in harder than he had expected. *That bed would sure feel better than this floor. He's sound asleep so he won't bother me*, he thought, stripping out of everything except his shorts and socks. *So long as I keep my socks on, I'm not sleeping with him because I never sleep with my socks on*, Jay rationalized to himself as he crawled into the bed. He carefully lay down on top of the sheet so that it became a divider between them.

The light from the late morning sun streamed in through the window, rousing Jay. He looked across the bed at the gently snoring Phil. He jumped out of bed, pulled on his pants, grabbed a blanket and curled up on the floor on the other side of the room pretending to be asleep.

"Jay. It's time to get up," Phil called. "It must be afternoon already. We need to get on the road."

Jay got up and headed down the hall to the bathroom. "I'll be ready before you are," he said.

Within half an hour they had checked out of the hotel, had a sparse breakfast of toast and coffee, three aspirins for Jay's unhappy head, and were getting ready to mount the motorcycle.

"I don't want to wear a helmet," Jay protested.

"It's the law."

"What do I care? I need fresh air and freedom. Besides, from the way my head feels I don't think it would fit into a helmet."

"It's your life," Phil said, buckling up his helmet and getting on the bike. "Climb on, and remember to relax. We'll have to bank to go around corners, but I won't let it tip."

They roared along the highway and up the steep incline out of the valley. Jay looked back and admired the breathtaking view of the verdant valley with the meandering river snaking its way between the rolling hills.

"That's so beautiful," he yelled into Phil's ear above the throaty rumble of the engine. "I don't know why I didn't see it before. I must have been asleep."

"Or pretending to be asleep so you could ignore me. Enjoy it while you can. We'll be hitting the flat prairies soon enough," Phil tossed back over his shoulder.

An hour brought them to a roadside gas station displaying the sign, "EATS." Another burger and fries for Jay and a bowl of tepid tomato soup and limp garlic bread for Phil served as lunch.

"You know what we forgot?" Jay asked.

"What?" Phil asked.

"We were going to check on finding my father."

"While you were busy getting drunk and chatting up the local girls, I did ask around. The mechanic recalled hearing of a Nobby McNabb who went to the west coast somewhere years ago but that's all."

"Thanks for asking, anyway. Could I drive the Harley for a while?" Jay asked with unusual meekness.

"No problem if you have a driver's licence and promise to do as I tell you. And you should wear the helmet."

"I did alright following instructions when I helped with the dinner, didn't I?"

"You did so well that I'm going to reward you by paying for your lunch. A loonie should be enough tip," Phil said.

"She gave us good service. Maybe leave her two."

As they got up from the table, Jay scooped up the coins and dropped them into his pocket.

Jay climbed onto the motorcycle with Phil on behind. Phil snapped on his helmet and handed the other one to Jay. Jay frowned, shook his head and hung the helmet back on the luggage rack. Without waiting for instructions, Jay started the engine. "How do you shift gears?" he asked.

Phil explained as Jay eased out onto the highway. Soon they had left the station and the speed limit far behind.

Phil shouted a few times into Jay's ear to slow down, but the twin demons of power and control had taken possession of Jay.

Jay was too preoccupied with his newfound feeling of omnipotence to notice the blue and red flashing antlers on the car behind them. After a couple of miles the cruiser pulled up beside the cycle and the officer waved Jay over to the shoulder.

"Licence and registration, please."

Phil handed over the registration.

"Your driver's licence, please," the officer said to Jay.

"I don't have one with me," Jay answered, looking straight ahead.

"You have one at home?"

"I'm a hick kid from up north in Oakridge. We don't have cars there."

"No helmet, no licence, and going 130 km/hr in a 100 zone. Those are serious offenses." The officer looked at Phil, "Come with me."

Phil got off and went with the police officer to the cruiser car. Several minutes later they returned and stood by the bike.

"No helmet costs you fifty bucks and about a hundred and seventy–five more for the speeding. And speeding also gets you two demerit points."

"How can you give me demerit points when I don't even have a licence?"

"That's easy, kid. We wait until you get one and then you start off your licence with that many demerits. Or if you get a suspension, then when you get a licence it's immediately under suspension and you have to wait until the suspension time is over before you get to use it. You may think you can get away with stuff by being stupid, but we have ways of waiting for you to grow up. In your case that apparently could be quite a while."

"I'm sorry. Honest. It wasn't on purpose."

"Well you'd better start thinking before you drive. If I ever catch you breaking the law again, I'll write you up so that you'll be in a retirement home before you can even apply for a licence. Now if you'll let this guy do the driving and promise me that you'll do whatever he tells you to do, then I'll let you off this time. But only this once, and it's only because I think that maybe you didn't know any better."

"Yes sir, I'll be good. You'll see."

The officer and Phil stood near the cruiser car, out of Jay's earshot. "See you at the Club this weekend, Phil?"

"Sure thing," Phil replied.

Jay and Phil put on their helmets and Phil started the bike.

They had rejoined the highway after bypassing the two–industry farming community of Portage la Prairie when Phil pulled off onto a dirt side road.

"Hey. Where do you think you're going?" Jay shouted into the back of Phil's head.

Phil ignored the question until he had wheeled down a poplar–lined lane and into a farmyard.

"I want to get some saskatoon berries. The people here have a few acres of them and they should be ripe about now. I'll bet you've never eaten saskatoons."

"You're right about that. We never ate berries at home. There were lots of berries around but we didn't know which ones were poisonous so we didn't eat any of them. My mother always said it was better to be safe than sorry about that sort of thing."

"They're like blueberries only a bit smaller and a lot tastier."

I've never eaten blueberries either, so that doesn't help me much, Jay thought to himself.

Phil added, "You probably haven't eaten strawberries either. We should get some at one of the U–Pick places down the road. After all, Portage la Prairie calls itself the Strawberry Capital of Canada."

"Well I don't suppose that you've ever eaten fish livers, have you?" Jay said in an effort to appear less naive. "They're excellent with a bit of vinegar, but you have to catch the pickerel in the winter or early spring while the water is icy cold."

"I'm vegetarian, remember?"

"Oh yeah. I keep forgetting because you seem so normal."

"Actually, I am normal. I choose not to eat meat or fish. Vegetarian is how I choose to eat, not what I am."

On the door of the house a hand–printed sign read, "We're out behind the barn picking berries."

A dozen big bushes, heavily laden with clusters of dark blue berries like bunches of miniature grapes, grew out of the newly mowed grass. Further out in the field newly started bushes enjoyed the labour–intensive luxury of cultivation.

"Hi, Helen," Phil called to the lady busily picking berries into an ice cream pail.

"Out for your yearly saskatoon fix, are you?" the lady replied.

"You know you grow the best berries in the country. It looks like you could spare a litre or two."

"I don't suppose you want to pick them yourself?"

"I'd like to eat some right off the bush, if you don't mind," Jay said.

"Go right ahead. Eat all you want while I put some in a plastic bag for Phil here. Have you finally come to your senses and bought a car instead of that infernal machine you used to ride?" she said with a wide grin.

"Don't make fun of my Harley. It's not just a machine. It's part of me. It's my past, present and future. I wouldn't be the same without it," Phil said lightheartedly.

"I guess you plan to have it buried with you, then, do you?" she countered.

Jay gingerly pulled a single berry off and put it into his mouth. It was warm from the hot summer sun and released its sweet, sharp juice as he bit into it.

"These berries are good," he said thoughtfully selecting another one for picking.

"This is how you do it," the lady said. She stripped a handful of the berries off in one pull and tossed them into her mouth. "You need enough to completely fill your mouth to get the full effect."

Jay collected a handful and stuffed his mouth full. "You're right. They're awesome," he sputtered around the berries.

The motorcycle followed the highway toward Winnipeg through a chessboard of yellow canola, blue flax, and green wheat fields. Clumps of trees and farm yards dotted the landscape like misplaced chess pieces. The heavy sweet fragrance of canola and clover alternating with barnyard odours teased Jay's nostrils.

Phil turned abruptly off the highway down a dirt road leading to a deserted farmhouse. A big tree in the front yard was covered with clusters of dark reddish–purple berries. He dismounted and began to fill a bag with the almost–black berries.

"I know the fellow who used to live here before he retired from farming and moved into Portage. He won't mind if we help ourselves to some."

Jay stripped two bunches and stuffed his mouth with a self–satisfied look. No sooner had he bitten into them than his eyes bulged wide and his face contorted in agony from the astringent effect on his mouth. He bent over, spewing the berries out on the ground. "What do you think you are doing to me?" he shouted angrily as best he could through his puckered mouth and lips.

"I didn't tell you to eat them. They're called chokecherries. They make exceptionally good jelly, but they're way too tart for eating like that."

"Tart, nothing. They're deadly!" Jay exclaimed. "You should warn a fellow."

"I guess that's why they're called chokecherries," Phil said.

Phil and Jay sat around the kitchen table picking over their newly acquired supply of berries.

"Tell me more about Scotty," Jay ventured.

"You could say we were soul mates. We seemed to know what each other was feeling without having to say a word. When he died, a part of me died too. I started missing more and more days at work until they called it a nervous breakdown and put me on sick leave. I should have rented out his room because I certainly could have used the money, but I couldn't bring myself to lose any more of him. I didn't want to desecrate his memory."

"What about the poem?"

"Scotty wanted to leave something to be remembered by, so he wrote poetry. He wrote that poem a few weeks before he died. I wanted to type it out for him, but he insisted that he needed to write it out in his own hand. He was always independent that way. He was like you in a lot of ways."

Phil continued, "I used to talk to Scotty all the time as if he were still around. That is, until Cam told me that people were beginning to say things about me. They were saying that I was going crazy because I was talking to myself. But you understand, don't you? I wasn't talking to myself. I was talking to Scotty. So I made that little shrine and kept his room as a place where we could be together to talk in private whenever I wanted."

"I know how that is. I used to talk to my dog even after he was dead. He was my only friend even though he never talked back. I suppose that makes me crazier than you because at least you were talking to a person."

"It seems so unfair that he didn't get to live out his life. At least he got to choose his time and place of death. That's something only the lucky few of us get to do. And he didn't die alone. I feel sorry for the homeless on the street. Living on the street is an acceptable personal choice; dying alone on the street is an indignity to the soul."

Phil sat staring thoughtfully into space.

Jay broke the silence, "I don't understand about the quilts in the photo. What have they got to do with Scotty?" Jay asked.

"Each panel of that quilt is made in memory of a person who died with AIDS. The panels were designed to be the size of a coffin because the early victims of the disease were cremated as a health–safety precaution. This gave each one a symbolic grave. Eight panels are sewn together to make a quilt."

"But there must be thousands of quilts in that picture."

"More than 43,000 panels, from all over the world. There are more than 500 from Canada alone. The first quilts were displayed in front of the White House in 1987 to impress upon the government and the world in general that thousands of men, women and children were dying from AIDS–related diseases and that little research was being done to stop this epidemic."

"And they still do this?"

"Every year there are more of them. These quilts represent only 12 per cent of the deaths in the U.S. alone. In 1995 the number of U.S. deaths peaked at 49,500 for that year."

"You know a lot about this."

"It became very important to me."

"So Scotty died of AIDS, then?" Jay asked.

"I guess you could say that, although nobody dies of AIDS as such. The virus weakens your immune system and makes you defenseless against other diseases. But yes. You could say he died of AIDS."

I probably shouldn't ask this, but I have to know, thought Jay. "So Scotty was gay, then?"

"How would anyone know for sure unless he told them? We think he got the virus from sharing needles during his drug period, but it could have been some other way," Phil replied.

Phil continued, "That's what scares me the most, because we used to share everything, including the same needle sometimes. It seems stupid now that I could have been so careless, but it never occurred to me at the time. He didn't seem like the kind of guy you had to be careful around. I still get twice–a–year tests and I'm always negative. But they say it sometimes takes years for the virus to show up even though the person can infect others during that time. It's a constant worry for me. That's why I'm so touchy about anyone using my personal stuff. I don't want to take the chance that I might accidentally infect someone. I'm spooked about it. I guess maybe I go overboard about it sometimes, but I can't help myself."

"Maybe I shouldn't stay here then. I don't want to end up getting AIDS." Jay stood up as if to leave.

"Hang on, Jay. You couldn't get AIDS from me even if I did have it. Not unless some of my body fluid or blood got into your system. That's why you must never use my razor or any of my personal things. So long as you don't do something stupid there's no danger from me or Steve or any gay. You're just getting scared and overreacting to the situation."

"You're telling me not to overreact. You're the one who wanted to throw out all those neat clothes I got from Steve."

"You're right. Steve gave them to you and you should be able to do whatever you want with them. I guess I panicked. But it made me feel better that they got a good washing and disinfecting. Not for the AIDS virus, of course, but for whatever they might have picked up."

"That's fine with me. But if I'm going to stay here with you then you had better learn to stop trying to push me around. I don't have to stay here, you know." Jay threatened. *I can always go and stay with Steve,* he thought, without giving any consideration to the implications of such a move.

"I don't mean to be pushy. It's just that having you here has brought back such a rush of memories that they confuse me. I couldn't do anything to save Scotty. I want to do a better job of looking after you."

"Well, I don't like being looked after. That's one reason I left home, and I don't plan to have somebody like you giving me orders."

"It's nice having you here, Jay. You can stay as long as you want. At least until you get a job and get established in a place of your own."

"Well, in that case I'll stay. So long as you don't start setting rules for me. I need to come and go as I please and to do whatever I want," Jay demanded.

"Fine then. You're big enough to look after yourself. I'll try not to act so much like your mother. Now give me your dirty clothes and I'll get the laundry done tonight."

10

THE PASSING PARADE

"Do you know anything about interventions?" Jay asked Phil.

"I've been involved with a few. Why do you ask?"

"Becky wants to do one with Jimmy to try to get him off drugs. The situation's more than she can handle. He just about killed himself last week. Again. She asked me to be part of it but I don't know anything about this sort of thing."

"It can be effective if everybody's sincere and willing to be tough."

"So we get together and tell Jimmy we want him to quit?" Jay asked.

"It's more than that. You have to make him realize how much you care about him and that what he's doing is hurting you."

"That's easy enough, because it's true."

"The tough part is that you have to convince him that you're not going to let the situation continue. If he doesn't change then you're no longer going to have anything to do with him," Phil said.

"You mean not even hang out with him?"

"That's right. He has to realize that this intervention changes his life whether he wants to or not. From that moment on it's either his friends or the drugs. He has to choose."

"Isn't that like the Amish punishment of shunning where the whole community behaves as if the individual no longer exists?" Jay asked.

"How do you know about the Amish?"

"Volume one of the World Book, remember? It's the only volume we had so I memorized it."

"Oh yeah. The difference is that the intervention isn't as a punishment; it's a clear picture of the consequences of continuing with a behavior pattern. It's like giving the person a chance to look into his future."

"I don't think any of us know enough to carry it off. We'd appreciate your help."

"We'd have to meet first so that everyone understands that the discussion is between each person and Jimmy. There can be no discussion between others in the group because Jimmy will try to seize onto anything to try to sidetrack the process."

"I'll talk to Becky and set it up."

Phil and Jay returned home from the intervention.

"Do you think it worked?" Jay asked

"You guys were amazing. I didn't know you could be so open and emotional, Jay."

"It was horrible. Poor Jimmy felt that we were all ganging up on him. And we were. I hated it. Are you sure this was the right thing to do? If I were Jimmy I think I'd go out and shoot myself."

"He knows that you're all on his side. And that you all care about him. That'll give him a lot of strength."

"You did a super job Phil. I wish I hadn't lost it toward the end," Jay said. "I haven't cried since I was a baby."

"Maybe you didn't notice, but we were all crying at the end. It was a good thing."

Phil noticed the answering machine's demanding blink.

"Check the messages, please, Jay," asked Phil. "I'm going to the washroom."

When Phil returned, Jay was sitting with a thoughtful look on his face, gnawing a thumbnail.

"Any messages?" Phil asked.

"A wrong number. Nothing to worry about."

Phil looked from Jay to the machine. He pushed the replay button. "We know where you live. We'll be coming to get you," the machine intoned.

"I told you it was a wrong number," Jay said.

"It sounds to me as if it could be Tony."

"How could he find me so fast?"

"Get real, Jay. He probably investigated you before he hired you. Drug dealers are not stupid. Those guys have to know who they are dealing with if they expect to stay out of jail. Did you think he'd trust an unknown guy with hundreds of dollars in drugs? He probably knows what color shorts you wear."

"If it is Tony then what do I do?" Jay asked. "It's all your fault that I am in this mess, you know," he added, glaring accusingly at Phil.

"My fault?"

"Yes. You made me come to your stupid dinner party. Then you fed me liquor to which I was not accustomed. And then you wanted me to go help you pick up your stupid motorcycle. If you had left me alone, then none of this whole thing would ever have happened."

"I'm sorry if I'm messing up your life."

"Well you are. Now I have to get out of here before Tony comes to get me. Just when things started to work out for me, you had to go and mess it up. I'll be back to pick up my stuff as soon as I find another place to stay."

"Jay, hold on. Let's…"

Without looking back, Jay slammed the door behind him.

Back on the street, Jay started walking slowly along the now familiar route toward the downtown area.

This is crazy. I have nowhere to go, Jay thought. He pulled out his wallet and counted the bills. *Eighteen dollars. Great going. Eight weeks in the big city and I have a grand total of seven dollars more than when I arrived. And on top of that there's a drug dealer out to get me, whatever that means.*

A black van with dark tinted windows turned the corner and moved down the street toward Jay. He sprang into the nearest walkway and cowered behind a hedge. The van crept past his hiding place and stopped a few car lengths down the street. The backup lights went on. He raced along the walkway, through the back yard and down the alley.

This is smart, he said to himself sarcastically as he ran. *If those are Tony's goons, they'll see me easily. A startled rabbit has a chance to escape because it is faster than the hunter. But they can drive faster than I can run so that makes me a rather slow rabbit. My best chance would be to hide.*

Jay darted down the lane until he saw a fenced backyard with a shed flanked by bushes. He vaulted the fence and dashed to the shed. Its door was unlocked and slightly ajar. Jay squeezed through the opening and into the building. A knothole afforded him a limited view of the lane. He settled down to out wait the hunters. Soon the van appeared, moving slowly down the lane. Jay's heart pounded and he held his breath. The van seemed suspended in time, less than ten feet from his hiding place. The urge to desert the shed and flee grew stronger by the second until it became overwhelming.

I mustn't let myself get trapped in here. If they stop, I'll make a run for it, Jay promised himself. The van stopped. Two men got out, one carrying a baseball bat. Jay tried to get up, but fear made his feet refuse to obey.

"He's got to be around here somewhere," one man said. "Jump over the fence and look around."

"You're the athlete. You jump over the fence."

"He's not here. I told you he's not here. He runs like a deer. By now he could be at the bus depot buying a ticket for the first bus out of here. If he has any brains, that's what he'll be doing."

"If we don't find him, Tony will be unhappy."

"So we'll tell Tony we found him and beat him up good. He'll never find out anything different."

"You have some kind of death wish? Tony always finds out what goes down. And you know he doesn't take kindly to people who mess with him. Get in. We'll check the bus depot."

The van slowly drove down the street, leaving Jay huddled in a corner of the shed waiting for darkness.

I have got to get somewhere far away from here where nobody would think to look for me. I could go to Steve's place but Tony will probably check Phil's friends. North Main Street might be good. It's the sort of neighborhood that Tony leaves to the gangs. He likes to keep a nice, clean, respectable image.

Jay kept to the back streets and alleys as he worked his way north toward the older section of the city. The streets changed from a compass–point grid into an angling, meandering, confusing area with three and five way intersections. The streets seemed to have been built more to follow the ancient bison trails than with any thoughts about automobile traffic. Brick and stone buildings preserved since the turn of the century were characteristic of the Exchange District. The area catered to the artistic community as well as housing upscale restaurants interspersed with offbeat commercial enterprises.

Jay moved toward an over–amplified outdoor public address system which was broadcasting an amateur stand–up comedy routine to all those within a three–block radius. Gayly decorated umbrellas anchoring helium–filled balloons surrounded the stage. An exotic mixture of sweet, pungent aromas from the variety of ethnic fast–food vendors mixed with the odor of deep–fried snacks. Sellers of jewelry and trinkets vied with roving magicians and other buskers for the attention of the crowd. The trees sported colorful banners and large paint-ed monkeys looking down through wooden eyes. The crowd overflowed the streets like a miniature Bourbon Street at Mardi Gras. Except, of course, that with typical Canadian inhibition, the consumption of liquor was carefully con-trolled in one tent–covered pavilion set up like a Bavarian beer garden sur-rounded by an impenetrable fence. Unwittingly Jay had happened upon the annual Winnipeg Fringe Festival. A four–piece band competed with the P.A. sys-tem for the attention of the crowd. A clown wandered aimlessly about in the fes-tive atmosphere idly juggling assorted fruits and vegetables.

This is perfect, Jay said to himself. *Nobody could find me here.*

Jay wandered into the midst of the milling crowd and soon got caught up in the holiday atmosphere of the event. He noticed a girl in her early twenties dressed in a long shapeless black skirt, white blouse and filmy black shawl look-ing like a misplaced Halloween witch. She sat on the curb eating a hotdog and staring pensively into the street. Her long straight black hair framed her unnatu-rally pale face and partially hid the three inch diameter golden astrological disks dangling from her ears. Jay bought a hot dog and sat down an arm's length from her on the curb. Eventually her gaze drifted in his general direction and their eyes met.

"Hello. This is my first time here. Any suggestions as to what one does for fun?" he asked.

The girl looked deeply into Jay's eyes but didn't reply.

"I could use some company," he added. *Those goons will be looking for a guy by himself. She would make a perfect camouflage for me,* he thought.

"I am picking up mixed vibrations from you. Your aura is disturbed. Tell me about yourself."

Jay slid over to sit closer to the girl. *There. Now I blend into the setting.* "My name is Alex. I'm here with my parents, but they went off on their own," he said.

"Your name can't be Alex, and you are not here with your parents."

"What do you mean? You can't tell me what my name is or isn't, or who I am."

The girl continued as if Jay had not spoken. "The name, Alex is number 5 in the Kabala Numerical alphabet. Number 5 people are charming, courteous and easy going. That is not you. I sense a conflict between your earthly body and your inner soul that has nothing to do with your parents. They are not here."

What do you expect when I have people dedicated to the forcible separation of my body from my soul? Jay said almost out loud.

"You are a person who seeks total freedom and have a hunger for knowledge. This is typical of a 3–person. Thus, your cosmic name could be Truro." The girl continued to look into Jay's eyes with an unblinking stare. "Yes. I will call you Truro."

I'll play along with this game, Jay thought. "You are right. I'm suffering from turmoil. Perhaps you can help. What is your name?"

"You may call me Tanya. It is my name to those who dwell on this celestial plane. I can help you reach a higher state of inner harmony, but only if you will be honest with me. Lies create bad karma and will cause our auras to be out of harmony."

"To be honest with you, there are a couple of guys looking to beat on me. I have no place to go and no place to stay tonight," Jay said.

"Come. Let's go to one of the performances to take your mind off yourself. That way your inner conflicts will resolve themselves and your true path will be revealed to you. I have free passes."

Girl, you are some fruitcake. But what the heck, you're the best option I have at the moment for staying out of sight, thought Jay. "Great idea," he said, "lead the way."

The room they entered had been made into a makeshift theatre by the addition of a raised platform at one end. Four dozen seats faced the platform and three banks of stage lights hung precariously from the ceiling. Jay and Tanya took two seats in the back row. Five teens on stage sang their original a capella composition. The tune was light and the lyrics funny. Jay's mind drifted to thoughts of Sue. *She'll be wondering what happened to me because I always phone her in the evening. Maybe I can find a pay phone when the performance is over.*

Jay's arm slipped easily around Tanya's shoulder. Their two mouths met in a casual kiss which quickly ignited into a fire fanned by the winds of raging adolescent hormones. *Was that metal that banged against my teeth?* Jay thought, pulling his head back in surprise.

A bit of judicious exploration convinced Jay that metal was definitely involved in the kissing activity. His exploring tongue reported a metal post with smooth round balls on each end like a miniature barbell attached to Tanya's tongue in some manner. It was totally fascinating, and in a weird sort of way, pleasurable.

"Do you wear braces?" he asked.

"No. Don't be silly," Tanya replied, leaning over to continue the kissing. *I wonder if all young people in Winnipeg come complete with metal parts,* Jay said to himself. *Maybe they are some sort of metallic transmission devices placed there as the result of alien abductions.*

"What was that in your mouth, then?"

"Oh. You mean my tongue ring?" Tanya stuck out her tongue.

"Why do you do that to yourself?"

"It feels good. I like to play with it. Sort of like a little soother that's always handy."

Jay's hand found its way up under Tanya's blouse, motivated more by his new found curiosity in metal than by passion. To his immense relief he discovered no metal parts other than the bra hooks.

I could get to like this, Jay thought while the fresh, slightly apricot fragrance of Tanya's hair drifted up to his nose.

Two hours later they were sitting in the same spot where they had met, with the sound of a five–piece band playing jazz in the background.

"I still need a place to stay for the night," Jay said.

"You're a cute guy. Why don't you go over to the hill and you'll get picked up by somebody who's looking for company for the night."

"The hill?"

"The grounds around the Legislative Buildings. That's always a gay pick–up area in any capital city. It's where the male hustlers hang out."

"Oh, you mean where the Golden Boy is," Jay said.

"I see you're already acquainted with that area."

"I've seen it in the distance. I have no intention of getting picked up by some queer that wants to have sex with me. I'm no homo and I'd rather starve than make money that way."

"A lot of the older guys are looking for companionship or trying to relive their youth. They don't recognize what they want or need, so they settle for random sex."

"You may be right. I've been living with this older guy for the past couple of weeks. He treats me like his nephew. I didn't know there were other guys like him around. I thought that he was just uniquely strange."

"No. There are lots of lonely men in a big city. But there are also lots of real weirdos that will mess with your head, or your body, just for kicks."

"Great. So it's kind of like some sort of fast–food promotion scam. Sometimes you get a free burger but more often you end up spending more than you intended."

They sat in silence, their eyes roaming over the crowd. Jay broke the silence. "Phil has a friend named Steve, who seems to like me. He said I could stay with him anytime I want, but I can't do that."

"You say you can't, but it sounds more like you chose not to."

"He's gay. I couldn't spend the night with a fag."

"Why are you afraid of him?"

"Afraid? Me? I am not afraid of anything," Jay said with indignation.

"Then go and stay with him if you aren't afraid of him. Or maybe you dislike him for some reason?"

"I think I might even like him if he weren't gay. He's a nice enough guy. He gives me things and he is friendly to me but it makes me nervous to be around him. I'm afraid he might try to do something and I wouldn't know how to react. Besides, he doesn't respect my personal space. You know what I mean?"

"Oh yes, I know. But it's all in your head. It has everything to do with you and nothing to do with Steve. You must strive to achieve inner peace before you can be comfortable with those around you."

The crowd began to thin out.

"I have to go now," Tanya said. "My parents will be starting to worry again."

"You live with your parents? I thought you were a free spirit." Jay's eyebrows raised and his forehead wrinkled.

"I leave home when the family scene gets too intense. That way my parents miss me and are glad to see me when I come back. Besides, it's hard to be a free spirit if you have to worry about where your next meal is coming from."

"I'd like to see you again. Could you give me your phone number or something?" Jay asked.

"No. If it's our destiny to meet again, we will. If it's not, then we won't. One cannot control one's own fate, nor the fortune of another. We are simply playing out the roles that were predestined by the stars at the time of our birth."

"Yeah, right. Are you saying that if someone is going to punch my lights that I should stand there and hope that my stars will arrange for him to get hit by a truck before he hits me? No thanks. I'll be responsible for creating my own destiny." Jay was startled to hear his own voice saying out loud the words that he had intended only for himself.

Tanya got up and started across the street.

"Ciao, Truro. Put aside your negative thoughts and be at peace with the universe. Only then can your true destiny be fulfilled. I have a feeling that we will meet again soon," she called back to Jay.

"Bye, Tanya. May the force be with you, too."

Jay left the Fringe Festival and continued his trek to the North Main area. He scrutinized the girls, looking like cranes with their long, thin legs and tight black skirts, as they shamelessly posed on street corners displaying themselves to best advantage.

Somehow I doubt that providing companionship is foremost in their minds, he thought.

Jay wandered past a small park with its benches occupied by individuals in various states of sleep. Across the street and down a back lane, a row of men dozed with their backs against the buildings at the edge of a secluded parking lot. He sat in an empty space against the building and casually inspected his surroundings.

"Wanna snort?" An unshaven vagrant in baggy tattered trousers and an equally tattered, but not matching, suit jacket held out a brown paper bag toward Jay.

"Thanks," he said, accepting the bag and its contents. He lifted the bottle to his mouth and pretended to drink before passing it back.

I'm not that destitute yet, I hope, he said to himself. *It never hurts to be sociable but I shudder to think what might be in that bottle.*

He looked around at the telltale signs of substance abuse among the general debris: empty Lysol cans, squeezed–out glue tubes, plastic bags, hypodermic syringes, heat–blackened tinfoil, a variety of empty liquor bottles and the ubiquitous solvent cans.

The man handed the bagged bottle back to him. Jay pulled down the bag to read the label.

Hmmmmm. Shooting Sherry. It may not be Phil's Napoleon Brandy, but at least it has a name. Jay tipped up the bottle and took a sip. *Not bad,* he thought. Another pull on the bottle sent a sweet stream of warmth through his mouth to the emptiness of his stomach.

"Thanks for the hospitality, my friend," he said, passing the bottle back to its owner. The man nodded a curt acknowledgment. "Where do you guys sleep?" Jay asked.

"The Guiding Light Mission down North Main has a shelter that we use when it's cold or wet. But they don't allow booze, or smoking or anything like that. I'd rather sleep out here even if it's uncomfortable, than go there and lose my freedom. At least here a guy can do what he wants."

Jay got up to stretch. He found that even in that short time his body objected to the hard concrete. *That park would be better than this. It's probably not as safe as being in a group like this, but I can look after myself.*

Jay found his way back to the park and an empty bench, but found it as hard as the parking lot. He went across the grass and through a flower bed, stepping carefully to avoid the plants, to a dark spot under the trees. *I think that maybe Phil should have given me more advice,* Jay thought to himself.

The moist, earthy smell surrounded him while the plaintive cooing of a morning dove calling to its mate lulled him to sleep. He felt relaxed and at peace with the world. In his thoughts he was back home sleeping under the stars. Sue was far from his preoccupied mind.

A police car sped down the street, its siren wailing, less than 15 feet from where Jay slept. Its passage went unnoticed.

Jay woke before dawn. He checked his back pocket for his wallet. It was gone. *That was stupid of me. Next time I'll remember to keep it in a side pocket. At least it didn't cost anythinsg.*

The incessant daytime roar of the traffic had dwindled to intermittent swishes as the occasional car went by. The sky was empty and quiet without the usual roar of landing aircraft. The air felt fresh and brisk. The noisy, big–city life had evaporated into the darkness to recuperate for its return with the early morning dew. Jay lay with his eyes closed trying to remember his home in Oakridge, surrounded by the sounds and smells of the virgin forest. Soon he was fast asleep again.

"Move it, fellow." The words were accompanied by a firm tap on the shoulder with a nightstick. Jay sat upright with a start. "You can't sleep here. This is a park, and you're trespassing. These flowers are for people to enjoy, not to be trampled by bums like you."

Jay looked up to see a uniformed figure standing over him pointing to a set of footprints and flattened flowers.

"I'm sorry. I didn't know. But honest, I didn't step on the flowers. It must have been the guy that stole my wallet that did that."

Jay got up, brushed the dust off his clothes as best he could, and gingerly tiptoed through the flower bed to a park bench.

"If I catch you here again, I'll run you in for vagrancy."

The sunrise lit up the eastern sky for a brief few minutes of intense glory. Jay's muscles ached and his mouth felt fuzzy from sleep.

Jay looked down at his soiled clothes. *Sometimes I don't think I'm gaining,* he thought. *Great. Not even any money for a cup of coffee or bus fare to go anywhere. As if I had anywhere to go.*

Jay walked aimlessly along the deserted street. The pawn shops, seedy hotels and wholesale stores were still closed and firmly guarded with locked metal grid gates. Jay sat down against a brick wall. His eyes refused to stay open in the daylight.

I'd better not go to back to sleep or some rummy will steal my shoes, too, he thought. In spite of his intentions Jay dozed off into a fitful sleep. The sidewalk filled with two opposing streams of people flowing purposefully to work. He looked up as a middle–aged businessman pause in front of him. Their eyes crossed for a moment and the man held out a coin toward Jay.

Instinctively, he reached up and took it. The man was immediately swallowed up by the stream of humanity and disappeared.

Great. A loonie. At least now I'm not broke. Jay looked up at the people flowing past him. Most of them stared straight ahead or looked away as they moved over to the outer edge of the human stream. The realization that people saw him as a beggar gradually crystallized in Jay's mind. A wave of disgust over what he had become in their eyes settled onto his shoulders and sat there like a huge weight. He slowly got to his feet, shook himself as if to dislodge the oppressive weight and started walking. *I've gotta get a grip here. This whole thing is outta control,* he thought to himself. *I can't even think straight.*

Jay entered the stream of people heading down North Main street toward their jobs in the business and financial district.

11

THE KINDNESS OF STRANGERS

North Main changes to South Main where it intersects with Portage Avenue. The corner of Portage and Main is generally accepted to be the geographical center of the city. Its fame is not because of its proximity to the juncture of the Red and Assiniboine Rivers which are historically important fur–trading and exploration routes. Nor is its fame because of the Toronto Dominion Bank Building, with its thirty–three stories making it the tallest building in Manitoba. Its fame is because the cold winter winds blowing down from the north across this intersection make it seem to be the coldest place in the world

Perhaps this is why the city council decided years ago to prevent pedestrians from crossing the intersection. They erected concrete barriers along the curb and signed an agreement with the property owners to maintain the obstruction of the intersection for at least 99 years.

And so they had to build an underground passage beneath the intersection. What should have been the easy task of going underground on one side of the intersection and surfacing on the other soon became complicated by the construction of an extensive subterranean Concourse. The area quickly grew into a small subterranean city whose main function seemed to be to trap the unwary who fell into its clutches and prevent their escape back to the aboveground world. Myriads of fluorescent suns provide intense shadowless light, disorientating the senses and confusing a person's sense of direction. Once entrapped, hapless tourists wander aimlessly for what seem to be hours through the maze of walkways, high rise bank buildings and mini malls, trying vainly to find their way back to the surface.

Cryptic signs promise an escape to the real world above, but in fact lead only to other areas of small shops, or a return to previously visited areas via a circular tour of concrete structures. It has been said that if you stand still in the Concourse for fifteen minutes, half the population of Winnipeg will pass by. This is probably an exaggeration. It would only seem that way.

Jay arrived at the corner of Portage and Main. Not seeing any way to cross the street, and not noticing the steps leading underground, Jay took the line of least resistance. He turned at right angles, blissfully unaware of the bustling civilization directly beneath his feet and of his narrow escape from its grasping tentacles.

Soon he arrived at the area known as The Forks, where the junction of the Red and Assiniboine Rivers had made this an important gathering place for First Nations peoples and early settlers. More recently, the area had been developed to attract tourists to this, the New Orleans French Quarter of the north. Stores and upscale restaurants held little interest for Jay in his current financial situation and depressed state of mind. He did, however, happen upon a well–kept, gravel path along the side of the river which held promise of some solace and peace of mind.

The air was pleasant and the scenery soothing. Jay paused often to listen to the water and to let the sounds of nature wash his soul clean of the events of the past night. He was surprised to discover after an hour of strolling along the path that he had arrived on the grounds of the Legislative Buildings.

Oh, no - hustlers' heaven, he thought sarcastically. *Fate must have brought me here to solve my financial problems. If I get picked up then I can afford to eat and maybe get a place to sleep for the night. Yeah right. As if I'd ever consider that to be a possibility.*

Jay wandered slowly around the grounds of the Legislative Buildings and the river pathway, waiting for something to happen. A girl left her half–finished bag of McDonald's french fries on the bench when she walked away. Jay wandered over and casually sat down beside them.

There's no point in letting them go to waste, he rationalized to himself. *And leaving them here would be littering.*

When he had finished devouring the fries, Jay crossed the bridge to Osborne Village. It was as if he had been transported into another world. The street was alive with Jello–coloured hair, body jewelry and shiny black, body hugging clothing. Outdoor patios offered an open invitation to sit and snack. Small stores offered an array of unusual goods for those with the money to afford them. Jay soon determined that this wasn't the place for him.

Returning across the bridge, Jay met a youngman, as Steve would call an attractive young man who is cruising, with startlingly spiked hair, walking toward him. Three paces after they had passed each other Jay turned his head to have another look at the man's green hair. As he turned to look over his shoulder, the youngman also turned to look at Jay. Jay quickly looked straight ahead and kept walking.

He sat on a bench, gazing at the sunset through half closed eyes.

"Hi there. Mind if I join you?" It was the youngman whom he had met on the bridge.

"It's fine by me," Jay replied, trying to keep from staring at the man's hair. *How did he get here so fast? He was headed the other way a couple of minutes ago.*

"You got a place?" the youngman asked.

"No. Do you?" *Not that it's any of your business, but I guess it doesn't hurt to be friendly.*

"What about the river bank?" the youngman asked.

"I slept in the park last night, but I hadn't thought about the river bank," Jay said. *Why are we talking about this anyway?*

"The river bank's quite safe this early in the evening, and I know a good private spot where no one will see us so long as we're quiet about it. I'd never go there after dark. There have been too many guys bashed around here lately. It isn't even safe for straights in this area anymore."

"Yeah, that's right," Jay said without actually listening.

The youngman got up and walked toward the river area. Jay leaned back, closed his eyes again and let his mind stay empty in the faint hope that some useful thoughts might take up residence there.

"I thought you were coming." The mildly annoyed voice jolted Jay's eyes open. The youngman with the green hair was sitting on the bench again.

Wow, this guy sure does change directions fast, Jay said to himself. "You thought what?" he asked out loud.

"Are you coming or not?"

"What do you mean?"

"I thought you were cruising me. You are cruising, aren't you?"

"Maybe," Jay replied, thinking to himself, *That depends on what you mean by 'cruising', I guess.*

"You either are, or you aren't. Are you coming with me or not?"

"Will you pay me?" Jay asked. *I haven't a clue what this is all about but maybe it's worth some money.*

"I never pay. I'm not that desperate; I like variety," the youngman said with a snarl as he started to walk away. He stopped and turned back to face Jay.

"I get it now. You're trying to hustle. You must be from out of town."

"As a matter of fact I am. Does that make a difference?"

"This hasn't been a hustler hangout for years. Not since the people down the street got mad at us and petitioned the city to close off the street. With nobody driving by, the trade had to move."

"Where did it go?"

"Over there," the youngman said pointing north to the back lane running parallel to Broadway. "Good luck. You're going to need it."

With a wave, Jay walked across the Legislative grounds in the indicated direction.

The lane was ideally suited to its recently discovered use. On one side loading docks and boarded up doorways provided natural display racks for the youngmen lounging on them. On the other side, parking lots, vacant during the night hours, provided a conveniently anonymous place for transient customers to park for a few furtive minutes with their newly chosen partner.

Jay took a position against the wall in a poorly lit area so that he could observe the action without being conspicuous. A dozen youngmen stood alone or in temporary groups of two or three exchanging comments and jokes, then moving apart to stand in solitary expectancy. An intermittent stream of cars moved slowly down the four blocks of the alley before looping back along Broadway to renter the alley and repeat the circuit. The solitary drivers and youngmen exchanged casual looks. When two pairs of eyes locked, the car would stop. The youngman would leave his post to stick his head through the car window. After a few seconds the car would drive away, either with the youngman inside, or leaving him on the sidelines for the next round of play.

A flaming-red hatchback with darkly tinted windows flicked its lights. It drove up beside Jay's position and stopped. The power window slid down revealing a middle-aged face looking straight toward Jay.

It's now or never, Jay thought as he ambled over to the car and bent down to be on a level with the window. The two men looked into each other's eyes for a moment.

"Can I give you a ride?"

"Sure," Jay replied, thinking to himself, *Whatever you mean by that.*

"How much?"

"The usual rate," Jay replied with a faked air of confidence.

"I'm new at this. What's the usual rate?" the man asked.

Jay realized that he was clearly way over his head with the discussion. He mumbled, "Never mind," and escaped to the relative safety of the road's edge.

"Too bad," the man said. "Maybe later." The car eased forward to pause in front of a dark–skinned youth dressed in white pants and an open–necked shirt. The youngman went over to the car window for a brief chat before getting into the car.

Jay leaned against the building, shaking from nervous excitement, his stomach threatening to heave. He closed his eyes and concentrated on taking slow, deep breaths.

"You're new here, aren't you?"

Jay opened his eyes and saw a two–hundred–pound, six–foot–two, twenty–five–year–old husky male with dirty blond, closely cropped hair, standing in front of him. He was wearing a black leather jacket adorned with three–inch silver rings at the shoulders and a heavy silver chain hanging from his neck down across his bare chest.

"What makes you say that?" asked Jay. *Don't tell me I'm in trouble with the hookers' union now.*

"I haven't seen you here before, that's all. That, and the fact that you didn't make it with Sammy. Everybody goes with Sammy if they get a chance."

"He said he was new at this. You mean he lied to me?"

"Surprise. A predator that deceives its prey. He probably wanted to beat you down in price. He's a bit of a cheapskate, but he's safe and harmless."

"I'm new at this. I'm trying to make a few bucks so I can get a hotel room for the night and maybe something to eat. I'll get arrested if I sleep in the park again. Maybe this wasn't such a great idea either," Jay said.

"You're cute enough and thin. You'd probably make a hundred bucks if you're lucky and willing to stay out here most of the night."

"Is that what you do?"

"No. Most of the successful guys specialize."

"You specialize?"

The man spread his arms. "Look at me. What do you think? Leather, bondage and general rough stuff. I've got hoods, whips and that sort of paraphernalia at my place. Guys who are into that sort of thing pay a premium rate. I have regular customers that phone me. I'm only out here when I feel like a change or need some more customers. Even the regulars only stay for a few weeks at a time no matter how good you are. The johns are always looking for new faces."

"You got any suggestions for me?" Jay asked.

"You need something to make you stand out from the crowd. Look at you. There's nothing to make you stand out from any of the other guys out here."

"Could you tell me what to say? You know, when a guy stops for me."

"Usually you have to speak first. The johns are afraid that they might be picking up a plainclothes cop. They can be charged with soliciting if they offer to pay for sex. It can be awkward at first. You don't want to say too much in case the driver is a cop, and he doesn't want to say too much in case you're a cop."

"I'd just ask him if he's a cop."

"Yeah right. Like he'd admit it. There's no law against lying. But there is a law against entrapment. He can't make you an offer or suggestive comment unless you've already made the first move."

"So it's kind of a standoff with neither one wanting to make a move?"

"That's it exactly. Prostitution isn't illegal. It's only illegal to talk about it. You have to be careful, but if the driver says something suggestive to you then you know you're safe. Cops can't entice you and still make a case against you. That would be entrapment."

A limousine with official Manitoba pennants flying on each front fender turned down the alley.

"Now there's where you can make serious money, but his boss is fussy. It must be nice to have a chauffeur to do your shopping for you and make deliveries right to your bedroom door. That's class."

"You ever get busted?"

"Oh sure. It's not a big deal. They hassle you for an hour or so and then let you off with a warning not to get picked up again. But it's annoying because it makes me mad at myself for being so stupid. It doesn't have to happen if you play it cool."

"So what do I say if a car stops for me? You seem to be saying that I should speak first," Jay asked.

"I usually say something like, 'What are you looking for', or 'Can you give me a ride' or 'Something I can do for you', and let him take it from there."

"That's easy."

"So what do you do?"

"What do I do about what?" asked Jay

"I mean what are you willing to do with a guy?"

"I'm not sure what you mean. What are my choices?"

The man gave Jay a puzzled look. "Have you ever had sex with a guy before?"

"No. Is that a problem? It can't be too difficult to figure out what to do, is it?"

"The physical part is easy to figure out. The guy will know what he wants. But I'll bet you don't even carry protection."

"You mean like a knife or a gun?"

"That would be an idea. But no. I meant like a condom. Anyway, the biggest problem is how this life screws up your head and your emotions when you start selling yourself. You aren't merely selling your body, you're selling part of your spirit. In time it erodes your soul and leaves you less than human. Listen. You need to get out of here right now and get your head together. This isn't for you."

"Oh sure. I know what you're doing. You're trying to scare me away to cut down on the competition. If I go away then you'll have a better chance to score. You don't con me that easily."

"There was a time when I was sweet and innocent like you. Well, maybe not quite as sweet as you. I got into this business by accident and since then there's been no turning back. It's killed my emotions and it's draining my life force. It's good money, but I waste it because it has no value. Nothing has any importance. I have no life and no future. I'm nothing but an empty shell, repeating the actions night after night because I don't know what else to do. If I can save you from a life like mine, then maybe I'll have done at least one worthwhile thing before I die. And don't kid yourself, death could be as close as the next car that drives up. That's something we learn to live with."

The man took something out of his pocket and shoved it into Jay's shirt pocket. "Now get out of here before you do something really stupidly."

Jay turned and without any help from his brain, his feet automatically turned him back down Broadway toward the Forks. He absent-mindedly checked his shirt pocket and found a condom. *I guess it's the thought that counts.*

It was dark and there was a spattering of rain. Jay walked along beside the river until he reached a bridge. *At least I'll be dry, and maybe the rain will keep the bashers away.*

The traffic noise over the bridge soothed Jay to sleep.

12

BACK TO SQUARE ONE

Jay made his way down Main Street. A dingy restaurant housed in an eighty–year–old building caught his attention. In earlier times its ornately carved and brightly painted sign proudly proclaimed its name to prospective discriminating diners. Now, with the paint faded and peeling, the Red Dragon sign was but a sad reminder of those more prosperous times.

"You got coffee and toast for a dollar?" Jay asked. "It's all the cash I've got."

The wizened little man of indeterminable age and ancestry filled a cracked china cup with strong black coffee and put a piece of bread into the toaster.

"Let's see the money," he said, keeping a firm grip on the coffee cup.

Jay meticulously set his loonie on the counter. He laced the coffee liberally with cream and sugar.

"I need a job. You know anyone who's hiring?" he asked.

The man gave Jay a squinty look. "I could use a bus boy nights. It gets busy sometimes," he said. "But you look rather scrawny. Think you could handle it?"

"I'm tougher than I look. What does it pay?" *I wonder what a bus boy is. Maybe it's somebody who came down from north on the bus?* Jay asked himself. He sat up straighter and his expression became businesslike. "What are the hours and how much does it pay?"

"Six until midnight during the week and until two on Friday and Saturdays. We're open every day but you get one day off a week. I choose the day. You can have your meals free if you don't eat too much, and a hundred and twenty bucks a week."

"Is there any way you could provide me with a place to stay? Where I'm living now is rather far away," Jay asked with as much dignity as he could muster under the circumstances.

"There's a room upstairs. It's not much, but there aren't any cockroaches. The other guy living up there is always quiet. You can have it for twenty a week."

"How about an advance on my salary? I gave you my last dollar."

"Not in this lifetime, sonny boy. You do the work before you see the money. I've had experience with your kind before. As soon as they have a couple of bucks in the pocket they're gone."

"Not me. I don't have anywhere to go."

"And don't try stealing anything. Everything that isn't nailed down is engraved with my number."

"Your number?" Jay asked with sudden interest.

"Yeah. My Social Insurance Number. That way if anything is stolen, the police can get it back to me." He pointed to a nine–digit number scratched onto the side of the cash register.

Jay read the numbers to himself and thought, *that's nine digits, the same as 609561826.* "Does everyone have one?" he asked.

"Yep. You'll need to get one if you plan to work here."

"I'll look into that right away."

"You want to see the room?"

A long narrow flight of stairs led to a door at the end of the hallway. The man opened the door and Jay stepped inside.

The small windowless room was more like a closet than a bedroom. A naked 25–watt bulb dangled from the centre of the ceiling like a dead spider at the end of twisted, frayed wires. The bed was sway–backed and the mattress stained and sheetless. Within arm's reach from the bed, a painted wooden chair and an antique roll–top desk snuggled up against the wall. The back of the door boasted two hooks which served as the clothes closet.

"Bathroom?" Jay asked as they returned to the main floor.

"Downstairs in the restaurant. There's a pay phone down there, too."

"What would I be expected to do?" Jay asked as they went back downstairs.

"Clean the tables, wash dishes, sweep up after we close," the man said.

"Is that it?"

"Maybe help throw out a drunk now and then."

"I can handle that," Jay said, trying to put on his toughest expression.

"If you get to wait on customers you get to keep the tips," the man said with the hesitant laugh of one who isn't used to having an appreciative audience.

"What's the joke?" Jay asked.

"Nobody ever leaves a tip in a place like this."

"When do I start?" Jay smiled broadly, partly in appreciation of getting a job and partly as reward for his attempt at humor.

"Tonight if you want. Move in anytime after six. Ring the buzzer by the front door if it's locked. I'll give you a key at the end of the month…if you're still here."

Jay headed up the stairs toward his room.

"Hold on a minute. There's a pot of tea here for the guy upstairs. First door on your right. We call him R.B."

"R.B.?" queried Jay.

"His name is Running Bear, but we prefer to call him R.B." He paused, trying to maintain a serious look while a grin tugged at the corners of his mouth. "It avoids having the mental image of him running around without any clothes on. That's not a sight any of us wants to think about."

The grin won out and he gave a small chuckle at his joke. "By the way, my name is Han Sing. You can call me Han, or you can call me Sing or you can call me Han Sing. Just don't call me late for dinner." Han doubled over in laughter at having found new ears for his well–worn joke.

At the top of the stairs Jay heard a low, droning intonation from behind the half–open door on his right. He tapped on the door and leaned his head through the doorway but still could see nothing in the dim light. The sound stopped. Jay put one foot tentatively into the room.

A deep–throated growl signaled the presence of a large dog. Most people would have reacted with a hasty retreat, but Jay's all–encompassing curiosity took over under the masquerade of bravery.

"Good dog, nice dog, good dog," he cajoled, while thinking to himself, *I hope you aren't as vicious as you sound.*

A low, voice emanated from the dark recesses of the room, "Come."

Jay took two tentative steps into the room and stood holding the teapot until his eyes grew accustomed to the darkness. An ancient First Nation native sat cross–legged on the hide–covered floor. Rugs had been rolled up at the corners of the room, creating a circular space as much like a tepee floor as possible.

Two long braids of grey hair and a weathered–beaten, wrinkled face reminded Jay of a jack–o–lantern the week after Halloween. A German Shepherd lay at the man's feet with his head on his paws, apparently oblivious to Jay. The man gestured for Jay to sit.

"Nice dog you have," Jay volunteered apprehensively.

This opening conversational gambit hung in the air for a moment like a bad odor before dissipating into the darkness. *So now what do I do?* Jay thought to himself.

Jay was not familiar enough with the traditions of elder native people to know that they observe a period of silence until they feel comfortable with each other. He was more used to the white man who is so uncomfortable with silence that he fills it with the sound of his own voice even when he has nothing to say.

The old man got up and went to a wooden chest. He took out two cups, filled them with tea and offered one to Jay. They sat in silence, sipping the tea, and staring into space until their cups were empty. The man refilled the cups without comment.

Jay began to feel restless with the silence. *This is all very nice, but maybe I should say something. This would drive poor old Steve right out of his mind. That guy can't keep quiet for a second.*

The man sensed Jay's uneasiness. "Do not speak yet. To speak now would be like the wind blowing through long grass on a summer's day. Pleasant enough, but conveying no meaning."

Several more minutes passed in silence before the man said, "Thank–you for the tea."

"I was glad to do it. Nice dog you have," Jay ventured again.

"Arrow is a good dog. He was a seeing–eye dog in his younger days before his owner gave him to me. Now he thinks he's my guard dog, but all he can do is growl. He would never bite anyone. You live here?"

"I start work downstairs tonight."

"That is good honest labor. One must be connected with the world of work in order to be happy."

"I like the way you have decorated your room. It must make you feel right at home," Jay said.

"I live as much as possible the way my ancestors did before the coming of the white man. I keep to our traditional ways, and teach the wisdom and culture of our elders to any who will listen. The Indians of Winnipeg are my tribe. They call me their shaman."

"You say you are a shaman? That's another name for medicine man, isn't it?" asked Jay.

"Medicine man works with the spirit world to cure illnesses of the body. I mediate between the spirit world and the human world to reduce the conflict in a man's soul."

"How did you become a shaman? Is that something that is inherited from your father like English royalty?"

"It is not inherited and it is not only for men. Many women of our nation become chief or medicine man. Those individuals whose body is shared by both the male and the female spirit become our strongest leaders."

"If it isn't inherited then how does one get chosen?"

"My first vision came to me when I was twelve. After I told my family about it they knew that I was queer and would someday have powers to help my people."

"When you say you are queer you don't mean that you're..." Jay started to ask, and then stopped himself abruptly.

"I was not like the others of my tribe. Sometimes I could see events in the future. I could find game where no one else could. But I had no powers to heal. Healing powers come only after the rites of passage into manhood. I had to wait until a ceremonial dance for the opportunity to act out my visions in front of my people. Only then did my full powers begin to come to me."

"What kind of powers do you have, if you don't mind my asking?"

"I know much about people and the stress in their spirit. It is clear to me that there is uneasiness within you because the hurtful thoughts of others are direct-ed toward you. My oldest grandson, like you, was bothered by bad influences that needed to be laid to rest so that his spirit could grow."

"I don't understand."

"He was caught by the street life of the city. His friends only wanted alcohol and drugs. He forgot the teachings and the ways of our people. His heart was heavy and his mind confused. He did not know what to do and so he sought me out for help."

"Is there someway that you can help me, then?"

"If you are to receive help, you must have three things: a need, an emotion and knowledge. I see that you have a need. I feel you have a strong desire to satisfy this need. I can give you knowledge of how to ask for advice from the

spirit world. Nothing in this world happens by chance. All events are connected to each other. Every action is influenced by the world and every action in
turn influences the world. You must learn how to react to the pattern of things
that happen. The spirits can help you to see these patterns. Whether you are
native or nonnative, man or woman, good or evil, you have the right to ask the
spirits for guidance and help. They may come to you or they may not. It
depends on whether or not they find you worthy."

"Great. Then you can fix things for me?"

"Not me. Every person has the right to live in accordance with the way they
see the world through their own eyes and their own experiences. No one should
be forced to change. In truth, no one can be forced to change until they are
ready. For me to even try to fix things for you would be an intrusion on your
right to live your own life in your own way."

"So you are saying that there is nothing you can do for me?"

"It is not for me to decide. It is up to you and to the spirits."

"Would you help me to contact them?" Jay asked.

"I help all who ask. It is my duty. But we must wait until the time is right. One
cannot rush matters of the spirit or of the soul."

The wizened native shuffled toward the door. "My dog needs to go out for
his evening walk. My knees are tired today."

"You'd like me to take him?" Jay asked.

"It would be a favour to me, and to him."

"I'd be happy to do it."

R.B. held out a plastic sandwich bag to Jay.

"I'm supposed to pick up after him and put it in here?" Jay asked.

"It is the white man's way," R.B. said, illustrating by putting his hand into the
bag, picking up a tea cup through the bag and then pulling the bag over his hand
to enclose the cup.

"It is how the white man captured our nation and trapped our people. His
treaties were the plastic bag to keep his hands clean and protect his conscience.
We were trapped into living on reserves and made dependent on welfare
money."

"Anything else I need to know about Arrow?" Jay asked, changing the topic.

"He likes the fire hydrant or the telephone pole. Guide him to one."

"That's easy enough," Jay said.

"His joints are stiff. Sometimes he can't balance to lift his leg. You may have
to help him."

Jay and Arrow walked slowly down the street. Arrow barked and jumped in fright at every bush and garbage can along the way as its shadowy image registered on his failing retina. Jay guided him to a tree on the boulevard. After his initial bark and suspicious sniffing of the object, Arrow began to circle the tree purposefully.

So if you want to pee, then do it, Jay said under his breath. Arrow continued to circle and sniff. "Oh all right then," Jay said lifting Arrow's back leg. *I'm glad that nobody I know is around to see me playing nursemaid to a dog.*

Jay had turned back to the restaurant when he heard a voice.

"Yo. Is that you, Jay? Whatcha doing with that dog? I thought you liked girls."

Jay looked up in surprise to see Jimmy's grinning face. "What are you doing around here?" he asked.

"I'm on my way to see some friends. I thought you lived on the other side of town?"

"I've started work at the Red Dragon, a block down the street. I live there now."

"As a dog sitter?"

"Don't get smart. As waiter and bouncer. Drop in anytime and I'll buy you a coffee."

"I will. And thanks for what you said the other night. I'll try not to let you guys down."

"You gave me a real scare the night of that rave. You certainly convinced me to stay away from drugs," Jay said.

"See you later. Right now I've gotta go and take care of some other stuff. Have fun with your dog."

Jimmy took a few steps and then turned back to Jay.

"Do you have a few bucks you could throw my way? I need to buy some potatoes for the weekend and maybe…"

"Don't bother explaining. If I've got spare cash, it's yours. What you do with it is your business." Jay pulled a couple of folded bills out of his pocket and handed them to Jimmy. "But please don't use it for drugs. I couldn't handle the guilt if you killed yourself with my money." *Guess I'll have to lift a few more bucks from R.B.*

"That's a nice thing to say."

"I do mean it, Jimmy, Look after yourself. What you do with your life has a consequence on my life."

"Thanks. I'll pay you back when I can." Jimmy turned back down Main Street, throwing a wave over his shoulder.

Back on the street again after returning Arrow to R.B., Jay started walking aimlessly along the sidewalk. *I need to get back to Phil's place for some clean clothes. And do I need a shower! Maybe I could check with Steve and see if the coast is clear. He'll know what's been happening.* Jay went back into the Red Dragon. As he stood looking at the telephone, three problems confronted him.

First, he didn't have a quarter for the phone; second, he didn't know Steve's phone number; and third, he still didn't know Steve's last name. *This is like the first time when I tried to phone Phil except that time at least I had a quarter. I do need to get my act together. And the key for Steve's apartment is on my dresser at Phil's place.* Jay closed his eyes and concentrated on focussing his brain. *This will work. I'll go to Steve's to find out what's been happening, and then he can drive me to Phil's and get my stuff and then he will drive me back here. No problem.*

Having established a course of action, Jay headed off at a brisk pace in the general direction of Steve's apartment. *I'm sure I can find my way.* An hour and a quarter later he completed the forty–five minute walk and arrived in the entrance. He pressed the buzzer for Steve. Dusk was beginning to settle over the city.

"Yes," said a disinterested, disembodied voice from the speaker.

"Hi Steve, it's Jay."

"Come on up," answered the suddenly animated voice from the speaker as the door buzzed open.

Jay hopped into the elevator, rode up to Steve's floor and knocked on his door. *Who says I'm not smart,* he said to himself. *This is working out exactly like I planned.*

Steve opened the door and looked at Jay. His nose scrunched up with displeasure and he pulled his head back as if to avoid possible contamination.

"Good lord, what has happened to you. You look awful. Get in here before anyone sees you."

Jay took a step toward the door.

"Wait. You'll track dirt onto my carpet. Take your shoes off."

Jay removed his shoes.

"Oh no. Your socks are just as dirty. Hang on."

Steve hooked Jay under the arms and the back of his knees, hoisted him up like a baby and carried him into the living room.

"Put me down! What do you think you are doing?"

Steve looked around the room for a place to deposit his protesting armful. Finally he chose the bathroom as the least likely place in the apartment to suffer irreparable damage from Jays's grime.

"Get out of those clothes and into the shower. Ursh! You're a mess. Don't go anywhere. Don't touch anything. Don't even breathe until you get cleaned up."

"Aren't you glad to see me?" Jay asked plaintively.

"Maybe I should phone for an exterminator. You don't have bugs, do you?"

Steve handed a green plastic garbage bag through the bathroom door to Jay. "Here, put your clothes in this, and hand them back to me so I can wash them. Or maybe I should burn them. Your underwear, too. Use the shampoo and soap on the shelf in the tub. And use the green bath towel, but please try not to touch anything else until you've showered."

Jay handed the bag of clothes back through the door to Steve who took it gingerly between his thumb and first finger.

Steam quickly filled the shower and enveloped Jay in a warm protective cocoon. Shampoo and hot water cascaded down over his body as he luxuriated in the hedonistic relaxation of total isolation from the rest of the world.

Jay had dried himself before he realized that he didn't have any clothes to put on. "Steve," he called. No answer. "Steve, I need clothes," he yelled louder. Still no answer. He opened the door a crack and looked out into the empty hallway. "Steve," he shouted again, but there was only silence. *Oh boy, here we go again. Except this time I am the naked one. Why is it that we can never both stay dressed?* Jay said to himself.

Jay wrapped the towel around his waist and went into the living room. Steve was lying on the sofa with a drink in his hand, listening to his stereo through headphones and staring blankly into space as he mouthed the words to the song.

Yeah, like I am supposed to believe that you forgot all about me? You are such an irritating idiot, Jay thought to himself.

He walked over and stood in front of Steve. Steve looked up as if suddenly startled out of his thoughts but the grin on his face belied his surprise. Steve let his gaze moved languidly up and down over Jay's body from head to foot and back again.

"How's the ankle?" Steve asked.

Jay looked at him blankly. "What do you mean?"

"Your sprained ankle. How is it?"

"Oh yeah. It's fine. That was a long time ago. I heal fast." *Don't you have more to think about than that? You need to get a life.*

Jay scowled. "Do you have something for me to wear?"

Steve took off the headphones and got up. "Sure, wait a sec." He went into the bedroom and brought Jay a black silk dressing gown. "This should do for the moment. Sit down and tell me what's been happening with Phil."

Jay took the dressing gown into the bathroom to change. As he slipped into the robe, he discovered that the smooth feel of expensive silk against his body was surprisingly pleasant and somehow sensually erotic. He sat on the chair opposite from Steve, carefully closing the gown.

"I talked to Phil last night. He said you had left," Steve said.

"Did he say why?"

"No. He said that you had packed up and left. Did you guys have a fight?"

"Of course not. I needed to get away. I'm working at the Red Dragon now."

Jay discovered that the silk dressing gown seemed to have developed a mind of its own and persisted in trying to slip open.

"That's somewhere up North Main, isn't it?" asked Steve.

"On the other side of the underpass. You might say I'm now officially from the wrong side of the tracks. It's a seedy area, but it's a job and I have a room there. The people are nice to me."

"Getting back to Phil, he was in a fight with someone. He has a black eye and a bunch of bruises on his face. Do you know anything about that?"

Jay noticed that the dressing gown had dropped open. He gathered it up and folded it over his knees.

Jay's brow furrowed in thought. "He was fine when I left. Why not ask him?"

"He wouldn't say. At first I thought that maybe you got into a fight with him. But from the look of your face I know it couldn't have been you. You must have some idea what went on."

Jay discovered that the dressing gown had again dropped open over his right knee. He pulled it back over his knees and tried tucking both sides of it firmly down between his legs. He crossed his feet on the coffee table.

Noticing Jay's discomfort, Steve said, "Sorry about that dressing gown. I fell in love with that orange and yellow dragon design embroidered on the back when I was in China but I don't wear it because it's impossible to keep it closed. Silk is bad that way. Don't worry about it. I won't look." He smiled broadly at Jay.

Oh sure. I bet you wouldn't look, Jay thought.

"What are those circles on your feet?" Steve asked. "They look like cigarette burns."

Jay put his feet on the floor. "It's nothing."

"Sorry. I didn't mean to pry into your private life."

"Look, Steve. I do appreciate all you've done for me, and heaven knows I needed that shower, but I don't want to discuss this with you. I have a lot on my mind right now. And speaking of clothes, may I have mine back?"

"You're right, Jay. Sorry. It's just that I'm concerned about Phil. I'm never entirely sure what he might do since he had his breakdown. And I care about you, too, whether you like it or not." Steve got up to take the clothes from the dryer.

"I don't want you to care about me. Leave me alone. I can look after myself."

Steve handed Jay the clothes. "I seem to recall that you are the one who came here. I didn't force you." Steve went over to the liquor cabinet.

"You gave me a key to encourage me to come here. You gave me clothes and made me feel in debt to you. And you keep feeding me booze, telling me it is some kind of iced tea. You keep interfering with my life and trying to control me. I came to Winnipeg to be on my own but you and Phil keep messing things up on me. Especially Phil."

"Hang on there. I know you're upset about something but you aren't making much sense." Steve handed Jay a tall glass of Long Island Iced Tea.

"What I want is for you to stay out of my life and stay away from me."

Jay took the drink and emptied it without pausing for breath. Steve took the glass, refilled it and gave it back to Jay.

"I'm only doing for you what I would do for any of my friends. Or even a stranger, as far as that goes. You're the one with the big problem, not me," Steve said.

"Maybe you're right. And I must say that I hate it when you are right, because that would mean that I'm wrong. I am upset and I apologize for taking it out on you. And I hate apologizing, too. There's something I've got to do, even if it may be the last thing I ever do while still having the full use of both my arms and legs."

Jay took his clothes and changed in the bathroom.

"I'll come back when I've done what needs to be done. That is unless I'm in the hospital. Is that okay with you?" Jay asked.

"No. It certainly isn't okay with me if you go to the hospital," Steve said in an attempt to lighten the mood. "But of course you're welcome to come back here anytime you want."

Jay opened the door to leave.

"Hair," Steve said.

"Excuse me," replied Jay pausing in the doorway.

"Your hair. You can't go out looking like that."

"Well, you wouldn't let me use your hair brush. What did you expect me to do?" Jay said, not wanting to admit his oversight.

"Maybe ask for one. Come here. You can use this one." Steve reached into the bathroom and got a hair brush for Jay.

Jay struggled to bring a semblance of order to his hair. "You have nice hair, Jay. With a bit of styling and maybe a reddish–blonde tint you would look quite hot."

"Fly off with your ideas. You're not getting your hands anywhere near my hair. As a matter of fact, you are not getting your hands anywhere near my anything."

"It's only a suggestion. If you change your mind, say the word. My friends say I'm a good hairstylist."

On his way back to the Red Dragon, Jay detoured through the Fringe Festival area in hopes of seeing Tanya again, but she wasn't there. *Just my luck. Here I am clean and smelling nice, and there's no one around to appreciate it,* he thought.

Jay kept pushing thoughts of Tony and Phil out of his mind in a vain effort to avoid feeling guilty about his role in the recent events.

Jay left the light on when he lay down to sleep on the sheetless bed.

13

IF I HAD A HAT I'D BE HOME

Jay lay on his bed, staring at the ceiling. The words of the shaman echoed in his head and seemed to be calling to him. He got up and went down the hall to the shaman's door. As he stood with his knuckles poised to knock, he heard a low growl from Arrow. The door opened.

"You have made a decision. Come in."

The shaman went to the head of his bed to a bundle wrapped in hides hanging from a makeshift tripod of willow branches. He took down the bundle and tenderly unwrapped the first layer to reveal four circles of cloth each about a metre in diameter, a small leather pouch and an amulet. The amulet was an eight–inch circle of lovingly tanned buffalo hide with a beaded four–pointed star on one side and an eagle feather hanging loosely from the middle of the other side.

The shaman hung the amulet around his neck and said, "You need an offering of a cloth print and of tobacco. As your friend I give them to you now so that you may offer them to the spirits." He spread out the four coloured prints: scarlet, blue, white and yellow. Jay looked at them and selected the yellow one.

"Yellow is the colour of the Eagle Spirit. The Eagle goes with the Sun, with Autumn and with the development of the ability to plan ahead. A person will select the colour of the spirit which best can meet his needs. The eagle flies high and sees far. Its feather is sacred because it knows all that the eagle sees and can give good counsel if you know how to listen," the shaman explained.

"But I don't know how to listen to an eagle feather," Jay said, feeling rather foolish.

"Someday when your spirit is ready you may be given a feather, and when that time comes you will know how to listen to it."

"Will you give me a feather?"

"One must prove himself worthy of the feather to make use of its power. You are ready only for your first tiny step."

"Tell me what I must do."

"Prepare your offerings so that the eagle spirit may look on you with favour and allow you to share in its knowledge," he said reaching into the small pouch.

Jay stood in the middle of the yellow cloth circle while the shaman sprinkled tobacco in a circle on the cloth around him. After the ceremony the tobacco would be gathered up in the cloth and hung out in the bush, eventually returning to the earth through natural decay. For a shaman living in the city it might be weeks before someone going back to the reserve could take the package to an appropriately sacred resting place.

"First you must be purified. It is best to do four days of sweat lodge after four days of fasting, but we do not have time for this. The evil influences that may cause you great harm are already in motion against you."

"I think I've had the four days of fasting, if that helps any," said Jay in an effort to be funny. His attempt at humour went unnoticed.

"You must fast for a reason. Fasting alone does not purify your soul, although it may be helpful in purifying your body. We use incense for purification. It could be sweetgrass, or sage or sweet pine. Because you are not one of us, and have not done a sweat lodge, we must use the most rare and powerful smoke for purification."

The shaman lit a small piece of fungus which he had gathered from the bark of a diamond willow tree in the moist heat of autumn. It had then been carefully dried, with prayerful chants over his hot–water radiator during the early winter months. A small packet of tobacco had been left at the gathering site as thanks to Mother Nature for having produced the fungus and for leading the shaman to it.

While waving smoke from the smouldering fungus around the door in a clockwise circle, the shaman prayed softly in his native tongue. The smoke wafted around Jay. He was instructed to use his cupped hands to pour it over his head like water and to inhale and exhale the smoke slowly. The dog got up and moved to the farthest corner of the room.

"When you breath in, the smoke mixes with your thoughts and prayers. When you breath out, the smoke goes up to the spirits and carries your prayers with it. Your guiding spirit will know what you need."

"But how will I know what I should do?" asked Jay.

"The spirit may come or it may not. If it comes, it will be in the form of a vision or a dream to guide you."

Soft chanting accompanied by the beating of a rustic drum continued for several minutes. The pulsing of the drum took control of Jay's heartbeat and breathing. His breathing became shallow and rapid. Beads of sweat appeared on his forehead as he slipped into a semi–hypnotic trance.

When the ritual concluded, Jay went down the hall to his room and collapsed on his bed.

The aroma of the burnt fungus had permeated Jay's clothes. It filled his nose and every pore of his body. He drifted in and out of a fitful sleep as if from a fever.

He saw himself back home in the woods with his rifle. As he approached a group of three deer, he found he was unable to decide which one to shoot. With his rifle swinging back and forth, aiming first at one and then another, he tried to decide on his target. The deer approached him menacingly, their eyes red with anger. Panic overwhelmed Jay when he realized that he had forgotten to slip a cartridge into the rifle chamber. He felt a rush of anger at his mother for teaching him never to carry a loaded rifle. He turned and ran, stumbling and falling through the underbrush with the deer in close pursuit. Exhausted he fell and did not get up. One of the deer poised above him ready to pummel him with his hooves. High above them an eagle circled, its wings motionless as it floated through the air. Slowly the head of the deer took on the features of a man. It was a man that Jay recognized but couldn't identify. The man's features dissolved into the face of a wolf and the deer's body turned into the body of a wolf. The wolf turned from Jay and chased the other two deer away. Drifting motionlessly in the air, the eagle observed the drama below. A lone feather fell to the ground.

Jay sat up. His hands trembled and his body was moist with sweat. He leapt off the bed and ran to the shaman's room.

"I had a dream, but I don't understand it. I was about to be trampled by a herd of deer and I could not escape. There was an eagle, but it didn't help at all."

"Your vision was good. It shows you where your present path will lead you. You must take some action to avoid harm. The spirit of the Eagle is there to protect you if you chose to make a plan and to act upon it."

The shaman continued, "The spirits look favourably on you because I, too, received a vision from the Great Spirit. The veil of time pulled aside and I could see into the future. I saw you bullied and shamed by three men while your friends stood by. You were not hurt physically but you were embarrassed. You gave up your search for your proper destiny. Life became frustrating and short."

"So this is what will happen to me, then. I am not impressed to know how bleak my future is. It doesn't help me to know that I have no hope for the future," said Jay.

"What you do with knowledge is up to you. The spirits show the path you are following and where it leads. If you want to change the future, then you must change your actions. If you can understand how to react to the pattern of the events in your life then you can change the future."

"But what should I do? I don't know how to change events."

"Only you can live your life. Only you can find the path that is best for you. You must have faith in the Eagle Spirit. It will protect you when you act and it will direct you in finding your true path. The spirits of your ancestors will guide you if you open your mind and heart to them. If you do not act, then the spirits cannot help you and your future will unfold as we have seen."

Jay went out into the early afternoon sun.

The busy, early afternoon lunch crowd at the mall was one of Tony's favourite times to make his contacts. Jay spotted him sitting alone at a corner table against the wall. Tony was immaculately outfitted, as always, in an Armani double–breasted dark–blue suit and yellow, Italian silk tie. He delicately puffed on a cigarillo, held gently between his thumb and first two fingers. A styrofoam cup of coffee sat cooling in front of him. His hair was heavily moussed and professionally styled. Jay went over and stood across the table from Tony.

"Yes, please sit. We have been unable to find you. But I hoped that maybe you would come to find me. I like that you have come to me. Let me get us something to eat. The pizza here is quite acceptable," Tony said as he waved a finger in the air.

This is a food court, Jay said to himself. *Does he think you can signal for a waiter like in some high–class restaurant?*

Tony continued. "Tell me how things are with you. You have been in my thoughts lately. I worried that perhaps something unfortunate had happened to you. You have not been around and you have not even been seeing your girl-friend lately."

"You mean that you've had Sue's place under surveillance? How did you know about her anyway?"

"I was concerned for you. I take a personal interest in all my associates."

"I had to go out of town for a while."

Jay looked up at the man who arrived with a pizza in one hand and a styro-foam cup in the other. His suit looked as if it had been purchased ten years and forty pounds earlier. Its buttons and seams strained to control the man's muscu-lar bulk. He looked uncomfortable as only a wrestler in a business suit acting as a waiter could look. "Here you are boss. I hope that Pepsi is satisfactory." Without waiting for an answer he disappeared to the far side of the food court.

All these times I've met Tony here and I never once noticed that he had a bodyguard with him. How could I miss something so obvious?

"Let us eat before we discuss business," Tony said taking a piece of pizza and pushing the rest toward Jay. "I know you usually like pepperoni pizza and Pepsi."

"How could you possibly know that?" Jay asked.

"I have people who tell me things that might be useful to me. Knowledge is power. You did not show me much respect when you told me your name was Joe. I am not so easily fooled."

"Joe is my middle name," Jay lied.

"It is of no importance. Enjoy the pizza."

Jay concentrated on his pizza in silence for a few moments. "If you had a beef with me, then you should have dealt with me. You had no right going around beating up on my friends."

"I see my little bantam rooster has some fight in him after all. I like that," Tony said.

It's not a rooster you are up against this time, buddy, it's an eagle, Jay said to himself, *and you'd better not ruffle its feathers.* "Where do you get off having your goons beat up on Phil?"

Tony picked up his coffee. His gold ring with its brilliant solitaire diamond looked bizarrely out of place against the flimsy styrofoam coffee cup.

"And he has loyalty to his friends. Another good quality in a man."

"This isn't about me. I'm here to talk about you. Where do you think you get off beating up on innocent people?" Jay was getting angrier by the minute at Tony's condescending attitude.

"But a bit impatient. This is not a quality I admire. But I overlook it for now." Jay stood up and started to walk away.

"I will explain. We waited for a period of time for you to contact me. When you didn't, I sent my boys to your friend's place to find you. They meant you no harm. I wished only to understand your motivations and feelings toward our business dealings."

"So why did they beat up on my friend?" Jay asked, sitting down again.

"When they ask about you, your friend Phil, he goes wild, slams one of my boys against the wall and starts throwing his fists about. They only try to persuade him to calm his anger. It is unfortunate, but sometimes a person gets hurt under such circumstances. But enough about him. Am I to understand that you no longer wish to work with me?"

"That's right. It was wrong to quit without telling you. But I should never have become involved in this kind of activity in the first place."

"Did we not have an agreement that should be honoured?"

"We didn't sign anything. There's no legal contract."

"I recall that we agreed to certain things. You would do me some favours and I would repay you for your kindness. Contracts are not necessary between people who trust each other." Tony leaned over, putting his face close to Jay's. He stared intently into Jay's eyes as if to implant the information directly into his brain. "I like you. You would do well working for me. But I will respect your wishes. I trust you will respect mine."

"And your wishes would be…"

"That you not discuss my business with others. There are those who do not wish me success in my efforts to make an honest living. It would make me unhappy if I discovered you to be one of those people."

"You live your life and I will live mine," Jay said.

"It pleases me to hear you say that. I will tell my associates that you do not wish to be further involved with us. They will listen to me." Tony drew deeply on his cigarillo and blew a cloud of smoke off to the side. "And your friend, Phil. I could have use for a man like him. You may tell him what I have said. The impression he left on my boys will not soon be forgotten," Tony said with the hint of a lopsided smile.

Jay left the mall and filled his lungs. Although the air was smoggy and filled with gasoline fumes, it felt like a breath of air fresh from the forest. He headed down Portage Avenue toward Main Street.

At the Red Dragon a group of men sat huddled over their half–empty coffee cups, engaged in recounting the exploits of their younger years, which became more vivid and adventurous with each retelling.

Jay sat at the counter. "Any chance of getting something to eat?"

"The stove's turned off until supper time, but I can get you a plate of left-overs from lunch," Han Sing replied.

"Anything would be fine. I can't seem to get filled up today."

The man disappeared into the kitchen and returned with a plate of lukewarm assorted Chinese food. "You starting work tonight?"

"I'll be here. But I'm going to take a nap first. I don't have an alarm clock or anything, so give me a shout if I'm not down by six."

"If you're not down here on time, I'll set R.B.'s dog after you," Han Sing said with a laugh.

"Why is that so funny?" asked Jay.

"Because Arrow's blind, that's why. And he doesn't have any teeth left that are any good."

I don't think that's funny, thought Jay, *This guy seems to have a strange sense of humour.* "Arrow is a good dog. He's my friend, and I don't want you making fun of him," Jay said defensively.

Jay finished his makeshift meal and went up the stairs. In front of the shaman's closed door he raised his hand to knock, but decided not to bother him. *He probably knows everything that happened already,* he thought.

Back in his room, Jay lay down on the bare mattress. As he stared up at the light bulb, it seemed to sprout wings and take on the shape of an eagle sur-rounded by a globe of white light. As he dozed off, the eagle left the cord and began to circle on motionless wings, illuminating the room with its glow.

YOU'RE THE CUSTOMER

"Work time, sleepyhead." The voice intruded into Jay's mind, pushing sleep aside. He sat up on his bed and tried to put the events of the day into some semblance of order. Fortunately, he started with remembering the most recent events first and realized that he needed to go down to work. If he had started with the earliest events of the day he might never have made it to work at all.

"I'll be right there," he shouted back in the general direction of the stairs.

The restaurant was almost full. Four men sat at their usual table eating supper. A party of eight teenagers had pushed three tables together to accommodate their plan of sharing a variety of dishes.

I guess I should appear useful, thought Jay. "Should I have an apron or something for clearing tables?" he asked Han.

"It's up to you. You look good the way you are if you don't mind taking the chance of getting your nice clothes dirty. Go around the tables and gather up plates when they are finished and refill their coffee if they ask. Wash the dishes if you have time, or wait until later, whatever you like."

Jay quickly got into a routine of clearing one table while getting an order from the neighbouring one so that each trip to the kitchen served double duty. As the evening wore on, the restaurant gradually emptied. Jay was careful to tidy and wipe the empty tables thoroughly. *Phil would be so proud of me,* Jay said to himself.

"I can handle this end now, Jay. You go to the back and finish washing the dishes. Do what the cook tells you. He loves bossing people around," said Han.

Great. As if that's what I always wanted. Somebody to boss me around, Jay thought while he said out loud, "Okay boss."

The last of the dishes had been put away and the kitchen wiped clean when Han came into the kitchen with a sombre look on his face.

"Jay, there's a guy out front who looks like he's been in a fight and might be looking for trouble. He's big and looks tough, but could you go throw him out, please?"

Jay took a deep breath and mentally steeled himself for the unpleasant unknown. "Sure thing. I'll try not to hurt him."

The only person in the restaurant sat with his back to the kitchen. As Jay walked toward the man, he thought he heard Han's laughter from the kitchen. *He thinks it's funny that I'm going to get killed?* Jay thought as he approached the man. *Wait a minute. That guy looks a lot like Phil.*

Phil turned around in his chair. His face looked as if it been used as a punching bag. Through puffy lips that muffled the words he said, "Hi Jay. How are you doing?"

"Phil. It's good to see you. I would have phoned you but I didn't have the number. How did you find me?"

"Steve told me. You know how gays are about spreading the latest news or gossip. If there isn't anything exciting happening, they make something up. A gay without his cellular phone is like a baby without its soother - restless and cranky."

"Are we still friends?" Jay said looking at Phil's face in general and his left eye in particular which had swollen almost closed.

"Of course. Why wouldn't we be?"

"No reason. I left rather suddenly, that's all," Jay said. "Can I get you a steak to put on that black eye of yours?"

"No thanks. It'll fix itself in a little while."

"I guess you'd want to put tofu on it instead of a steak anyway, wouldn't you?" Jay said with a grin. "So what is new with you?"

"Not much. A couple of guys came looking for you but I told them you didn't live with me anymore. Then they left."

"And that's all?" Jay asked.

"Yeah. What did you expect? By the way, Sue's been wondering what happened to you lately. Maybe you should call her."

"You're right. She's used to having me call at least once a day. Maybe she thinks I don't like her anymore."

"I took the liberty of telling her that you'd had some things to work out and that you'd get back to her. I hope you don't mind my interfering with your life."

"No, that's great. I appreciate your help. Are you sure you are not angry with me?"

"Why would I be angry with you?"

"From the looks of you I would say that you probably have good reason to be angry at me. I would guess that the reorganization of your face is because of me," Jay said.

"Not completely. If it hadn't been those two goons, it would have been someone else. Those punks just happened to be in the right place at the right time for me to work out some of my frustrations. I need a good fight now and then. Your situation chose the time and place for me."

"Apparently you did a good job. Tony was more impressed with you than with his own boys. He says you can work for him anytime you want," Jay said.

"You talked to Tony? That took guts. Tell me about it."

"There wasn't much choice. I'm not going to spend my life running and hiding, so I told him that if he didn't leave me alone I would send you to beat him up personally."

"Don't be funny. It hurts me to laugh. Seriously though. Are things settled?"

"Sure. He wanted to be sure I wouldn't try to make any trouble for him with the law. He did say that he could use you in his organization anytime."

"Not my sort of thing. My temper would get me in big trouble. I'd end up killing somebody. But I do like a good rumble now and again. It lets the evil spirits out of my head and makes room for my gentler spirit to develop," Phil said. "Are you coming back to stay with me, then?"

"I have a job here with a place to stay right upstairs. That way I don't have to get up so early to go to work."

"You work days?" Phil asked.

"No. Nights from six to midnight. It's a marvellous arrangement because I can still go to all-night parties and stuff and sleep during the day."

"So you're moving out on me. That leaves me with an empty room. I won't have any use for it with you gone."

Jay looked dejected. "I'm sorry, Phil. I know that you went to a lot of trouble for me, what with fixing up the room and like that. And I haven't done anything to thank you, but I do have to get on with my own life." He looked up with the expression of a puppy needing approval from its master and said, "You can come to visit me here anytime, you know."

"I'd like that, Jay. Maybe you'll come to visit me. I'll keep your room for you so you can sleep over anytime you want. By the way, why don't you come home with me now and you can get some of your things. Maybe tomorrow we could go to the YMCA. A good workout and some time in the sauna would get me back to feeling somewhat human."

"That would be great. I miss having a shower handy. Maybe I could stay there overnight," Jay said. He looked at Phil expectantly, "If you don't mind, that is."

"That would be great."

"I feel rotten about taking advantage of your generosity and then running off on you like this," Jay said.

"I only did what I wanted to do. You never asked for anything. You let me look after you for a while and I liked doing it. It made me feel more useful than I have since…" Phil slipped into silent thought.

"Since Scotty died?" Jay finished the sentence.

"Yes. You've been a big help in getting me over my depression. I think maybe now I've finally laid him to rest in my mind and I'm ready to get on with my life."

"I wish I could have taken Scotty's place for you, but I have to make my own way in the world."

"Nobody can take the place of another, and shouldn't try to. You've helped fill the void that he left, but his memory will always be there. He will always be a part of me, just as you will always be a part of me, too," Phil said.

Jay changed the topic before it became uncomfortably emotional. "You wouldn't believe the things that have happened to me since I saw you last. There's this great shaman guy, called R.B., who lives next to me upstairs. We call him Running Bear because he goes around without any clothes on," Jay said with an expectant smile which suddenly vanished. "No, wait a minute, that's not right. It should have been the other way around. It was funny when Han told it."

"You never were good with jokes, were you? Besides, you know it hurts when I smile."

"Anyway," Jay continued, "he's going to teach me all about native religion and the Sweetgrass Trail and the Medicine Circle and how a person's character is determined by his actions and all sorts of things like that. He has his room set up so it is like a circle with hides and blankets all around the edges and on the floor."

"That's probably because natives understand that things in nature and in life are circular, and that life–energy must flow. When the natives were put onto reserves, the white man put them into gray square boxes. The corners of the buildings prevented the circular flow of their life force and energy. Their spirituality and culture got caught in the corners where it withered and died."

"Doesn't it bother you that he has animal hides around his room and probably a selection of dead animal parts as well? Someone must have killed the animals to get them," Jay asked.

"Those animals will have died knowing that they had fulfilled a part of the cycle of nature. The bounty of nature is a trust given to us by God, to be passed on from generation to generation. If it is used wisely then it will last forever, but one must be careful not to exploit it or it will be unable to sustain itself and the planet will eventually die."

Phil continued, "The spirit of a wild animal is released from its body during the contest for survival. If the hunter wins, then the animal's spirit is freed to join with the spirit of the hunter.

"Slaughterhouses are different. The animals are trapped in pens filled with the odour of hostility and fear. They are frightened by the sharp shadows cast by the corners of the chutes as they are herded in to slaughter. This causes adrenaline and hormones to be released into their blood stream. Because they can neither run nor fight to cleanse their system, these chemicals remain in the animal's flesh and organs. It is these chemicals that cause physical and emotional sickness in the people who eat the meat.

"That is why the Jewish people require that a rabbi be present at the death of animals. He ensures that the animal is hung up when it dies so that all the blood is drained out. Only then do they consider the meat to be fit to blessed and made kosher or fit to eat."

"If you keep talking like that you're going to turn me into a vegetarian," Jay said.

"It's the same when a person dies in an unnatural or violent death. Their spirit may not have time to be released naturally from their body before death. Then the tormented spirit is destined to wander the earth as a ghost or apparition until it can find its proper rest."

"I must introduce you to Running Bear. You two would have a lot of things to discuss," Jay said.

"I think we would. You do know that you should give him a gift, don't you?"

"No. I hadn't thought about that. He didn't say anything about being paid."

"A shaman will never ask for payment. It is part of their belief that they must help anyone who asks. But it is expected that people who are helped will show their appreciation through some sort of a gift, just as the shaman leaves a gift to the spirits for their help. It's always customary to give a gift of tobacco to an elder or a teacher as a sign of respect. If you wanted to make it extra special, you could also give some bark from the red willow tree."

"Yeah sure. Like I always carry red willow bark around with me."

"Red willow bark is sacred. It likes to grow in wet areas so it's rare to find it on the prairies except near a river. It's abundant in the muskeg of the Cross Lake area. That's fairly close to where you come from. It is such a beautiful sight to see the blood–red bark rising out of the white, frozen landscape in the winter."

"I've never seen red willow where I used to live. It's mostly all big trees."

"Natives often mix the red willow bark with tobacco as a ceremonial smoke. If tobacco or red willow isn't available, the elders smoke a mixture of dried sumac leaves, dogwood and bearberries. They called it kinnikinnick."

"How do you know so much about this anyway? You sure don't look like a native."

"I've spent a lot of time with native people over the years. Besides, a person can't live in Winnipeg all his life without picking up a few clues about the native culture. After all, Winnipeg has the largest native population of any region in Canada. Winnipeg could become Canada's biggest Indian reserve if they wanted to make one here."

Phil continued, "And I do happen to have some red willow bark at home that I gathered two years ago when I stayed with some native friends in South Dakota. The red willow tree is sacred to the aboriginal people because its spirit is a great teacher. When a person smokes it, his breath mixes with the smoke and makes a direct link between him and the Great Spirit, which they sometimes call the Kitche Manitou."

"I guess there is a lot more that you could teach me, too."

"Not as much as your shaman friend. You are lucky to have met him."

"He said that I should participate in a sweat lodge ceremony to purify my spirit, but I don't know anything about that."

"A formal sweat lodge is usually built from willow branches stuck into the ground in a circle and curved over to make a dome to support a covering of hides. Then hot rocks are brought in and showered with water to make steam. Sometimes a simple one is improvised by a circle of people crouching around hot rocks while they hold the edge of a tarp. In a city like this there is no place where a proper sweat lodge can be made and kept sacred."

"So what do they do, then?" asked Jay.

"Most wait until the summer and then go to one on their reserve. I have heard of a person in Winnipeg who has built a sauna in his basement as a sweat lodge. It has a circular floor and domed ceiling. The floor is covered with sage brush for purification and it is reserved for use only in sweat lodge ceremonies under the direction of a holy man such as your shaman friend. That's what I have heard. I don't know if it is true or not."

"Is there anything else I could give R.B. as a gift?"

"Nothing that you can buy in a store. I'm sure he would like some sweetgrass or copal or blue vervain or even cedar to make a ceremonial smudge. But Safeway doesn't sell these things. It's the things of nature that would be most important to him."

Jay changed the subject, "I know what that number is."

"You mean the one about your dad?"

"It's his Social Insurance Number 609–561–826. And 609 is what they use for Manitoba."

"I'll bet Cam can trace it through the Internet. He's a real genius with computers."

"I'll phone him from your place."

"Are you ready to come with me now, or do you need to get back to work?"

"You go ahead and I'll get there on my own. Unless you want to sit around here until I get off at midnight," Jay said with an expectant look.

"I'll get the bike and meet you in front when you get off work."

It was five minutes to midnight. "You might as well be on your way. I'll see you tomorrow. Remember you owe me five minutes," Han said with a chuckle.

Jay left the restaurant and stood waiting at the curb. A dishevelled man, staggering from an excess of drink, stumbled up to him and mumbled, "Got any change for a cup of coffee?" The man continued his erratic path down the sidewalk without pausing for a reply.

As a matter of fact, I don't, Jay said to himself. *And even if I did, I think that you need more than a cup of coffee.*

Phil wheeled his Harley over to the curb. "Hang on. I feel like a fast ride."

Oh boy. I sure hope that Eagle Spirit is still on duty. I think I'll need his help more with Phil than I did with Tony.

15

SO SUE ME

"Hello. You must be Sue's mom," Jay said to the middle–aged lady as she swung open the oak door, inviting him into the marble foyer. Her freshly done make-up and hair contrasted with a faded beige bathrobe that had acquired the status of a cherished friend.

"And you must be Jay. It's so good to meet you at last. George, come down here and meet Sue's new boyfriend."

George was neatly attired in a double–breasted grey pinstripe suit. His trimmed moustache and old–fashioned hairstyle presented the image of a successful businessman. He held out his hand to Jay. "Nice to meet you, young man. We have heard so little about you. Sit down and tell me."

"Tell you what?" Jay asked as he let go of George's limp hand and sat down.

"Tell me all about yourself, of course. Where do you come from? Who are your parents? What do they do for a living? Sue is my daughter, and these are things I need to know if you're going to be dating her."

Oh no. I'm in big trouble now. How could I be so stupid as to come here without a prepared story, Jay thought to himself as he took a deep breath and hoped that some sensible words would come out of his mouth.

"Oh for heaven's sake, George, give the lad a chance to get comfortable before you start interrogating him. Where are you and Sue planning to go tonight, Jay?" Helen asked.

"We were thinking..." Jay began to reply without any idea how the sentence would end.

"I'm not going to interrogate him," George interrupted. "But I do feel that we have a responsibility to know something about the person who is dating our daughter. After all, you remember what happened with her last male friend, don't you?"

"Let's not bring that up again. It wasn't our fault that he turned out to be married. You're not married are you, Jay?"

"Heavens no," Jay replied.

"Maybe you'd like a drink, Jay?" Helen suggested.

"Yes, please, I'd love one." *Oh no. That was much too eager. It sounds like I'm desperate.* "A glass of water would be nice." *There. That was smooth. First impressions are always so important.*

"Would you look after that please, dear? I have to finish dressing," Helen said as she headed up the spiral staircase.

George returned from the fridge with a bottle of Perrier, a glass for Jay and three fingers of Scotch for himself.

"Thank–you, sir," said Jay. *Woops. That was a bit too formal.* "I like your house. It has a great ambiance." *Did I say ambiance? He'll think I'm a total geek, or some kind of a phony.* "Did you buy it new?" *O.K. Now that was a stupid question. Maybe I should keep quiet and guzzle Perrier until Sue shows up.*

"We designed and built it ourselves."

"You build houses?" asked Jay.

"Well, I didn't build it with my own hands, if that's what you mean. I hire people to do that sort of thing. I don't suppose that your parents are the sort of people who have to work with their hands to make money, are they?"

"Oh no. Neither of my parents has ever worked a day in their lives as far as I know." *Well, that's certainly true enough.*

"That's good. Our family has been in the investment business for three generations. We let our money do our work for us. And what about you? What do you do besides dating my daughter?" George asked pointedly.

"Right now I'm getting experience in the restaurant industry. I plan to open a chain of restaurants in a few years." *That sounds like a good plan. Maybe I should think about doing that,* Jay said to himself. "Maybe you'd like to invest in it when I get things organized."

"We invest only in established businesses. If you have enough collateral, send me a copy of your business plan and I'll look it over. We don't stay wealthy by taking risks with our investments, you know."

"I totally understand. In what sort of things do you usually invest?" Jay asked.

"Mostly real estate. Our family members are all shareholders in a single company that deals with all our financial matters. Decisions are made by the company, not by any one individual. We invest in whatever looks good from the company perspective."

"So the money isn't yours then?"

"Of course it's ours. It's managed by us through the organization for us. We get tax benefits that way."

"Sort of like democracy."

"Excuse me?"

"Management of the money for the money and by the money," Jay said with a grin.

"That's a cute thought. I see why Sue likes you."

"What you are saying is that you are paid as a shareholder of the organization, is that right?" Jay asked.

"That's right. We received the money from the previous generation, and it is our duty to preserve it for the next generation. We make a good living from the profits of our inheritance, but we don't consider it to be ours to spend. It is a trust handed down to us for safekeeping. Do you golf?"

The question caught Jay off guard. The words popped out of his mouth without effort or thought, "Of course. It's a great game."

"What's your handicap?" George asked.

Oh great. Other than my big mouth I haven't a clue what he means by a handicap, Jay thought to himself. *Maybe I can pretend I didn't hear the question and change the topic.*

Helen interrupted Jay's thoughts as she swished into the room in a formal, off–the–shoulder dress accented by a necklace with a massive pendant diamond hanging low over her throat.

"It was nice meeting you, Jay. Sue will be down in a minute. Make yourself at home. Come on George. We don't want to be late."

"You aren't wearing that necklace, are you?" George asked.

"I was planning to. Doesn't it look nice with this dress?"

"It's too flashy. Wear something plainer."

George glanced at his gold–plated Rolex watch. "You'd better hurry. We're going to be late."

Helen went back upstairs while George poured himself another drink.

"Ninety thousand dollars for a necklace and she wants to wear it to a dinner party. I don't need to have people passing judgment about me and my money because of that," George said to no one in particular.

"Ninety thousand…" Jay exclaimed involuntarily.

"Diamonds are a good investment. They keep their value in times of inflation. But wearing them can seem pretentious. Now a fancy watch is something else," he said, showing Jay his watch.

"Wow. That's a handsome timepiece."

"Notice how smoothly the second hand moves? That's how you can tell it's a genuine Rolex. With cheap imitations the hand jumps from second to second. If you can afford a nice watch, you deserve to have the time flow by without any jerks interfering in it."

I wonder if that's a shot at me, Jay thought. "Something like that must have cost a thousand dollars," he exclaimed.

"A thousand would about cover the tax on it."

Helen returned wearing a triple strand of pearls and went straight to the door. With a glare at her husband she said, "Is this better? Now let's go or we'll be late for the appetizers."

Jay got up and went toward the door with them.

"Maybe we could get together for a round of golf sometime," George said to Jay as he and Helen went out the door.

"That would be splendid. I can be available anytime. Thanks," Jay called after them from the doorway. *I wonder how long it takes to learn to play golf? Maybe Phil can teach me this weekend.*

Sue skipped down the stairs and slipped her arm around Jay's waist at the door.

"Bye," she called as Helen and George climbed into their Mercedes.

"What do you have planned for us tonight, Jay?" Sue asked.

"I thought I'd leave that up to you."

"But it's so manly when you make the decisions."

"Maybe you could give me another driving lesson, then."

"We can do that on the way to wherever you decide we should go. Besides, if you would learn to parallel park, you'd be ready to take your test anytime."

"Why do you keep nagging me about parking? I don't need to parallel park. I can always drive around until I find a double space."

"But you need to be able to do it for your test."

"Maybe the guy will forget to ask me to do it. Besides, if I need to do it I'll do it when the time comes. It's no big deal."

"So how come when you try it, you end up in the middle of the street or on the sidewalk?"

"It's because you make me nervous. I can do it anytime if you're not around."

"Sorry I make you nervous. Come on, let's go drive downtown. Maybe we can catch a movie or something."

When they got to the car, Sue opened the driver's side.

"I thought you were going to let me drive," protested Jay.

"Not unless you plan to learn something. Besides, if you got into an accident I'd be the one in trouble. You don't have anything to lose."

"Sure I do. They might hold off giving me my licence for six months or a year. A cop told me that."

"Since when are you so friendly with the police?"

"No big deal. Phil got stopped on his bike one time, so I asked the policeman. I like to know those kind of things."

"That's still no big deal. You don't have a car anyway."

"Stop saying that. I'll have a car soon enough. I haven't decided yet what I want." *And I need to get a credit rating so I can lease one. It would take me twenty or so years to save enough to buy one.* "Besides, I need to have a photo ID."

"You aren't old enough to buy liquor."

"No, but I'm going to the United States and you have to have identification or they won't let you across."

"You're not planning on going with Steve, are you? I didn't think you liked him. Besides I'd expect him to take one of his comrades."

"You mean one of his gay friends?"

"I meant someone more his own age. But yes, that too, I guess."

"If I don't go with him, I'll go with someone else. Maybe you'd like to come with me," Jay said.

"To San Francisco?"

"Well, maybe to Grand Forks first. Anyway, get out of the car and let me drive. I'll be careful."

Jay climbed in behind the wheel of the white Mustang and zoomed down the driveway onto the street.

"You'd better do up your seat belt," Sue said.

"I don't use it in the city. It's a nuisance. And it's not going to be any help in a little fender–bender anyway."

Jay's was the first car away from the green light. He turned to Sue, "Let's go downtown to the Cineplex and see what's on."

Jay regained consciousness one thought at a time. *Why am I sitting here pushing on the brake pedal when it's already right to the floor? Why is there a smashed–up car in front of me? Why is there blood running down my face?*

Sue's voice tried to be reassuring. "There's an ambulance on the way. Don't try to move until it gets here."

"Are you hurt?" he asked.

"I'm fine. You hit your head on the steering wheel and you're bleeding. We need to get you to the hospital."

Jay leaned back and closed his eyes. The next time he opened them he saw Sue and a doctor looking down at him.

"Nice you decided to join us," Sue said.

"Where am I?"

"You've been here in the hospital since yesterday," the doctor said. "You've suffered a minor concussion, but the X–rays and tests look good. I'll check on you again in the morning, and you should be able to go home tomorrow."

"There's a gentleman here who says he needs to see you," a nurse said from the doorway.

A man with a briefcase came over to the bedside.

"I'm Stenwich, of Stenwich, Stenwich and Funk. I'm here about the accident."

"And why should I talk to you?" Jay asked.

"Because if you don't, you'll be in bigger trouble than you are now. We know that you hit my client's car so that makes the accident your fault. If you would please sign this paper I think we can avoid any problems that could be rather expensive for you." The lawyer held out a packet of several sheets of paper folded back to the last page. "Just sign here."

"I'll have to read it first."

"It's only a formality. Sign it, and then I'll leave it for you to read when you are feeling better."

Jay took the pen and leaned over to rest the paper on the night stand for support.

"Wait a minute, Jay. Let me see that paper," Sue said.

Sue took the paper and quickly glanced through it. She handed it back to the lawyer.

"He's not signing this paper. It says that he takes full responsibility for the accident. I was there. I know that the other guy went through the intersection long after the light changed, and there were witnesses there that will testify to it."

The lawyer handed the paper back to Jay.

"You're not going to let your girlfriend tell you what to do, are you?" he asked Jay.

"You bet I am," Jay retorted. "If I have to choose between you and her I'll choose her. She's the most important thing in my life." The lawyer took the unsigned paper and left.

Jay looked up at Sue. "I'm sorry I've made such a mess of things, Sue. Your car is a wreck and that guy seemed to think there could be trouble. I don't have any money and I've probably lost my job because I didn't show up for work. I wouldn't blame you if you never wanted to see me again because I'm such a loser and for being so stupid."

"That's sweet," Sue said.

"What's sweet? My smashing up your car?"

"No, silly. Saying that I'm important to you."

"Well it's true. I love you more than anything. But what about the car?"

"Don't worry about it. Lie there and get some rest," Sue said.

"But how am I going to fix this mess I've made?"

"It's all right, Jay. I phoned my dad and he's looking after things."

"How can he do that?"

"He'll make some calls. He has people who owe him for past favours or who work for him, and they'll do whatever he asks. Believe me. A couple of phone calls and everything is looked after. You don't have to worry about anything."

"But what about your gorgeous car? It's a wreck. I've got to get it repaired for you somehow."

"We don't repair things. My dad said that a new one is going to be delivered to our house by noon tomorrow. I needed a new car anyway. I hope it's a dark blue one this time."

"But my job…"

"The restaurant has been contacted and they know you won't be in for work until next week."

"You mean that when I leave here my life carries on as if nothing had happened?"

"That's about it. Little accidents are not a problem with us. My dad puts in a call or two to his lawyers or accountants and the problem disappears. It's one of those little perks you get when you have lots of money. I'm glad that you're all right."

Sue went over and gave Jay a little kiss on the cheek. "Now try to get some sleep. I'll be here tomorrow to take you home."

Sue left as Han Sing stuck his head through the doorway.

"Can I come in?" he asked.

"Sure," Jay replied. "I certainly wasn't expecting to see you here."

"Running Bear said I should check to see if you were all right or if you maybe needed some of his hocus–pocus medicine. He would have come himself but he doesn't like to leave Arrow alone."

"Tell him thanks for his concern, but it's nothing more than a little bump on the head. I'll be fine. By the way, can the restaurant get along without me for a day or two? I may have to rest up a bit before I can go back to work. I suppose you'll have to dock my pay for the time I miss."

"Don't worry about it. Some guy in a suit with a brief case told me to keep paying you and to hire someone to work in your place. He gave me two hundred bucks and a business card and said for me to call if that didn't cover expenses until you got back to work. I've hired myself to replace you and that guy'll be paying me your wages until you come back, so don't hurry. By the way, I doubled your salary, starting yesterday," Han said with a self–satisfied grin.

"It seems that everyone is a lot better off without me, even me."

A voice over the intercom announced the end of visiting hours. Jay rolled over and was immediately asleep. Half an hour later a hand on his shoulder gently roused him.

"Time for your medicine."

Jay swallowed the pill.

"What's it for?" he asked.

"It's your sleeping pill," the nurse replied as she turned off the light on her way out of the room.

16

THE MESSAGE IS THE MEDIUM

"Come on you guys. Take it easy with the booze. We should try to get in the right mood before Tanya gets here to lead us."

Tiffany was having trouble getting the group to take the seance seriously. Jay sat patiently at the table with Steve and Cam. Becky and Jimmy were off in a corner enjoying each other's company and a bottle of vodka.

"I don't know how we got into this, Cam," Steve said.

"You are being such a wet blanket," Cam replied. "It was as a favour to Phil that we're here. Just because he wimped out at the last minute is no reason for your being so bad–tempered about it. The spirit world is sensitive to bad vibes and bitchiness, you know."

"This is all your doing, Jay," Steve said. "I hope it's worth the effort."

"I did mention it to Phil but it was his idea to invite you, not mine. I think he wanted to have you here for support in case he contacted Scotty. If you're not happy here, why don't you leave? Phil might have needed to have you here but we don't. We can get along quite fine without you," Jay retorted.

"Where's Sue?" Cam asked.

"She had to go with her parents to a family dinner."

"I would have thought that you'd be going with her," Cam said.

"They don't seem to want to accept me as part of the family."

"But you get along with them, don't you?"

"Sure. So long as it's just them and me we get along fine. But if anyone else comes to visit I get sent to the kitchen. I hate that. Even though it does give Sue and me a chance to be alone together. It makes me feel like a second–class person."

"How's the job going, Jay?" Steve asked.

"Great. I got my salary doubled. I get more than two hundred a week now."

"So that's how much an hour?"

"About five dollars."

"That's not even minimum wage. He must have been ripping you off before. You could have forced him to pay minimum wage, you know."

"Yeah, sure. All that would have happened is that I'd have ended up without a job. I know he hired me because he felt sorry for me. He didn't need the help. Besides it includes a room and meals. He's good to me, and I like the people there. They are all so genuine."

"I have bad news for you," Cam said. "That number you gave me isn't your father's Social Insurance Number."

"How do you know ?"

"I checked the number and it isn't a valid S.I.N."

"You can do that?"

"It's complicated, but I found a formula on the Internet to check for internal consistency with the last digit."

"Thanks for trying. The number must be something else."

Jay moved over to sit with Jimmy.

"How's your dog?" Jimmy asked.

"He's not mine, but we go for a nightly walk together. You can come by to see him any time you want. I think he likes you."

"I've been wanting to talk to you. You've been so good to me, what with money and everything. I don't have any cash, but I'd like to give you this watch as payback for what I've borrowed from you." Jimmy handed Jay a gold watch.

"Wow! That's totally awesome," Jay exclaimed. "But where would a guy like you get a watch like that?"

"It doesn't matter where I got it. I was going to pawn it and give you the cash, but then I thought that you're the kind of guy who likes nice things. You want it, it's yours."

Jay slid it onto his wrist and held it out at arm's length to get the full effect. "It's exactly what I've needed to make an impression on Sue."

"Glad you like it. You've been such a good friend to me and have always accepted me for what I am. And you had a lot to do with making that intervention thing happen. It made a big difference in my life and I want to do something special for you."

"I'll think of you every time I look at it."

"I'd like that. There aren't many people that think about me. Sometimes I wonder if my life is worth anything."

"Maybe now that you're off drugs you'll see what people really think about you. It's hard to make sense with a guy who's high all the time, you know."

"I'm hanging in there. I think of what you said when I'm tempted, and it helps me have some willpower. It's not easy you know, when nobody cares about you, and you have no job."

"Becky loves you."

"She puts up with me. She's always been too nice a person to throw me out on the street. I think she's liking me better now."

"There's the gang we hang out with. You've got more friends than I do and I'm happy."

"You have Phil and Steve. Those guys look after you. They care about you."

"They're more trouble than you could imagine. But maybe you're right. They do give me a feeling of stability. I'm going over to Steve's tonight. Maybe you'd like to come and get to know him better."

"No thanks. He's not my type."

"He's not my type either, as far as that goes. But he's an OK guy. I wish he weren't gay."

"That's more than enough to turn me off on anybody as a friend. Aren't you worried all the time about what he's thinking or what he might do?"

"I used to, but not anymore. Besides, I may get a free flight to San Francisco with him at Christmas."

"That would be awesome. But I'd never do it with a gay guy."

"I'm not, as you say, doing it, with him or any other guy."

"That's not what I meant. I meant that I couldn't be comfortable travelling with someone like that."

"Hi Jay," Becky said, sitting down at the table. "What are you two plotting about so seriously?"

"Just boy stuff," Jimmy said.

Tiffany went to answer the knock on the door. "Come in. We're all here. I think a couple of us have already made contact with some spirits, even if they are from a bottle. I doubt that you know anyone here except me. That should make it exciting. Everybody, this is Tanya. She'll be our spiritual guide this evening. Let's get started."

Tanya fixed each person in turn with an expectant look as they went around the table giving their names. Tanya gave no indication that she had ever met Jay before. Jay remembered her as the girl that he had met at the Fringe Festival. *There can't be many girls named 'Tanya' around. She has that intense look I remember. I'm sure that's who it is, even though she is so much sexier as a blonde with makeup,* Jay thought. *This could be fun if I don't let on I know her.*

Tanya's gaze continued to move around the circle without any glimmer of recognition. *I'll bet if you had your head on my shoulder again you'd remember me,* Jay said to himself with a sly smile, remembering the night at the Fringe Festival.

"Let me see what psychic energy I can read from each of you," Tanya said. "It will help us to understand each other better." She looked at Jimmy and said, "You are confused about your future, but I see this changing."

"Does this mean that I will get a job or that I will move back with my parents?"

"I'm sorry. I can't look into the future without the help of the spirit world. We would have to use Tarot cards or I Ching or some other means to reach into the future."

Tanya continued clockwise around the table, turning to Becky. "I feel strong energy from you. You are a practical person who likes to get things done. I sense that you are a skeptic. You are withholding your psychic energy from us."

"And Jay. I see powerful forces being channelled through Jay. You have been through some difficult times. There have been financial difficulties, personal conflicts and most recently an accident of some sort. I am getting strong but mixed vibrations from you."

"Is there anything else you know about me?" Jay asked.

"There is. But this is not the time for such things."

Tanya directed her attention to Steve. "I see travel in your aura. Perhaps you will soon go on a trip, or maybe you have some business connected with travelling. I also sense hostility flowing between you and other members of our group."

If I have to sit here beside Steve, you can bet that there will be hostility flowing, Jay said to himself.

Cam's turn came next. "You are a private person. Your aura is totally hidden from me. You like working and living in a solitary environment, but seek periodic social interaction. A certain amount of secrecy is important to you."

Tanya spoke to Tiffany, "As always, you're a powerful psychic force. You are a help to me with my sessions. I had thought to give you each some sort of psychic reading, but there are such powerful psychic forces concentrated here tonight that I'd like to try to direct this power into group self–exploration. Please cross your arms and hold the hand of the person next to you. Close your eyes and let your mind go blank. I'll try to get in tune with all of you together."

The group sat in a circle with their eyes closed, clasping hands until Tanya said, "This is not good. Too much energy is getting lost. Jimmy and Becky, your energy is flowing to each other instead of to the group. Cam and Steve, you are also sapping each other's energy. Let's try changing the seating arrangement to break the connections. Becky, if you would change places with Steve that should do it."

Tanya looked around the newly formed circle approvingly. "That feels much better. Now, without crossing your arms this time, join hands and look into the centre of the table. We must focus our psychic energy away from ourselves onto the centre of the table."

Jimmy took Steve's hand. "Hi. I don't think we've met. I'm Jimmy."

Steve's left eyebrow raised as he looked warily at Jimmy's straggly, unkempt appearance. "I'm Steve."

Tanya continued, "Close your eyes and concentrate your thoughts inward toward yourself. Breathe in slowly. Hold your breath and slowly let it out. In...out...in...out. Concentrate on your breathing. Feel the new air filling your lungs...the spent air leaving your body. Be aware of the pressure of the chair you are sitting on...the warmth of the hand you are holding...your chest rising and falling as you breathe...concentrate on drawing fresh air into your lungs and exhaling the used air."

"Now I want you to lie on your back on the floor and focus your thoughts and energy onto yourself as you continue your deep breathing," Tanya continued. "Concentrate on the big toe of your left foot. Try to imagine that you are your big toe. Feel how crowded it is in your shoe...feel the pressure of the shoe against your big toe...feel how hot and stuffy it is in there. Now visualize your feet encased in a red light, swirling in a clockwise motion. Let the light move up your legs to your spine. Gradually it turns orange and then yellow when it reaches your stomach. It is still swirling as it continues to rise up into your chest and turns green when it reaches your heart. It is moving upwards toward your throat and is now turning blue. See the swirling light as it moves up to reach your face and turns indigo. As it covers your face, it turns violet. The light is now expanding and lightening in colour until your entire body is encased in a protective ball of white light. You have now awakened the fiery serpent of your psychic energy.

"Imagine yourself lying on the grass, in your favourite place, with the sun beating down on your face and a gentle breeze caressing you. Remember this as your happy place. Now visualize yourself rising out of your body so that you are floating directly above yourself. Look down on yourself as you are lying there. You see yourself, safely enclosed in a force field of white light. Examine the details of your face. You may ask yourself a question that has been bothering you and you will receive an answer. Or maybe there is something you feel like saying to yourself as you are lying there."

Tanya paused for a few minutes, and then said, "When it feels right for you, open your eyes."

The members of the circle remained with their eyes closed, engrossed in their own personal question and answer discussion period. Eventually, one by one, they opened their eyes and looked around. No one spoke for a long time.

"Would anyone like to share his or her experience?" asked Tanya.

"I found it relaxing, but I couldn't think of a single thing to ask myself," said Tiffany.

Jimmy spoke next. "I couldn't believe it. I really floated and could look down on myself. It made me feel so confident."

"Remember that happy place you experienced. You can go back there whenever you need to, just by relaxing," Tanya said.

Steve gazed around the group. "When I looked down on myself, I saw an angry person who hides his anger quite well. I realized that over the years I have become heterophobic. I resent the freedom that straight people have for P.D.A."

"What's P.D.A.?" Jimmy asked.

"Public display of affection. We can't hold hands or flirt in public the way everyone else does. So I try to make straights feel uncomfortable the way they make me feel. I think otherwise I'm a nice enough person."

"Did you get some guidance from the channelling?" Tanya asked.

"I didn't get any real answers, but I realize now that I need to change my attitude," Steve answered.

Becky said, "I'm not quite sure what to make of it all. It was much more real than I had expected. I'd like to try this again sometime, Tanya."

Tanya responded: "What you have experienced was low–trance channelling with yourself acting as the medium. Let me try to explain. In your everyday life you use your conscious mind to deal with sensations and experiences in what you consider to be a rational manner. In reality most people are in fact trying to make their conscious experiences match with the forgotten events from their past that are stored in the subconscious mind, but that's another story. Most people do not realize that there is another level of consciousness which contains all the feelings, thoughts and memories inherited from your ancestors. I like to call this level the preconscious. It is what the psychiatrist, Jung, called the 'collective unconscious'."

"You don't mean that the preconscious contains the memory of everything that has happened to mankind since the beginning of time, do you?" asked Becky.

"No. Not all mankind. Only all your own ancestors back to Adam and Eve. Your preconscious will not be the same as mine because we have had different ancestors from some point in our heredity."

"How could something like that be transmitted from generation to generation?" asked Becky.

"How can the knowledge of migration be transmitted from generation to generation of geese? Or how do salmon know where to go to spawn? They don't tell each other legends or stories. There is no way that they can possibly learn something like that from their own experiences. It must be transferred through some sort of genetic coding that we don't yet understand," said Tanya.

"Does that explain why great inventions are often developed at the same time by people who don't know each other? Like the telephone was invented in Canada and in England at almost the same time," Becky asked.

"Yeah. Like several coloured comics have the same idea at the same time," Jimmy jumped into the conversation, sidetracking it severely. "They'll have turkey dinners all at the same time, or golf or football and like that."

"If the migrating instinct works for geese and salmon, I suppose something like that could work for people," said Tiffany, trying to get back on topic. "You mean that if a person learns how to tap into this knowledge they can be guided by the wisdom of their ancestors back to the beginning of time, and not only the ones that they have known?"

Tanya continued, "That's right. Most people rely on a medium to make this contact with the preconscious. Some people think that channelling through a medium is a way to contact their dead departed friends or relatives. This, of course, is nonsense. It is not the departed people themselves who are being contacted, but rather, accumulated knowledge which has already been coded into the person's brain. Some mediums go along with the idea of contacting the spirit of a departed loved one because it is what people want to think. Most channellers will say that someone is speaking through them. That's only because it is easier for most uninitiated people to think of a single entity speaking rather than accessing the accumulated memory of past generations."

Cam spoke up. "I am not one to be believing in any supernatural kind of thing. It is only what I can see or feel that I believe. However, it was indeed pleasant enough to be imagining I was a fey thane lying on a grassy knoll in bonnie Scotland. But it was nothing but a fancy little meditation thing. It makes a person feel good because it relaxes the brain and turns off the worries of the day. For some reason I kept thinking about California."

"If it relaxes you, then it is a good thing." Tanya suggested.

"And maybe when the brain cells are freed up they are able decode the preconscious information," suggested Becky.

"You're saying that a person can contact only their own ancestors. That means that I wouldn't be able to contact my dead sister?" asked Tiffany.

"That's right. You might think that you are contacting her because her preconscious and yours will be identical, and so you would be able to think like she did," said Tanya.

"This means that people don't need to be dead in order to be contacted so long as they have the same ancestors."

"That's right. That's what people call mental telepathy. You can think the same as other people with similar preconscious memories and thus feel that you are reading their minds."

"This is getting a bit too technical for me. Whatever the explanation, I did learn something about myself tonight," said Steve.

"And I feel better about myself than I have since I was a kid," added Jimmy.

"What about you, Jay?" Tanya asked.

"I'm sorry, but I'm confused. There has been so much happening to me lately that I'm no longer sure of what is real and what is not. It became obvious to me that I've been stealing from my friends, emotionally as well as financially. My lack of moral values is disgusting. I feel that I owe you an apology, Steve, but I have no idea for what. I feel vaguely guilty about how I've been reacting to you."

Steve replied, "You haven't done anything for which you need to apologize. If you feel guilty, maybe it is because of what you have been thinking."

"Sometimes I do think too much," Jay conceded.

"It's time we went home," suggested Tiffany. "Thanks for a great evening, Tanya. We must do this again. Soon."

"Yes, thanks Tanya. Do you want a ride home with Cam and me, Jay?" Steve asked.

"Sure, if you don't mind," replied Jay. *It's late and I'm tired. Of course I'll accept a ride from anyone, even a fag,* Jay thought to himself. As soon as the thought entered his mind, Jay realized what had happened. *Steve was right. My thoughts keep labelling him when there is no reason for me to be doing so.*

"I'd appreciate a ride with you," Jay reworded his statement. *Because you are a generous person and have been a good friend to me,* he forced himself to think. *There, that feels better.*

Jay walked to the door. *I don't care about his being a fag.* The thought jumped into his mind. *Now why did I even have to think about his being gay? I do have to get a grip on my thoughts.*

"Goodnight, Tanya. I'd like to do this again," Jay said.

"I told you our paths would cross again," she answered.

Jay stopped abruptly. "So you do recognize me."

"Of course. I recognized you the moment I saw you, but I thought it would be better for this session to ignore our past little adventure."

"That's what I thought, too," Jay lied. "But couldn't we at least exchange phone numbers and maybe see each other again?"

"That must be left up to fate. Besides, your girlfriend might not be pleased."

"How do you know about Sue?"

"The stars tell all," Tanya replied with a smile. "Bye for now, Truro."

As they walked toward Steve's Lexus, Steve handed the remote to Jay. "Do you want to play with the door lock?"

"Sure." Jay pressed the button and smiled with pleasure at the car's audible response. "It still likes me."

Jay handed the keys back to Steve when they got close to the car.

"You drive," Steve said, declining to accept the keys.

"You're kidding, aren't you?" Jay asked.

"You have a learner's permit don't you?"

"Well, yes. But I've got to tell you something. I've already smashed–up one car."

"Phil told us about Sue's car. He said it wasn't your fault. Accidents happen. Go ahead. I trust you."

Cam climbed into the rear seat. Jay started the car and leaned back into the seat to luxuriate in the anticipation of driving the fine automobile. With an exaggerated display of caution, he put on the signal light and shoulder–checked for traffic before easing the car away from the curb and out into the sparse late evening traffic.

"Straight ahead at the next intersection?" Jay asked.

"Gaily forward, I prefer to say," Steve replied with a smile. "That was an interesting evening," he added.

"I learned a lot about you," Jay said. "And about myself as well."

"You are hung up on my being gay, aren't you?"

"No. I accept that you are, and I try not to think about it," Jay lied.

"Do you succeed?"

"No, I guess not. But I can't control my thoughts."

"I know what you mean. It's like being told not to think of a green elephant standing on the street corner. The harder you try not to think about it, the more you do think about it."

"So what am I supposed to say about your being…" Jay's voice dropped off into silence.

Cam's voice from the back seat said, "The first thing you need to be doing is to realize that gay is not a dirty word. Neither is fag nor queer. It is quite all right to say the words instead of dropping off into an embarrassed silence. It's what Steve is, the same as you are young or male or thin or whatever. It is nothing of which to be ashamed. It is only derogatory if it is said in a manner to make it such, or if the person saying it is embarrassed by saying it."

"My mom taught me that you shouldn't call women girls or Italians Wops or native aboriginals Indians or blacks…oh darn. I'm not entirely sure what one should call blacks these days. Anyway, isn't it wrong to call a homosexual person gay?"

"It all depends on how you do it. One rule of thumb is that if you are using it as an adjective it is likely to be derogatory. If you are using it as a noun then it is more likely acceptable," Cam said.

"Oh great. Now I have to check my grammar rules before I can say anything."

"It's not that hard. Assume for the sake of argument that I'm gay. Then if you are calling me a gay accountant that is unacceptable because you are using the word gay as an adjective that seems to imply that I am less of an accountant because I'm gay. If you are saying that I am an accountant who is gay then my status as an accountant is not limited by my being gay. You can either say I'm an accountant or you can say I'm gay. But don't try to say both at the same time."

"I must admit that I would be more embarrassed to admit that you are an accountant than I would be to say you are gay," joked Steve.

Cam continued, "It's like people calling you a teenager. If it is important that you be designated as such then it is fine to say it. But if someone says that you are a teenage driver that assumes that there is something sinister about your being both teenage and driving. Otherwise, both terms wouldn't be used together."

"I think that the big issue is more a question of why is it that you have to think of a person as either gay or straight. Do you think of Phil as being gay or straight?" Steve asked.

"He's not thin enough to be gay," Jay said.

"Now that's a real stereotype. What do you really think?"

"I've never had any reason to think about that sort of thing because it doesn't matter to me. I guess he could be either." Jay thought for a minute. "But if he is one I'm surely glad I moved out when I did."

"And why would that be?"

"I couldn't live with a guy that's gay?" Jay asked.

"But maybe you did," Cam countered.

"If I didn't know it then it would be all right. Nobody else would know either. The problem with you two is that you are so obvious. If anybody sees me with you then they will assume that I'm one, too."

"So that's what concerns you? You're afraid that people might be thinking you are gay? And supposing that they did?"

"I don't want anyone looking at me and thinking I'm one of those."

"One of those?" challenged Steve. "You are calling us 'those'? As in there are the normal people, and then there are the others like us? Do you realize that you keep referring to gay people as one of those kind of people? You speak about us as if we were objects instead of people."

"That's not true. I don't have any trouble using the word."

"And what word might that be?" asked Cam.

"I don't have to say it. You know what I mean."

Steve interrupted. "That's enough, both of you. Drop the argument right now before Jay gets into another accident and smashes up my car."

"I want to be hearing him say the word," Cam persisted.

Jay pulled over to the curb and turned off the ignition. "I don't need to take this," he said as he got out of the car and started to walk down the street.

The window of the Lexus slid smoothly open. Steve leaned across the seat and called out the window. "Get back in the car, Jay. It's late and it's a long way to the Red Dragon. We both promise to get off your case. Please, get back in the car."

The rest of the ride to the Red Dragon was long and uncomfortably silent. The first light snow of winter was turning the street lamps into halos of light in the darkness and blanketing the grass in a coat of white. Jay got out of the car and went into the building without any parting word.

BYE BYE SUE

"Did you know we will have been going steady for four months next week?" Sue asked Jay.

"That means I'll be buying you another monthly anniversary present. What would you like?"

"Surprise me. You know I always like your presents."

"Maybe I'll take you out to a special restaurant for dinner."

"That would be nice, but I like to have something I can hold. Something I can put under my pillow at night so that I will dream about you."

"Do you actually dream about me?" Jay asked.

"Well, I think about you when I'm dropping off to sleep. That's kind of like a dream."

"I think about you all the time, too."

"Do you want to go out or stay in tonight?" Sue asked.

"You know I always like to stay in so I don't have to share you with anyone," Jay replied.

"I rented a movie."

"Great idea," Jay said snuggling up closer to Sue. "What's the movie?"

Sue moved over to the other end of the sofa. "It's one I thought you'd like. It's called 'Ghost', with Patrick Swayze and Demi Moore."

"Oh good. I like that one. It is such a sadly romantic story. I've always like ghost stories."

Jay put the tape in the VCR. "Why are you looking at me like that?"

"Do you always associate the supernatural with romance?"

"You're not referring to that seance are you? You can't still be mad at me about that, can you?"

"Well, you could have invited me."

"I didn't think you would want to go."

"Or didn't you want Tanya to know that you have a girlfriend?"

"I had no idea Tanya would be there. How do you know about Tanya, anyway?"

"From what I heard you were hitting on her and trying to pick her up after the seance. Did you get her phone number?"

"Who's been talking to you?"

"The stars know all, don't they? Maybe you'd like me to call you 'Truro', like Tanya does."

"I bet it was Steve. He's always getting me into trouble."

"It doesn't matter who told me. You should have told me about her yourself."

"There's nothing to tell. Why can't we forget all about it?"

"I need to know if you have gone out with her since the seance."

"Of course not. She didn't give me her phone number, so how could I?"

"I suppose that's the only thing that's stopping you from seeing her, is it?"

"Why do I feel that I'm not going to win in this discussion? Maybe I should go home now."

"If that's the way you feel about it, maybe you should."

Jay walked over and opened the door. A swirl of snow and cold air blew into the foyer. *If I walk out that door, I'll have a fifteen minute walk to the bus stop. I guess rich people who live on Wellington Crescent never need buses. If I stay, Sue will probably give me a ride home.*

He closed the door and turned back to Sue. "We shouldn't be fighting like this. I do love you, so maybe we need to work on more open and direct communication. Now, tell me. What's bothering you? It isn't Tanya at all, is it?"

Sue sat quietly for a few minutes. "No. You're right. It isn't Tanya. It is about us. I wanted to hear you tell me that I am more important to you than anyone else."

"But you know you are. I'm always telling you that you are my best and only girl. There must be something else bothering you."

Sue sat quietly again. "It's my dad. What with Christmas coming on, I think he'd rather that I had a different male friend for Christmas dinner."

"Is it about the car?"

"The car was nothing to him. The company collected the insurance and the company bought a new car. It means nothing to him and it means nothing to me. It's only a car. It isn't even our car when you come right down to it. It's the company's car, not ours."

"Then it must be me. I thought he liked me. We always seem to get along. We're even planning to go golfing together when spring comes."

"Oh, he likes you as a person all right. But he liked you better before he found out you live in a grubby little room above a rundown restaurant. And you don't come from a wealthy family. You are a waiter."

"Wait a minute there. You make it sound as if being a waiter is what I am. I'm a lot more than that. I'm a person who happens to be working as a waiter to buy food." *Good grief. I'm beginning to sound like Cam. 'I'm not a gay waiter, I'm a waiter who is gay.' Maybe it does make a difference.*

"And to buy little presents for his best girlfriend," he added with what he hoped was an endearing look.

"Dad liked you better when he thought you could play golf together."

"I'm willing to play with him. What did my not having money have to do with playing golf? Phil said he knew where I could borrow some clubs. So why couldn't we golf together?"

"You don't understand. He'd have to introduce you to his friends. You know. Like, this is Sue's boyfriend. He's a whatever and his parents are something or other. He doesn't have anything to fill in the blanks and that would be embarrassing. Appearances are everything to him."

"I still don't see what this has to do with anything. We're not going to be playing golf now that there is a foot of snow on the ground, so why are we talking about it?"

"We're talking about Christmas."

"We are?" Jay asked. "What has Christmas got to do with golf?"

"My dad would have to introduce you to the other family members who will be around here at Christmas. He wouldn't know what to say."

"Are you saying that you are ashamed of me?"

"Of course I'm not. But you aren't my dad's kind of people. You haven't any formal education, you don't have any money and you have no plans for the future."

"I told him I plan to open a restaurant some day."

"I meant realistic plans, not a pipe dream."

"It's not a pipe dream. At least not a dream from an opium pipe. Maybe it's an Indian peace pipe dream; those dreams do come true, you know."

"Whatever you say. You lost me on that one."

"But we love each other. We can't break up simply because your father doesn't know how to make idle conversation. You need to stand up for your rights, for us."

"It's not that simple for me. You don't realize the pressure that having a responsible position in society puts on the whole family. Our family's reputation is the single most important thing in my dad's life, both personally and professionally."

"I guess this means we are breaking up," Jay said.

"At least until after Christmas. I do love you, Jay, but I've got to have some other boyfriend for the sake of the family appearances."

"You mean you're going to start going with somebody else just for Christmas?"

"That's about it. I can't be without a boyfriend, because he'd have to explain that. He wants a nice neat picture–perfect daughter that causes him no worries. But we can still see each other the rest of the time."

"You mean I'd be your wrong–side–of–the tracks boy–toy? No thanks. If you're too ashamed to be seen with me then it's over."

"Can I at least give you a ride home?"

"I don't need any favours from you or anyone else. I'd rather walk." Jay walked to the door and opened it.

Sue walked over and stood beside him. "Don't be angry, Jay. You'll always be in my thoughts. And we can get together again after Christmas."

After a brief parting hug, Jay went dejectedly down the steps onto the snow–covered sidewalk.

"Wait. I should return the presents you've given me," Sue called to him.

"No. I want you to have them so you will remember the good times we've had. And to remind you that I will be back, but it will be on my terms, not on your father's. You'll see."

Jay's usual route home to the Red Dragon led past the shops and restaurants of Osborne Village and over the bridge across the Assiniboine River. Tonight his mind was so preoccupied that he didn't realize he had turned before he crossed the bridge until he found himself in front of Steve's apartment.

He rang the buzzer. "Yo," the buzzer said back to him.

"Can I come up?" he asked the grill on the wall.

"Who is it?" inquired the buzzer.

"Me," Jay responded.

"Who?"

"Me. Jay."

"Come on up. I didn't recognize your voice. You sound tired."

The inner door unlocked with a click and Jay went up to Steve's apartment.

"I haven't seen you since the seance," Steve said from his doorway.

"I'm sorry to barge in on you like this, but I don't feel like being alone tonight," Jay said.

"Sounds like girlfriend trouble to me. You've come to the right place."

"What would a gay like you know about women?"

"A lot. Most of my best friends are girls. Sometimes I get a bunch of gals and gays together for a hen–party so we can badmouth straights for being so insensitive, unemotional and generally uncaring about people. And by the way, thanks."

"Thanks for what?"

"That was the first time you ever called me gay to my face. Thanks for finally accepting me for who and what I am."

"Is your being gay the same as my being a waiter?" Jay asked.

"Quite a few gays are waiters, but that doesn't mean that you have to be gay because you are a waiter." Steve saw the look of confusion on Jay's face. "But that isn't what you meant, is it?"

"Not at all. I meant, is a person only what they do? Or is a person something more than what they do to put food on the table?"

"I'm not sure that we are on the same wavelength, but let me explain something that might help. Gay is what I was born and what I am because of the way I think and feel and react. Being homosexual is something I can choose to do, or choose not to do. But I cannot choose whether or not to be gay."

"You are saying that being gay and being homosexual are two different things?"

"They can be. Usually the two go together the same as being straight and being heterosexual go together. But they don't have to, particularly in situations where there is strong societal pressure, like for ministers or teachers."

"This is all somewhat interesting, but that's your problem. I have problems of my own."

"I'm sorry. Of course you do. That's why you're here. It has to do with Sue?"

"Yes and no. It's her father. He considers me to be a second-class citizen and not a person worthy to date his daughter because I am a waiter."

"Well, aren't you?"

"I work as a waiter. A waiter is what I do. It is not what I am."

"Then that is your choice. I know people who are waiters, or hairdressers, or bankers, and that is all that they are because they chose to make it their whole life. Sometimes I'm afraid that I am becoming nothing but a travel agent because that is all I do and think about. Then I have to have a serious talk with myself to remember that it is only my job, not who I am. I am a total person. A person who works as a travel agent."

"You mean that if I keep on working as a waiter, then maybe that is all that I will become? You certainly are one smart fag."

"Phil gave me some good advice once. It's kind of a prayer of some sort. It went something like, 'Give me the serenity to accept the things that I cannot change, the courage to change the things I can, and the wisdom to know the difference between the two'. I've found it to be helpful in dealing with being gay in a straight society."

"I'll try to remember that. By the way, was it all right that I called you a fag?"

"You didn't call me a fag. You called me smart. If you had called me a fag that could be hurtful because it puts me into a category. Once you name a stereotype you have depersonalized everybody who is included under that name, and this gives licence to treat them as less than individuals."

"I don't get it," Jay said.

"It's the same as calling someone a girl. If I say to someone that she is smart for a girl then that's a putdown. If I say she is a smart girl then that's a compliment. There's nothing wrong with the terms fag or queer themselves. It is in how it is used. We use those terms ourselves all the time, like in the parade chant, 'We're here, we're queer, get used to it.'"

"We seem to be back to you again. I'm the one with the problem, remember?" Jay glanced at his wrist. "It's getting late and I've got to get some answers."

"Is that a Rolex?" Steve asked. "I've never held one before. Could I wear it for a while?"

"Sure. Anything to get back to me and my life."

"So then tell me. What's your problem?"

Jay sat deep in thought. Finally he replied, "I'm a nobody in a world full of somebodies. I don't have a life that is going anywhere. I work at a crummy job that barely pays me enough to live on. All I do is work, go out and party, come home and go to bed. There doesn't seem to be much future for me."

"Let's think about you for a minute. You are obviously intelligent, and you're kind of fun to be around, at least when you're not in one of your bitchy moods."

"Thanks, I guess. I suppose that next you're going to tell me I'd be good looking if only I weren't so ugly."

"Well, yes. That, too. What have you got for education to get a good job?"

"Not much. I never did attend school much. I tried to learn by reading. And speaking of that, could I borrow some of your books sometime?"

"Sure. You have a key, unless you've lost it."

"I've still got it, but I never feel comfortable enough to use it. It wouldn't feel right to walk into your place."

Steve gave Jay an understanding look and nod. "It's all right to use it whenever you want. I kind of think of you as my little brother."

"Thanks. I'd think of you as my older brother if only you weren't..."

"If I weren't what?"

"I'm sorry. I don't know what made me say that. Sometimes my mouth doesn't seem to be connected with my brain."

"Forget it. I should be used to that sort of thing by now, but it still gets to me," Steve said, before returning to the previous topic. "Did you know that a person like you can get a Grade Twelve equivalency just by studying and then writing the exams?"

"No classes?"

"There are special classes you can take if you want to, but you're bright enough that you could do it on your own. Then, when you pass, you can take university night school or evening classes to work toward a degree. There's nothing stopping you from becoming whatever you want. You have to make up your mind what you want to do and then do it."

"Would you help me? You know, find out where to get the exams and classes and maybe help me study? I don't have a clue about this sort of thing, but I'd like to try it, if you would help me."

"I'd like to help you. I don't have a family to make me feel useful and needed."

"You sound like Phil. What am I? A surrogate son for everyone who needs someone to mother?"

"I guess you'll have to include Cam in there, too. He phoned to tell me that he found out something that might be interesting for you. 609–56–1826 is a valid United States Social Security Number. I don't know what made him think to check that."

"Oh great. So he isn't even a Canadian. That increases the possible population by a factor of ten."

"And 609 is one of the numbers reserved for California."

"That Cam would make one great private eye. I owe him for this."

"Not only that, but it's likely that in the fifties the digits 609 were assigned to San Francisco."

"Anything else?"

"There are only six McNabb's listed for all of San Francisco. He has addresses and phone numbers."

"Now all I have to do is get there somehow and look them up."

"You could phone. He has their phone numbers."

"I'd rather be able to look into his eyes so I would know if he's telling me the truth."

Midnight had long past before Steve retired to his bed. Jay went into the spare bedroom. The rows of books caught his attention and held him captive until the morning sun shone in through the window.

WHO'S GOT THE TIME?

Jay was going through the usual Monday routine of waiting on tables and letting his mind wander to thoughts of his future. He checked his wrist for the time. *Great. Steve kept my watch. I suppose he thinks I'll have to come back and get it. That guy comes up with more ways to get me into his apartment. Well, I'll fool him this time. He can keep it until he feels guilty enough to bring it back to me.*

"Is your name Jay?" The question jarred Jay back to reality. He set the two cups of coffee down in front of the customers, noticing with surprise that they were police officers.

"Why do you want to know?" he asked, stalling for time to get his brain back in gear.

"We ask the questions. You give the answers. Are you Jay or not?"

"Yes, I am. But I'm not saying anything more until you tell me what this is about. I have rights, you know."

"We're investigating a robbery on Wellington Crescent and we think you might know something about it."

"You've got the wrong guy. I'm strictly legal."

"You know a Sue Parkington?"

"Yeah. I guess so. At least I used to. You mean her place was broken into?"

"Would you mind showing us around your room upstairs?"

"You got a search warrant?"

"Not yet. We'd like it if you'd cooperate. It would make it easier for all of us. Unless, of course, you have something to hide. We can always get a search warrant."

Jay called back to the kitchen, "Hey, Han. I've gotta step out for a minute, okay?"

The officers stepped into Jay's room. A quick glance convinced them that there were few hiding spots. A look in the dresser drawers and under the mattress seemed to satisfy them that there was nothing of any value in the room.

"Would you mind emptying your pockets?" the shorter one asked.

Jay pulled out his wallet, a dirty handkerchief, and a keychain. With a flourish he turned the pockets inside out

"Satisfied?" he asked.

"You wearing a watch?"

Jay's heart skipped a beat but he kept his face impassive. He pulled up his shirt sleeves to reveal bare wrists.

"See. There aren't any stolen goods here. I've got to get back to work now, so you guys had better leave." Jay said.

"Not so fast. You could have stashed the stuff anywhere. We think it was an inside job because the alarm system didn't go off. Your girlfriend told you the code, didn't she?"

"Did she say that? Even if she did, that doesn't mean that I did anything wrong. Maybe they forgot to turn the alarm on."

"We'll need to get a statement from you. You want to come down to the station on your own or do you want to come with us now?"

"I've got to make a living right now. I'll go tomorrow," Jay promised.

"That'll be fine. But remember that it's like American Express. You know. You can't leave town without it."

The other officer screwed up his face in mock pain. "Please excuse my partner. He thinks he's a comedian."

When Jay's shift finished he went immediately to Phil's apartment.

"I'm in big trouble," Jay said to Phil. "Sue's parents got robbed and the cops think I did it because it had to be someone who knew the surveillance code."

"She told me about it. Did you know the code?"

"Of course I did. Sue always wanted me to turn it on when we went out. She liked me to look after her that way. She'd never remember to do it herself."

"If you didn't do it then you have nothing to worry about."

"Oh yes I do. I know who did it. And it's all my fault. I told him the code."

"You told him the code?" Phil said, his face blank with incredulity.

"Well, not in so many words. We were talking one day and I used Sue's code as an example of how unimaginative people are in choosing them. I had no idea he'd remember anything like that let alone use it."

"That doesn't prove he did it, though."

Jay looked down. "He gave me a Rolex a couple of days ago. I'm so stupid. I should have known right away that it was stolen. I even knew that Sue's dad had a Rolex."

"That's not good. If the police find it on you, you're dead meat. As a minimum they'll have you for possession of stolen goods. Where is it now?"

"Would you believe it's at Steve's?"

"You're kidding. Oh great. We've got to get it back before Steve gets caught in the middle of this mess, too."

"You're right. They probably wouldn't question him, but if they did he'd have to tell them it's mine. But what will I do with it when we get it back? I can't give it to the police because then I'd have to say where I got it. I'm not sending my buddy back to jail."

"If he's guilty then he has to take the consequences."

"Maybe if I could convince him to give all the stuff back, then they'd go easy on him."

"I don't understand why you are so concerned about protecting a hoodlum like Tony. He'll either hire a high–priced lawyer and get off, or he'll have one of his goons take the rap for him."

"I'm not talking about Tony," Jay exclaimed. "I'm talking about Jimmy."

"Jimmy? You think Jimmy got away with a quarter of a million dollars in jewelry?" Phil said.

"I guess so. He's the one who had the Rolex."

"Come on. I'll go with you to Steve's."

"Thanks. I can use some moral support."

"You need more than moral support. Sometimes I think it isn't safe to let you out of the house alone."

"Maybe you could keep the watch for me, Phil," Jay said.

"Sorry. I'm not holding stolen goods for anyone. You need to give it back to Jimmy. He's the one that should have to deal with it."

Phil and Jay sat on Steve's sofa.

"You guys want a drink?" Steve asked.

"No thanks," Phil replied. "We just dropped in to pick up the watch that Jay left here by accident. You know how easy it is for that to happen."

"Yeah, sure." Steve got the watch out of the table drawer and held it toward Jay. "That's a very fine piece of jewelry. I'm surprised that you can afford luxuries like that."

"Yeah, it's nice enough. It's not hard to buy stuff on credit," Jay said.

"Even if it's second–hand?" Steve asked, looking pointedly at Jay. "That watch must be at least ten years old. I didn't know that you could buy stolen goods on credit."

Phil interjected, "Drop it, Steve. We don't have time for this right now. Give him the watch and forget you ever saw it or us. I'll explain later."

Jay and Phil stood on the sidewalk outside Steve's apartment.

"I'm not going to the police station with you. I know people there and I don't need to be associated with whatever is going down here. You're on your own now," Phil said.

"I'm going home to get some rest. I'll go down there tomorrow and make my report."

Jay walked into the police station, looking as tired as he felt from a sleepless night trying to think of a nonexistent solution to his dilemma.

The officer on duty looked up drowsily at Jay. "Identification, please."

Jay reached into his pocket for his wallet and discovered that he still had the watch. *Keep calm,* he said to himself. *They're not going to search me, so all I have to do is keep from pulling it out and waving at them.*

"You're here to make a statement about the Parkington robbery?"

"That's right. They told me I had to come down today."

"Well, sir, this is your lucky day. They caught the perp red–handed with the loot early this morning and he's safely locked up. So we don't need anything from you right now. Sorry for the inconvenience. We'll contact you if we need anything else."

"What about the alarm?"

"The owners probably forgot to turn it on. It happens all the time."

"But what about the watch…," Jay started to ask. *Shut up and get out of here. For once try to keep your big mouth from getting you into trouble.*

"Excuse me, sir. You had a question?"

"No. Have a nice day."

On the way home, Jay stepped into the mall to settle his frayed nerves. Jimmy sat at their usual table.

"You're not in jail," Jay said, stating the obvious.

"Should I be?" Jimmy replied, furrowing his brow and squinting his eyes.

"But they told me that you were."

"Well I'm not. Who said I was?"

"Never mind. If you're not in jail, then who is?"

"A lot of people, I would imagine, but I don't think that's our concern. You know you're not making any sense, don't you? What's with you anyway?" Jimmy asked.

Jay placed the watch onto the table and pushed it over in front of Jimmy. "You stole this from Sue's place, didn't you? Admit it."

"I don't know what you've been smoking, Jay. My grandfather gave me that watch a month ago. He said that he felt guilty about having expensive possessions at a time when I was barely making enough money to keep my life together, so he gave it to me. He says that he came into the world with nothing and he'll go out with nothing, but he'd like the watch to be like a family heirloom. Besides he didn't move around enough to keep it wound."

"What does moving have to do with anything?"

"It's a Rolex. Your wrist movement keeps it wound."

"Oh. Why don't you keep it?"

"If I wore it, I'd get mugged within a day. I thought it would be best to give it to you."

"You're lying, aren't you?"

"No. I lie to most people, but I'd never lie to you, Jay. Not about anything important."

"That's touching. But don't you need the money?"

"I'm using you as an informal pawn shop. He said I could pawn it if I needed the money, but it wouldn't be fair to him to give it up like that. If I pawned it for what I could get I'd spend the whole wad in a week and then I'd still be broke. And the watch would be gone forever. This way I'll borrow money from you whenever I need it. It cuts out the middleman, so to speak. And it keeps the watch kind of in the family."

"So then are you giving it to me?" Jay asked.

"Sure. It's yours whether you loan me money or not. I know we're buddies and I can always count on you. I'm trying to repay you for what you've done for me in the past. And maybe prepaying you for what you might do for me in the future."

"Now you're starting to confuse me again. Are you expecting something from me?"

"Of course not. I don't want anything. It's your friendship I value."

"You wouldn't be upset if I pawned it to get some cash to go to San Francisco for Christmas with Steve, then?"

Jimmy chewed on his bottom lip and looked down at the table. "I didn't know that you and Steve were…you know…like…wanting to spend Christmas together. Is that why you and Sue broke up?"

"Whoa, there. You're dropping off the deep end. If I do go with him, it's only because he has an extra free ticket."

"Don't get uptight. It's your life."

"You're not suggesting that I'm gay, are you?" Jay asked.

"It seems that there is always something going on between you and Steve. One never knows these days about who is what."

"Trust me. There's nothing between me and Steve. You wouldn't believe how little there is between him and me."

"But you're going to spend Christmas with him. And in California, no less."

"I'd be going for the trip to see if I can find my father there. Steve'll probably find someone else to go with, anyway."

"Tell him I'll go."

"You'd leave Becky at Christmas to go to California?" Jay asked.

"I'd do anything to get to California."

Jay put the watch back on the table. "Here. Pawn this then and buy yourself a ticket."

Jimmy handed the watch back to Jay. "I couldn't go alone. I'd be too afraid."

Jimmy thought for a minute and added, "It's a nice dream, but that's all it is. Some things are better in the imagination than they would be in reality. Send me a postcard. That's the closest I'll ever get to California."

"When I get back, we'll go on a trip together. The two of us. Maybe we could go to Vancouver or maybe Montreal for a week," Jay said.

"I'd like to go to Montreal. There are such exciting things happening there, and the people are so intense. But we'd have to go before they form their own country."

"That won't happen soon. Those guys are so emotional and excitable they'll never get their act together enough to separate."

"I've got a question for you. I saw in the newspaper that they will be holding the Gay Games in Montreal. You must know all about that sort of gay thing. So tell me. What kind of games would be gay games?"

"You're putting me on, right?"

"No. Seriously. What kind of games are gay?"

"As far as I know they are ordinary sporting events."

"So what can they do to make something like the pole–vault gay instead of straight? I don't get it."

"Maybe we should use some other example," Jay said with a grin.

Jimmy missed the attempt at humour. "Use any example you want. How can the sports be different?"

"It's not the sports that are different. It's the people that are different. The games themselves are the same as the Olympics, but the competitors are gay so it becomes the focus for a big gay party."

"So what's the point? Why is it such a big deal?"

"It's an excuse for gays to get together with each other. It's like teenagers hanging out in the mall together or men joining the Masonic Lodge. People feel more comfortable when they are part of a group where they know how everyone else feels about things without having to ask. It's like my being here in Winnipeg. When I meet someone from up north it's as if we were bosom buddies because we've had the same experiences. We laugh at the same jokes."

"So why aren't there Black Games and Native Games and Hindu Games and like that."

"Maybe there are. How would I know? Or maybe they have other things instead of athletic competition for bonding. How do you expect me to know all this sort of stuff anyway?"

"Well, have a good time in San Francisco, if you go. If you don't go, have a good time anyway, wherever you are," Jimmy said, walking back out onto the street.

I LEFT MY HEART

From the cab window Jay could see the airplanes on the tarmac. His heart pounded in anticipation.

"You have your driver's licence for identification?" Steve asked.

"Sure do," Jay replied. "I don't know how I can ever thank you for this. I thought you were just stringing me along and that you'd end up taking one of your gay friends and leave me at home."

"Don't feel too grateful. None of my friends wanted to spend Christmas away from home. I usually try to be away at Christmas and New Year's Eve, but I hate flying alone. It can be such a depressing season when you don't have any family to share it with," Steve said.

"I know the feeling. Phil's going away to be with family and most of the other people I know have plans. Maybe I should have gone home to Oakridge to be with my own family but we never did celebrate Christmas much anyway. I'd rather have them come to Winnipeg sometime so we could do it up right."

"It's too bad that you and Sue broke up. You made such a cute couple. For a pair of straights, that is."

"It's only a temporary thing until I find a way around her father. I plan to marry that girl. You watch me."

"That would be lovely. I envy guys that can get married."

"You could get married. I sure you could find a nice girl who would…" Jay stopped abruptly. "I'm sorry. I wasn't thinking."

"That's O.K. Gay guys do get married, but a church wedding isn't always easy."

"Now I'm confused. If you got married would you be the bride or groom?"

"That would depend on the dynamics between my partner and me."

"You mean sexually?"

"You are such a typical straight sometimes. For you everything revolves around sex."

"Sorry. Again."

"It would depend on the relative strengths of our feminine and masculine sides emotionally."

"Being straight has its advantages. At least I know I'd be the groom."

"No wonder straights are so annoying. They're so totally simplistic," Steve said.

Steve put his loose change into the tray and walked through the metal detector after answering a few perfunctory questions from the security guard. The machine emitted an annoyed beep. The official waved a hand detector around Steve. The wand beeped insistently as it moved up around Steve's legs. "Do you have something metal in your pocket?" the official inquired.

Steve's face betrayed his embarrassment. "Uh, yes," he stammered.

"Put it in the tray, please."

Steve leaned over for a whispered conversation before turning and going back the way he had come.

"Where's he going?" Jay asked the official.

"He'll be right back. He had to go to the washroom."

Now that's weird, Jay thought as he watched Steve's back disappear back down the hallway. *Maybe they don't have washrooms after you go through customs? Maybe I should be going, too.*

Jay was still weighing the relative merits of a trip to the bathroom when Steve returned. He put his coins and a two–inch diameter silver ring in the tray. The metal detector remained silent as Steve walked through and picked up his belongings on the other side.

"What was that all about?" Jay asked as they continued toward the flight gate. "Why didn't you just put the ring in the tray in the first place? It's no big deal. It's only a jacket ornament."

"I was wearing it."

"What do you mean you were wearing it? I didn't see it anywhere."

"It's a C–ring. I totally forgot about it," Steve said. "That was stupid of me."

They continued to the plane with Jay running 'c' words through his mind until he hit on a possibility. He wondered if a C–ring could possibly be what he thought it might be, and if so, why and how anyone would actually wear one.

The plane waited for permission from the tower to take off. Jay adjusted his seat belt for the fifth time, making it snug but not too tight. The engines roared as the plane lumbered down the runway, gathering speed for its leap into the still dark sky.

Jay looked out the window. "I've never travelled this fast before in my life, have you?"

Steve looked at Jay and grinned.

"Oh. Of course you've flown before. I meant on the ground."

"I've gone faster than this in my car," Steve said. "But not on the highway."

"On a race track?" Jay asked, looking at Steve with surprised admiration.

"Practice runs. I've never competed in a real race."

"Maybe you could take me, sometime?"

"Why not? You seem to have attached yourself to me as if I were your guardian angel."

The plane rose gently off the runway as if testing gravity's control of it, and then rose sharply into the emptiness of space. Jay looked out the window. The white landscape was broken by clusters of Monopoly–sized buildings and pin-points of light. Unbroken strings of lights stretched out in all directions from the city, like carelessly dropped Christmas lights in the predawn darkness. Soon there was nothing to see but a layer of clouds.

This isn't at all like flying; it's more like sitting in the living room watching TV, Jay thought to himself. He looked over at Steve. "I've been wondering about Phil. Has he always been a vegetarian?"

"Only for the past few years. There's quite a little story about what happened before he gave up meat. Phil used to pride himself on his macho image. He fancied himself to be some kind of real outdoors, primeval, macho hunter type of guy who kept bagging bigger and better trophies. When he finished high school, he had enough trophies to cover all the walls of his apartment, and still have more left over than he could give away."

"That's funny. I didn't see any mounted trophies there," Jay said.

"Let me finish the story. After he moved here, he went on a hunting trip. He couldn't find anything to shoot, so in frustration he took a random shot at a pigeon hawk that happened to be gliding overhead. As luck would have it, he hit the bird. I doubt that he intended to kill it. Anyway, he had it stuffed sitting on a branch with its head forward and its wings half spread and hunched forward as if ready to attack. Maybe the taxidermist got carried away with the mood of the pose, or maybe the hawk's soul returned into its new glassy eyes. Whatever the reason, the hawk's eyes took on a hostile, menacing gleam as if it resented having its life abruptly snatched from it for no useful purpose. Phil couldn't keep it in the same room with him. He said that it made him feel guilty. I took it to my place for a while but its eyes kept following me, so I had to give it back to Phil."

"About that time Phil stopped hunting and developed an aversion to eating meat. He gave all his stuffed animal heads and trophies away except for the hawk. He couldn't bear to have it around but he couldn't give it away, so he told Scotty to keep it in his room. Scotty said that he admired its wild, free spirit and that he understood the hurt and anger in its eyes."

"So it's still in the apartment somewhere?"

"No. That's the weirdest part of all. During Scotty's illness, he asked Phil if he could have the hawk buried with him. He said he wished that he could have been more like it when it was alive. During the funeral the hawk sat on the coffin, guarding the bed of lilies, and looking like a miniature of the eagle seal of the United States government. After the funeral, they reopened the coffin and Phil put the hawk in with Scotty."

"That's a bit bizarre."

"Very. But Phil was having his nervous breakdown then, so we went along with it. He said that Scotty and the hawk were kindred spirits and that they should soar together into eternity."

"I don't know exactly what that means, but I think that if I had been Scotty I would have liked having a hawk soar with me into eternity, to be my companion through whatever follows after death. Do you ever think of what kind of creature you'd like to be if you reincarnated?"

"That's a dumb question. I never think about things like that. I have enough trouble dealing with the real world as it is," Steve said. "Do you have a plan for looking up your old man?"

"Cam gave me six addresses. I'm going to phone them and ask if they've ever been to Canada."

The pilot announced the beginning of the plane's descent. Steve turned to Jay and asked, "Do you have a place to stay?"

"Well, I'm a bit short of cash. Maybe we could share a room and cut down on expenses," Jay suggested hopefully.

"I reserved a room in a nice little apartment. You're welcome to share it with me if you don't mind that it's in the gay section of the city."

"Let me get this straight, if you'll pardon the expression. I'd be sleeping with a gay guy in a gay apartment in the gayest section of the gayest city on the continent."

"Right. And there wouldn't be a straight person within miles to hear your cries for help."

"How many beds?"

"One."

"Oh I get it now. You're trying to do it to me again."

"Do what?"

"Scare me."

"If you're scared it's because of what you have inside your own head. Would you expect me to be scared if I had to share a room with a straight man in Winnipeg? As far as you're concerned, that's all right, isn't it? But if it's gay instead of straight, then it's a big problem."

"You don't understand," Jay protested.

"Oh, I understand all right. You're the one who doesn't understand. You don't understand what it is like to be surrounded by people who wouldn't talk to you or associate with you if they if they knew your secret. You don't know what it is like to have to hide your real self every minute of every day and to live in fear that somehow, some day you will be found out."

"How is that different from my staying in a gay area? I won't be accepted if they know I'm straight."

"They might not share your views and life style, but they'll respect you as a person. It's highly unlikely that they'll take after you with baseball bats just because of your sexual orientation, unlike some of the neighbourhoods where I've lived. The worst that might happen to you is that you'll be ignored rather than being accepted with open arms."

"But I'd have to sleep with you. I've never slept with a man, and I don't intend to start now." Jay muttered under his breath, *OK, so I was in bed with Phil, but I had my socks on so that doesn't count.*

"I'm not going to jump you, if that is what you are worried about. We would be sleeping together with a small 's' not with a capital 'S', if you know what I mean."

"Sure, you mean platonically. I'm not stupid. I understand the terms. It's the idea I don't like."

"It's up to you. But you'll have to decide soon because we'll be landing in half an hour."

Jay lapsed into thoughtful silence. Eventually he asked, "Did you plan this whole thing just so you'd get to sleep with me? You've been hitting on me ever since we first met."

"In your dreams. What I've been doing is pushing you to make you come to grips with your homophobia. I must admit that you have been making some progress, but it is so very slow. Relax and forget about my being gay. I don't have any interest in you except as a friend who amuses me by being so naive."

Jay looked out the window. "Good grief. It looks as if we're going to land in the ocean. I sure hope the pilot knows what he's doing."

The plane flew in low over the San Francisco Bay and touched down smoothly a short distance from the water's edge. Within minutes it had docked at the terminal.

They picked up their bags and headed toward the car rental stands. "Do you want me to put you down as an alternate driver?" Steve asked.

"That's up to you. It's your party."

"It could be useful. When I'm on holidays, I sometimes get carried away with relaxing. It could be helpful to have a designated driver along with me."

"Are you going to rent a convertible?"

"I hadn't thought to."

"If you rent a convertible, I'll be your chauffeur whenever you want."

"You drive a hard bargain for a guy without any cards to play. I know that you love to drive now that you have your licence. You should be begging me, not the other way around."

Steve got into the Mustang convertible and adjusted the rear view mirrors. "On the prairie highways there are not many cars around, so you point the mirrors back along the side of the car to see into the distance behind you. For freeway driving you need to see the cars beside you, particularly in your back–corner blind spot. So your mirrors should point further out away from the side of the car. A lot of drivers never think of that."

The Mustang, with its top down, sped up to freeway speed and merged smoothly into the traffic.

"Wow. You sure know how to drive," Jay exclaimed as Steve expertly moved into the centre lane. "I'm glad you are doing this and not me. I'd be afraid I was going to crash into somebody."

"It's not difficult so long as you have nerve enough to keep up with the traffic speed."

"But wouldn't it be more polite to slow down and let others go ahead, like we try to do at home?" Jay asked. "Particularly when you're merging with the freeway."

"It's not a matter of politeness. It's a matter of survival by keeping the traffic moving. If anyone stopped in the middle of the freeway there could be forty–car pile up. Besides, the law is different here. The car coming onto the freeway has the right of way. The traffic has to move over or make room for it."

"That makes me feel a bit better. I thought you were being suicidal to speed into a solid wall of cars like that."

Jay leaned over and looked at the speedometer. "Are we really only going 75? It seems very fast."

"Miles per hour. That translates into about 120 kilometres per hour."

Twenty minutes on the freeway with cars driving bumper to bumper, weaving from lane to lane, brought them to the exit marked Civic Center.

"This will meet up with Market Street which is one of the main streets in the downtown area. It runs diagonally northeast–southwest and divides the city into the areas north of Market and SoMa, as they call the south of Market area. Generally speaking the area north of Market is the business, financial and tourist area. It's the area in which you would be most comfortable," Steve explained.

"Let me guess. Then our chosen accommodation will be south of Market, right?" Jay asked.

"You might say that. But we'll be driving so far down Market that it is past the distinction of north and south."

Steve pointed out the building called, "Under One Roof" at 2632 Market as they drove past. "I want to come back there to see the Names Project after we get checked into the hotel."

"Would that interest me?"

"Maybe. That's the project that makes and administers the AIDS quilt."

"You mean that Scott's panel will be there? Can we see it?" Jay asked with sudden interest.

"Not likely. They have a few panels on display and some that are waiting to be sewn into quilts, but the finished quilts themselves are stored away except for formal display occasions."

"So why do you want to go there?"

"They have a panel where you can write on the names of AIDS victims who don't have their own separate panel. I have a couple of names I'd like to add to it."

"I want to come with you when you go. Actually, I want to come with you everywhere you go. You can be my personal tour guide."

"Well, that's an offer I can hardly refuse," Steve said sarcastically. When he saw the look of disappointment on Jay's face, he added, "Sorry. It might be fun to do the tourist thing with you. I haven't been here for several years and San Francisco is one of my favourite cities."

The apartment was the top floor. A small, cluttered entrance hall exuded a friendly, homey warmth. Jay and Steve lugged their suitcases up the staircase to their room on the third floor.

"There are two beds," Jay exclaimed as he stepped into the room. Steve smiled but said nothing. "You knew there were two beds, didn't you?" Jay dropped his suitcase and glared at Steve.

"Which one do you want?" Steve asked, ignoring Jay's questions. "The one by the window or the one closest to the door so you can get away easily."

"The window." Jay looked out the open window. *No bars here. Not even any screen.* "Should I close the window to keep the mosquitos out?"

"No need. They don't have little annoyances here like flies and mosquitos. Just earthquakes."

"Great. I think I'd rather have mosquitos."

"Since we're going to be staying together, I have to tell you one of my rules. You don't ever touch any of my personal things like my razor or stuff."

"Yeah. Yeah. Phil explained all the about that sort of hygienic stuff, and it makes sense even if you aren't worried about diseases and such. Don't worry. I'm scared enough just staying in this place with you. I'm not likely to take any unnecessary chances."

Jay and Steve postponed their unpacking to set out on a quick tour of San Francisco.

"You might as well try driving," Steve said. "The traffic is light now and I'll be right here to guide you along."

The Golden Gate Bridge was their first point of interest. They followed the main route across the bridge through green hills dotted with luxurious mansions, looking like sheep grazing on the hillside overlooking the bay.

"You mean that this is the Golden Gate Bridge?" Jay asked.

"Yes. Isn't it a magnificent structure?"

"But I thought it would be gold. The Golden Boy in Winnipeg is gold. This is yucky dull reddish paint."

"I guess it's better for preventing rust. Besides, if it were gold leaf like the Golden Boy, people would scrape it off. I think the name means that it is the golden gate to the city, not a golden bridge."

"Why are there telephones all along the way? I wouldn't think that there would be a lot of people stopping to make calls. Especially since the signs say no stopping."

"They're for people who are thinking of jumping off the bridge and might want to talk to somebody. It's quite a popular location for that kind of activity."

The route took them to the movie–famous tourist town of Sausalito. They stopped to browse through the quaint arts and craft shops and to have a drink at an outdoor cafe looking out across the San Francisco Bay.

"No liquor for you, Jay," Steve said as he ordered a Long Island Iced Tea. "That's the price you pay for the fun of driving."

"It's worth it, believe me. This is the biggest thrill of my life."

The highway headed north working its way through the sites of several popular movies to the Sonoma vineyards and then to the wineries of the Napa valley. Steve indiscriminately tried all the varieties available while Jay toured the facilities and admired the scenery.

"This is one of those times you don't drink, Jay. You'll be responsible for getting us home safely."

"That's fine with me. I don't care that much for wine. Beer is more my drink."

By five o'clock they had toured enough wineries to convince Steve that they should head home. "We should head back to the city so we can see a few more sights before it gets dark."

They returned across the Golden Gate Bridge and drove down Lombard Avenue to Van Ness. "Go straight ahead, unless the steepness of the hill scares you," Steve said.

"Gaily forward, it is," Jay said with a grin. "I'm a pro at this sort of thing."

Jay had overcome his initial panic at seeing the cars ahead of him disappear abruptly into oblivion at the crest of the ubiquitous hills. But he wasn't prepared for the white–knuckle trip down the one–block length of Lombard Street, the world's steepest and crookedest road, having eight switchback curves on a 40–degree slope, all in a one–block length.

"You get a nice view of the bay from here," Steve said.

"You look. I'm busy," Jay replied through clenched teeth as he cranked the car around the curves.

They swung back through the Pier 39 shopping area and past Fisherman's Wharf. From far out in the bay Alcatraz Island invited them to tour the former federal penitentiary.

"We'll come back another day and spend more time here," Steve said. "If you're going to have the full tourist experience we need to ride the cable car and walk through Chinatown."

The club was busy for a Tuesday night. The tables were full with men and women roaming about aimlessly. Jay and Steve stood at the end of the bar, nursing their drinks.

"I can't believe that there is snow and probably minus thirty–degree temperatures back home," Jay said. "It's still like summer here."

"We're lucky. The rainy season has eased up for the moment. It can be miserable when it rains."

"At least it wouldn't be frozen rain." Jay thought for a moment. "Have you noticed that you seem to feel more at home here than I do?"

"What do you mean? I thought you were having a good time."

"Don't get me wrong. This has been great. But it's as if we are living in a little self–sufficient city and we make excursions from here into the real world. I'd like to move to a hotel in the downtown area for a while if that's all right with you. I want to spend some time where the action is."

"You mean where the straight action is, don't you?"

"If by straight you mean where there are some girls that I can hit on, then yes."

"There are lots of good–looking girls here," Steve said.

"Good looking, but they are either lesbos or what was it Phil called them? Fag hags?"

"So what's wrong with fag hags? I've seen you chatting up a few of them."

"They may be straight, but what they want is a heterosexual gay guy. You know, a guy who is tender and sympathetic and understanding and sensitive and all that sort of stuff. I need to hang out with some girls who are looking for a tough macho guy who wants some fun."

"Like you?"

"Like I used to be. Or like I used to think I was, anyway. Since hanging out with you I'm not so sure anymore. Sometimes I think you're mellowing me. I need to get to where people think like I do."

"Now that's a scary thought," Steve said with a smile. "But I do know what you mean and that's fine with me. It might even be better for me because I'm making some good friends here and I'd feel more comfortable having them over if you weren't here. No offense intended. You've been a great sport about things and a good roommate...for a straight guy, that is."

"Thanks for the compliment. I'd like to spend some time wandering through the stores and shopping. Gays aren't the only ones that like to shop, you know. Besides I've got to check out an address for my father. I phoned the other five, but the number for the one on Nob Hill isn't in operation."

"Tomorrow I'll drive you downtown to find a cheap hotel for you, somewhere within walking distance of Nob Hill."

HOME IS WHERE THE HAT IS

Situated on the corner, the hotel consisted of a floor of rooms above a popular bar and restaurant. In one direction an all–night bar catered to an ever–changing population of hookers and their prospective clientele. A few doors down the other street was the San Francisco Sheraton, a sophisticated hotel that had retained all its outward elegance as well as its hard earned reputation for pampering its residents with luxurious service.

"Tell me again, why do you think that this a safe place for me to stay?" Jay asked. "It looks a bit scary to me."

"Let me try to explain it. Imagine that you and I are in the woods together and we hear bears nearby. You'd be afraid, right?"

"Of course. If the bear chases us, we'd have to outrun it, and I don't think I can run faster than a bear."

"I wouldn't be afraid because I wouldn't have to outrun the bear."

"Why not?"

"I'd only have to outrun you, and I'm quite sure I could do that. The moral of the story is that if you want to be safe in the woods be sure that you can run faster than the person you are with."

"And the point of your story is…?"

"You need to be sure that there are others in the vicinity who are an easier target for predators than you are. In this hotel you would be safe because the hookers on one side provide a more vulnerable target for anyone looking to prey on the weak. The obviously affluent hotel on the other side provides targets for anyone wishing to prey on the wealthy. Why would anyone want to bother you? You are tougher than the hookers and obviously your pockets aren't bulging with cash."

"So I'm kind of a nobody?"

"Exactly. The trick is to be invisible. If you aren't noticed, then you are safe."

"Then why don't gays stay in the closet and be invisible?" Jay asked.

"For the same reason that you wouldn't spend your life locked up indoors. It might be safe, but it isn't what you would consider living. To be honest with you, being openly and flamboyantly gay is a bit of a rush. The element of danger is stimulating so long as it is under control."

The tiny room was sparsely furnished, and without a telephone or television. A bathroom and shower down the hall served eight rooms. But it was clean, inexpensive, and conveniently located within walking distance of the downtown area, and only eight blocks from the Nob Hill area, all of which were important factors for Jay. The street entrance locked automatically at all times and the wide stairway leading from the door up to the second floor gave no indication of anything at the top except a blank wall. Steve noted with satisfaction the lack of incentive for anyone to try to break in.

Jay went into the bar and paid his week's rent to the landlord who also served as bartender and bouncer.

Steve got ready to leave. "If you need anything or get in trouble, phone me. Otherwise, I'll meet you at the airport next Thursday."

"What if you want to call me?"

"I can't imagine why I would, but if I do I'll leave a message at the bar."

Jay headed uphill along Sutter Street toward the downtown area. *These hills are steeper when you're walking,* he muttered to himself as his ankles complained at the unaccustomed effort. *Why would anyone want to build a city on these hills?*

Four blocks from the hotel a man with a furry, grey face sat at the edge of the sidewalk, a plastic cup containing a few coins strategically placed in front of him. He had the layered look common to street people who are forced to wear all their belongings. His top layer was a heavy grey and white striped wool sweater and cap. On his lap a grey-colored cat, garbed in an identical knitted sweater and cap, sat in a most un–catlike erect position. Both cat and man stared straight ahead.

Jay stopped and said, "Hi."

Neither the man nor the cat paid any attention to Jay and continued to stare straight ahead.

"Nice weather," Jay offered hopefully. *There must be something about me that makes people not want talk to me,* Jay thought. "Aren't you hot in that sweater? I'm wearing a light shirt and I'm almost too hot."

"It gets cold at night," the man said.

"Do you stay out here all night?"

"No," the man answered. As if reading Jay's thoughts he added, "But if I did, I'd need it to keep warm."

"What about your cat?" Jay asked. "Cats don't need sweaters."

"He keeps me company."

Jay dropped a quarter into the cup and continued on his way. *That's weird,* he thought. *But he did get me to stop long enough to make a donation to his cause.* Jay looked back. The man and cat both sat motionless, staring straight ahead as if watching a show on a television set that only they could see.

Sutter Street leads directly into the Union Square section of San Francisco. A park bench invited Jay to enjoy the warm sun and look at the upscale stores and tiny hotels surrounding the park.

"Hello, big boy." The deep husky voice from behind the bench took Jay by surprise. "Mind if I join you?"

Jay turned toward the voice. A smiling face heavily made up with powder and blue eye shadow looked down at him through soft blue eyes.

She must be a hooker, Jay thought, *but what the heck, it's not as if I have much to lose and at least I'll have some female company.* "Sure, why not," he said.

With sensuously swinging hips the person flounced around the bench and stood in front of Jay. Jay casually let his gaze take in the short leather skirt, the long thin legs, the slender trim figure, the well–filled blouse and the high heels.

The bright red lips formed the words deliberately, "It surely is a nice warm afternoon. A cool beer would be right nice about now, don't you think?"

Oh yes. She's a hooker all right, expecting me to spend money for beer and goodness knows what else. "I'm not thirsty, but maybe one would be all right."

Jay stood up and immediately found himself with a firm arm around his waist escorting him out of the park.

"I know a nice quiet bar, honey. You stick with Felicia and we'll have ourselves a time you'll never forget."

Jay found himself being ushered to a tiny isolated table at the back of the dark, nearly deserted bar. There was scarcely room under the table for two pairs of legs and Jay found the closeness stimulating and enjoyable.

"What do you want, deary?"

"Beer," Jay said, and then added, "for now, anyway," going along with the mood of the situation.

"Two beers, please. I'll have mine in a large glass."

Two beers and twenty minutes of idle but provocative conversation later Jay noticed that the hand he was holding was at least as large as his own. Suddenly the pieces began to fall together. The deep voice, the slender hips and the large hands suggested only one thing.

"You're...a...a...a transvestite," Jay stammered in disbelief.

"No honey, I'm no drag queen. I'm a girl. Well, maybe not yet, but I'm going to be."

"You either are, or you aren't. I think you're a guy dressed up like a girl."

"I'm actually a transsexual. I'll be totally girl as soon as I have my operation."

Jay stood up. "I'm out of here. All I want is a nice, simple heterosexual girl. Is that too much to ask?"

"This is San Francisco, dearie. It's asking more than you might think. Don't dash off. At least sit and finish your beer."

"Let me try to understand this. Are you male or female?" he asked.

"Until I have the operation, you can take your choice. I'm whichever you want."

"You mean you're going to get it chopped off?"

"Not exactly. They turn it outside–in and tuck it inside so that it forms a..."

"Whoa. That's getting more descriptive than I'll ever need to know."

"Well, you did ask."

"Let me make one thing crystal clear. You are definitely not what I want. Chopped or unchopped or whatever, I don't want any part of this."

Jay sat for a moment contemplating the situation. His curiosity finally got the better of his desire to flee the situation. "So those are falsies?" he asked waving his hand in the general area of his companion's chest.

"They're totally real. Not implants, and no padding. It's all me. You want to check?"

"No thanks. But you weren't born with them, were you?"

"No. I had to take hormone pills to get my physical self in step with my mental self. As long as I can remember, I've known that I'm a girl trapped inside a boy's body. I happened to get born into the wrong kind of body. Damn chromosome error, I guess."

"So you plan to get 'it' chopped off, or whatever?" Jay asked with an inward wince.

"You bet. And 'them', too."

"Isn't that a bit drastic?"

"For some of us it's a big step. But for me it is something I have to do. I have to choose either my girl–spirit or my boy–body. They can't exist together."

"Couldn't you just dress and act like a girl? Or get therapy to become more male?"

"That would mean spending the rest of my life living a lie. I can't do that. If I'm not honest with myself my soul will, always be in torment."

"Isn't there some sort of middle ground in all of this?" Jay asked.

"Without the operation, my boy–body would survive but my inner girl–identity would have to die. I choose to sacrifice my body in order to save my identity."

"Do a lot of people switch sex?"

"Some of my friends who take the hormones don't plan to have the operation. For a working girl there is a big advantage in not having the operation."

"I can't imagine why they wouldn't make up their minds and become one or the other. Not that it has ever previously crossed my mind that this is some sort of a choice."

"Some guys like to make it with a girl who has a dick. If a working girl is going to make it in this business, it helps to have a gimmick."

I've never heard it referred to as a gimmick before, Jay thought. "I can't even begin to imagine how all that is supposed to work," he said, getting up from the table.

"Don't leave yet. I'll tell you anything you want to know."

"You've already told me way more than I'll ever need to know," Jay said, leaving the bar.

Is this what I left the Castro district to find? Jay muttered to himself angrily as he headed down Jones Street in the general direction of his hotel. He crossed Eddy Street to the Boeddeker Park which is a tiny recreational area designed to be a green place where people could shoot baskets, sit and watch the birds or generally hang out. Jay walked through the area and paused to admire the sculpture. It portrayed a soccer ball with a different ethnic face on each of the panels. A couple of boys wandered about lackadaisically bouncing a basketball, but most of the patrons centered their interest in the contents of their brown paper bags.

Wow. Heavy–duty black neighborhood, Jay thought to himself as he realized that his was the only non–black face in sight. He kept his eyes focused straight ahead. *Don't make eye contact with strangers, Phil said. I sure hope he knew what he was talking about.*

The man and his cat were still sitting where they had been earlier. Jay said, "Hi," but they either didn't hear or chose to ignore him. They continued to stare straight ahead at their invisible TV as Jay walked passed them toward his hotel.

A man sitting at the top of the hotel stairs nodded vaguely to Jay as he approached. "I'm Marco."

"You can call me Tom," Jay said. "Have you lived here long?"

"Ever since I quit working."

"When was that?"

"Oh, about 20 years ago."

"So how old are you, anyway?" Jay said looking at Marco carefully.

"Forty–two. I quit working after my twenty–fifth birthday."

"What do you do for a living?" Jay asked.

"I get a disability pension. I got a piece of shrapnel in the head and they had to put in a metal plate up here," Marco said, parting his hair on one side of his head to expose a bare patch of skin.

It looks like a bald spot to me, Jay thought. *But if you say there's a plate under there I guess I can go along with that.* "Does it hurt?" Jay asked.

"Not anymore. It did when I first got wounded and I used to get headaches so bad I couldn't concentrate enough to keep a job. After a couple of years the headaches went away but I never bothered telling anyone. So long as I don't get a job I keep collecting the cheques."

Jay tried to do some mental arithmetic. "That would be like ten or twenty years ago. Were you in the Gulf war?"

"Heavens no. Nothing that exciting. It was a freak accident. A shell exploded during a training maneuver and I got hit with a chunk of flying metal. That was back east. I moved out here for the weather. That and the fact that the social security benefits are a lot better in California."

"But isn't it boring, not working?"

"You're here on a holiday, right."

"Yes. Sort of."

"And you enjoy wandering around doing nothing except watching the girls at the beach and soaking up the sunshine."

"Well, yes. I guess so," Jay said, while thinking, *of course. The beach. That's where I need to go to find some foxy females.*

"I'm on permanent holiday. Call it early retirement, if you like. It suits me fine."

"Excuse me," Jay interjected. "I just remembered that I have to go somewhere right away."

Jay bounded down the stairs and out onto the street. *Oh great. I should have asked him which way it is to the beach. I'll ask the guy with the cat. He should know.*

He jogged up the hill until he reached the cat man. "Can you tell me how to get to the beach?"

"Sure can," the man answered.

Jay waited expectantly, but the man continued to stare straight ahead.

"So will you tell me how to get to the beach?"

"Sure will," the man said, looking at the styrofoam cup.

I get it. I need to pay for whatever I get around here, even directions. He tossed a quarter into the cup.

"The best beaches are down the coast toward Half Moon Bay."

"So I'd need a car to get there?" Jay asked.

"Yep."

"Well that's no help. Do I get my money back?"

"Nope." The corners of the man's mouth twitched slightly as if trying unsuccessfully to smile. "Besides, nobody goes to the beach in December. At least not to get a tan."

"Thanks for the advice. Maybe you could tell me how to get to Nob Hill." Jay tossed another quarter in the cup. *This is just like a slot machine. Except that I doubt I'm going to hit a jackpot.*

"Just keep walking uphill from here. You can't miss."

"I'm looking for a house on Clay Street. That's Nob Hill, isn't it?"

The man sat staring straight ahead.

"Gimme a break. I'm out of change," Jay pleaded.

"When you get to Jones, head uphill and you'll find Clay at the top."

Jay returned to his hotel to phone Steve and make plans for tomorrow.

21

THE ILLUSIVE TRAIL

Jones Street rose steeply into the distance until it disappeared abruptly into the sky. Jay's determination kept his feet moving steadily upward under the early afternoon sun. The leveled intersections gave brief respite from the climb until the peak was reached at Sacramento Street. As he reached the highest natural point of the city, Jay had an unobstructed view of the narrow passages made by streets cutting through the tall buildings as they dropped down to the water's edge.

Jay turned down Clay with its wall–to–wall apartment buildings, until he found the address that Cam had given him. The polished brass gate at the entrance and the well–kept exterior of the building gave a hint of the posh cosmopolitan apartments within. Jay looked in vain around the entrance for a listing of the apartment tenants.

"Can I help you, amigo?"

The voice of a middle–aged Hispanic standing behind Jay startled him.

"I'm looking for someone that lives here."

"What's his name?"

"I'm looking for a Mr. McNabb."

"Are you sure you have the right address? We don't allow solicitation or canvassing here."

"The Internet said he lives here."

"I don't care who said he lives here. There's nobody by that name registered."

"You're sure?"

"I've worked here for years. I know all the residents. There's no McNabb here."

"Darn. I've come all the way from Manitoba to find my father and you've never heard of him."

"Manitoba, Canada?"

"Yeah. Why?"

"I know a guy who said he came here from there. He worked with me up until last year."

"What was his name?"

"We just knew him as Nobby."

Jay's heart leapt. "That's the one. Nobby McNabb. So you actually did know him?"

"We used to work together cleaning up around here. He mostly worked out-side. I worked inside."

"What was he like?"

"He was a good guy to work with. Easy–going and always happy. He loved telling stories about his time up north."

"Like what?"

"Winters mostly. He'd talk about checking his trap line and about the bliz-zards that would drift snow right over the cabin so that he couldn't get out the door or see out the windows."

"That'll be him, all right. I remember times we had to shovel a tunnel through the snow to get out. If the door had opened outward, we'd have been trapped inside until spring. Did he say why he left his family?"

"I think the isolation got to him. What did he call it? Cabin–fever, or something?"

"I don't suppose he mentioned me?"

"He never mentioned any children. He talked about his...uh...your mother. That's all."

"Do you know where he lives now?"

"He said he liked Mexican food so much he was going to work his way to Mexico."

"So he's in Mexico?" Jay asked.

"Not likely. He liked to make jokes. I got a letter from him from somewhere near Los Angeles. Solvay, or something like that. He got a job on a ranch somewhere around there."

"Wow. That would be so exciting to live on a ranch with horses and cattle and stuff."

"He only wrote once so I don't know much."

"Do you have his address or phone number?" Jay asked.

"It would be at home somewhere. I could get it for you."

"That would be great. I really do want to find him."

"Sure. Check back with me tomorrow. I'll bring his letter and tell you some more stories."

"OK. Same time tomorrow. You have no idea how important this is for me. Thanks for everything. "

Later that afternoon the sun was beating down on the open car in a futile effort to keep the two shirtless men warm as they drove south on I–280. The freeway turned toward the scenic community of Pacifica snuggled against the brown Peninsula hills to the left. On the right the Pacific Ocean provided diverse intertidal areas popular with surfers and nature lovers who searched for ocean creatures in the water pools left by the receding tides.

"I wish Phil were here to give me some of his words of wisdom," Jay said.

"What's the problem? Maybe I can help," Steve suggested.

"I don't like myself a lot of the time."

"Is this from that psychic session with Tanya?"

"That started it. I met this unusual person yesterday. I don't think I was very nice to her."

"Let me tell you a little story."

"Oh no. Not another of your stories," Jay said with a big grin.

"I'm not a good chess player, but I'll bet you that I can play any two people at the same time and either win one game or make a draw of both games."

"So what's the trick?"

"You let one player make the first move. Then you use this move against the other player and take that players move and use it against the first player."

"I get it. You actually have the two players playing each other. You don't do anything. Very clever, but how does this help me? I'm not interested in playing chess."

"Really, Jay. Sometimes you can be so dense."

"Explain it to me."

"Most people spend their lives doing unto others as they have been done to. The events of their past determine their reaction to everyday events."

"So?"

"Do like in the chess game. When someone does something nice to you, pass it on to someone else. And then take their reaction and pass that on. That's how one creates good karma."

"But how does a person change something about themselves? Like Jimmy who's a thief? Or me who picks up things that aren't mine."

"A person has to get a clear mental picture of whom they want to be, and then act like that ideal person would act. A person becomes what they do."

"But what about getting therapy for bad things in your past? Isn't that a good idea?"

"It can't hurt, but don't expect the therapy to change you. People can use therapy as an excuse to avoid change. You have to accept yourself and your past for what it was. Decide how you want to be and then act like that. You become what you do."

Jay caught sight of a parasail floating high over the ocean near Half Moon Bay. "I'd love to do that," he said to Steve. "It would be an absolutely awesome experience. But I don't suppose you'd want to, would you?"

"What makes you think I wouldn't do something like that?" Steve asked.

"It doesn't seem to be your sort of thing."

"I work out with weights; I play tennis and racquet ball; I like to drive fast cars; I'm a macho guy. Why can't you think of me that way?"

"I know intellectually that you're a macho gay, but somehow I can never think of you that way."

"Maybe it's because people automatically think of gays as being wimpy?" Steve asked.

"Oh, no. We're back there again. Fine then. It's exactly the kind of activity I expect you'd like to do."

"It looks like fun. Let's do it."

"You're kidding again, aren't you?"

"I'll show you who's kidding," Steve said turning down a side road leading to the ocean.

"It's probably expensive, and I'm broke."

"My treat. You've been a good sport about everything. This would be a fitting way to end our little adventure."

"I wish you hadn't said that. I don't want to end up at the bottom of the ocean with a broken neck."

"Don't worry. You won't end up at the bottom of the ocean. The sail will keep you afloat. Now who's starting to wimp out?"

"I'm not wimping out. I can do anything you can do."

Fifteen minutes and a hundred and ninety dollars later they had convinced the parasail owner to let them try it.

"Hang onto the straps and pull on them to guide the sail," the man said as he strapped Jay into the harness "Let the air currents do the work."

Jay ran down the beach as the boat started to pull him into the air. The roar of the motorboat faded as he rose into the silent air. From his position high above the water Jay had a panoramic view of the area which inspired a feeling of omnipotence. It was as if he were alone in the world, untouched by the expectations of civilization.

Like a dog with its head out a car window savoring the wind, Jay lifted his face to let the fresh, clean air flow around him. *Now this is what I call flying. Like a bird floating through the air, free to go wherever I want,* he thought. *I wish Sue were here. She'd enjoy this.* Jay felt omnipotent and insignificance at the same time. He felt as one with the universe but at the same time totally isolated.

Back on the ground again, Jay and Steve relaxed in the sun recounting the excitement of the flight.

High above them, an eagle floated on silent, motionless wings. Throwing its head back, it opened its mouth in a soundless cry. A feather floated down and landed at Jay's feet. He picked it up, and examined it.

"Where did that come from?" Steve asked, looking up into the now empty sky.

"It's an eagle feather," Jay said. "R.B. said I might be given one, but I don't know what it means."

Jay stroked the feather, studying the rippling effect his finger made along its edge. Suddenly he stopped and turned to Steve, "I need a phone."

"We can phone from the hotel."

"No. I need one right now. I've got to talk to Sue," Jay exclaimed, running toward the building.

"What's the rush?" Steve asked.

Without answering Jay ran to the phone. Without thinking he automatically dialed the number.

On the second ring Sue's mother answered. "Oh Jay, thank goodness. We've been trying everywhere to find you. Nobody seemed to know where you went."

"What's the matter? Is Sue all right?" Jay asked.

"No. Sue's not well."

"What wrong with her?"

"We don't know. We found her unconscious on the bathroom floor. She's in the hospital now, but we don't know what the problem is."

"Can't the doctors say what's wrong with her?"

"Her dad brought in the best specialists he could get and two psychiatrists. The specialists say they need to do more tests and she won't tell the psychiatrists anything. She says you're the only one she will talk to. When are you coming home? We'll do anything to get you here."

"I'll be there on the next flight. Tell Sue I love her and to hang on until I get there. Tell her I'll be there soon and that then everything will be all right. I promise you I'll look after her."

Jay hung up and turned to Steve. "We've to go home right away. Something terrible has happened to Sue."

"Our flight doesn't leave until Thursday. We'll have to stay until then," Steve replied.

"Sue needs me, so I've got to be there for her. Can't we just change our flight?"

"Weren't you going to get some information about your old man tomorrow?"

"That can wait." Jay grabbed Steve by the shoulders and made a futile effort to shake him. "Listen to me. I've got to get to Sue. That's the only thing that matters now. What's the matter with you? Didn't you heard the feather crying? Get in the car. We're going to the airport. Now."

"It would cost a big chunk of cash to change the ticket," Steve said.

"I don't care. I'm going. Are you coming with me?" Jay replied.

"I'll stay here. But you go if you want."

"I have no choice. The eagle has spoken. I must listen."

"If it's that important to you, then take this and go," Steve said, handing Jay some bills.

Jay's eyes filled with tears of gratitude. He took Steve in his arms for a long, close hug. "Thank–you. Thank–you," he sobbed. "I've always been able to count on you. I'm so sorry I haven't been a better friend to you."

"Be a good friend to Sue and her parents," Steve said. "That's the best way to repay me."

Jay sat alone on flight 836 to Winnipeg, oblivious to his surroundings, his mind filled only with thoughts of Sue.

Appendix

PHIL'S FAVORITE RECIPES
(with commentary by Cam)

Being a vegetarian who loves giving dinner parties, Phil has developed a repertoire of recipes that are robust enough to satisfy his carnivorous friends while at the same time being animal–friendly and providing a balanced diet. Even non–vegetarians will enjoy these meals–just don't tell them that they are nutritious.

His biggest challenge is in accommodating his friends' innate dislike of tofu. Phil considers tofu to be one of the essential food groups because of its high protein content as well as being a good source of vitamin B12 and minerals. Besides the rather obvious ploy of chopping it up and hiding it in everything, he has developed some recipes that actually benefit from the use of tofu.

Cam has provided his practical (and sometimes cynical) comments and suggestions for shortcuts or variations throughout the recipe section. If you are the sort of person who says, "sizzle for a few minutes with a little oil in the frying pan" instead of "saute" then you'll find Cam's comments helpful.

ESSENTIAL SHOPPING LIST
(Assuming you have the usual pantry items, including mild onions)

LENTIL SOUP (pg. 223)
1 pkg (450 gram) split red lentils or 1 tin

PEANUT & LIMA BEAN LOAF (pg. 224)
1 pkg (450 gram) dry lima beans or 1 tin
2 cups peanuts, chopped
¾ cup low–fat yogurt

REFRIED BEANS (pg. 226)
1 pkg (450 gram) Romano beans or 1 tin

SPINACH & LIMA BEAN LOAF (pg. 228)
1 pkg (450 gram) lima beans or 1 tin
1 pkg (300 gram) frozen spinach (chopped)
½ cup low–fat yogurt

VEGETABLE MOUSSAKA (pg. 230)
½ cup soybeans
½ cup brown rice
½ cup pot barley
1 large eggplant
1 small can tomato paste
1 cup dry curd cottage cheese
¼ cup corn meal

MOUSSAKA TOPPINGS (pg. 232)
(Bechamel Sauce / Whipped Potato)

CREPES CHEZ PHIL(pg. 234)

RISOTTO (pg. 236)
1 cup fresh chopped parsley
1 cup frozen peas

TOFU "FRENCH FRY" SNACK (pg. 237)
10 oz pkg of firm or very firm tofu

TOFU LUNCH ON–A–BUN (pg. 238)
10 oz pkg of firm or very firm tofu
2 inches of ginger root

TOFU SALAD (pg. 239)
10 oz very firm tofu

TOFU SALAD DRESSING (pg. 240)
10 oz box soft tofu

VEGETABLE CHILI (pg. 241)
1 pkg (450 gram or 2 cups) red kidney beans
10 oz pkg of extra firm tofu
1½ cup mushrooms
1–5 oz can (156 ml) tomato paste
1 green pepper
1–550 ml tinned tomatoes including the juice

CASBAH VEGGIE–RICE PIE (pg. 243)
1 cup brown rice
250 gram (1 cup) 1% cottage cheese
6 cups packed, torn spinach leaves (or 2 pkg frozen)
1½ cups tomato sauce

¾ cup grated mozzarella cheese
½ cup light raisins

VEGGIE LASAGNA (pg. 245)
9 whole wheat Lasagna noodles
1 pkg firm tofu
1 cup (250 gram) 1% cottage cheese
2 cups tomato sauce
1 pkg (300 gram) frozen leaf spinach
¼ cup Mozzarella cheese
1 oz Parmesan cheese

LENTIL OAT BURGER (pg. 247)
2 cups lentils

DIPPING SALSA (pg. 249)
12 ripe tomatoes
3 green tomatoes
3 medium onions
1 stalk celery
4 green peppers

GREEN TOMATO PICKLE RELISH (pg. 250)
10–12 green tomatoes
8 cooking onions (or 4 Spanish)
1 bunch celery

VEGGIE MINCEMEAT (pg. 251)
5 green tomatoes (chopped)
6 apples (chopped)
2 cups raisins
2 cups currants

LENTIL SOUP

Pick over and rinse:
1 pkg (450 gram or 2 cups) split red lentils

Saute for 2–3 minutes:
2 medium onions, chopped
2 Tbsp olive oil

Dice, add to onions and steam for 10 minutes:
½ cup water
4 stalks celery
4 carrots
1 green pepper

Add the vegetables to:
8 cups water
¼ tsp salt
¼ tsp black pepper
rinsed lentils

Bring to a boil, then simmer 20 minutes.
Very briefly blend soup in a food processor—not too smooth.
Garnish with:
grated cheddar cheese or chopped parsley

Cam's Comments:
If you don't have red lentils, any other color will do. No need to be racist about it.

Phil likes olive oil because it is good for the cholesterol level, but any vegetable oil is fine.

A vegetable stock can be used instead of water. For added flavour OXO and BOVRIL sell cubes to make vegetable stock.

You might like to make it more tangy with the juice and the grated rind of a lemon.

This makes a nice sauce for the Peanut & Lima Bean Loaf (next recipe), if it is blended enough to be smooth.

PEANUT & LIMA BEAN LOAF

Soak overnight in cold water:
1 pkg (450 gram or 2 cups) dry lima beans in 6 cups water

Then cook beans until tender (2 hours). Boil until almost dry and mash.

Chop and saute for 3 minutes:
1 mild type onion (2 cups)
¼ cup olive oil

Add to onion and cook until tender:
2 cups celery, thinly sliced

Add to onions & celery and cook for 2 minutes:
2/3 cup whole wheat flour

2 tsp salt
½ tsp black pepper

Add to mixture and stir over low heat until thickened:
1 cup milk

Remove from heat and stir in:
1 beaten egg

Add to the mashed bean mixture:
3 cups carrots, chopped coarsely
2 cups peanuts, chopped
¾ cup low–fat yogurt
2 cups soft, whole wheat crumbs (2 slices)
½ tsp baking powder
½ tsp baking soda
½ tsp allspice

The mixture should be the consistency of thick cement. If it is too moist add dry bread crumbs. If it is too dry add more milk.

Spoon into three greased 8” x 4” loaf pans and bake 35–45 minutes at 375 degrees in preheated oven.

Cam's Comments:

Buy a tin of lima beans. Nobody will know the difference and you'll save a lot of time.

Don't let the dryness of the flour mixture scare you. Just keep stirring while it gets hot.

If you use a BIG pot for cooking the beans you can just keep adding these other things to it.

What would a gay accountant know about cement? A thick paste would be more like what I'd say.

I sometimes put cheese slices on the loaf before baking.

REFRIED BEANS

Sort for stones and rinse:
1 pkg (450 gram or 2 cups) Romano beans

Simmer 2 hours (until very soft) in:
6 cups water
2 bay leaves
1 tsp baking soda

Remove bay leaves and discard. Mash beans in remaining water until smooth.

Chop and saute for 5 minutes:
1 medium onion
1 green pepper
4 cloves garlic
3 Tbsp olive oil

Add and saute an additional 3 minutes:
½ tsp ground ginger
1 tsp ground coriander
½ tsp cayenne
½ tsp black pepper
½ tsp dried basil
½ tsp dried dill
½ tsp salt
½ tsp ground cumin

Mash the vegetable-spice mixture and add:
¼ cup butter

Continue to cook with frequent stirring for 30 minutes or until a thick, pasty consistency.

Cam's Comments:
You can use a tin of beans if you want to save time and effort. Pinto beans are excellent, but may be hard to find.

I never remember to add bay leaves and I never notice their absence. Besides, I'm always afraid I'll forget to take them out.

Frying the spices briefly mellows their flavor and smooths the taste. Yes, it really does! Even I notice the difference.

Margarine is fine in place of butter.

These are nice with tacos, lettuce, tomato slices, and stuff like that.

SPINACH & LIMA BEAN LOAF

Soak overnight in cold water:
1 pkg (450 gram or 2 cup) lima beans in 6 cups water. Then cook beans until very tender (2 hours)

Drain beans and mash.

Stir into mashed beans:
1 cup cheddar cheese, grated
2 eggs, beaten
1 tsp grated nutmeg
¼ tsp allspice
2 tsp salt
1 tsp cinnamon
½ cup low–fat yogurt

Layer into two 4 x 8 inch loaf pans:
two–inch layer of bean mixture
1 pkg (300 gram) frozen spinach (chopped or leaf)
another two–inch layer of bean mixture.

Mix together:
1 cup whole wheat bread crumbs
2 tsp olive oil
3 tsp sesame or sunflower seeds
juice of one lemon
grated rind of 2 lemons

Put mixture on top of beans in pans.
Bake 40 minutes at 400 degrees F in preheated oven until crisp and golden on top.

Cam's Comments:
A person would have to be crazy to spend all this time cooking lima beans when you can buy them in a can already cooked.

If you like your loaf lighter and fluffier, add half a teaspoon each of baking soda and baking powder.

Phil is always putting sesame or sunflower seeds in his recipes to "complete" the vegetable protein. A good chunk of meat also balances it out as far as I'm concerned.

It really is better with the "zest" of two lemons, but it's all right without it. I hate the look of naked lemons shriveling in my fridge.

VEGETABLE MOUSSAKA

Cook:
½ cup brown rice according to box instructions

Cook:
½ cup soybeans in ½ cup water until water is absorbed and then puree with more water if needed.

Cook:
½ cup pot barley in ½ cup water until water is absorbed.

Bake in 9 x 12 inch casserole at 350 degrees:
1 large eggplant (½ inch slices brushed with 2 Tbsp olive oil, covered in foil) until soft (15 minutes)

Saute in olive oil:
1 large onion, finely chopped
2 cloves minced garlic

Add to onion and cook briefly:
1 small can tomato paste   ¼ tsp pepper
½ tsp powdered ginger   ¼ tsp salt
1 cup dry curd cottage cheese   1 Tbsp white sugar
½ cup water (as needed to keep moist)   ¼ tsp cinsnamon

Mix the onion mixture, barley, rice and pureed soybean together with ¼ cup of corn meal and layer on top of eggplant

Sprinkle on top of mixture:
½ cup Parmesan cheese, grated
1 cup (2 slices) wholewheat bread crumbs

Pour on top of bread crumbs:
Bechamel Sauce or Potato Topping (see recipes following).

Sprinkle: 1 tsp each of basil and oregano on sauce or potato.
Bake at 375 degrees until golden brown and custard is cooked (45 minutes). Let stand for 30 minutes before serving.

Cam's Comments:

Pearl barley is OK but not as high in fibre.

Baking the eggplant separately makes it tender and it sort of disappears. For some people, this is the way they like their eggplant. You can skip this step if you like yours a bit rubbery.

The final mixture needs to be wet enough to cook properly. It should be sloppy but not runny.

The Moussaka freezes well either before or after cooking except for the Bechamel Sauce.

BECHAMEL SAUCE
(For Moussaka topping)

Melt 2 Tbsp butter in saucepan.

Whisk in 3 Tbsp whole wheat flour.

Add 1½ cups milk while over low heat and stir until smooth.

Heat until sauce is thick and smooth.

Cool slightly and stir in:
2 well beaten eggs
1 cup of 1% cottage cheese
1/8 tsp nutmeg

Spread over the top of Moussaka and sprinkle with Oregano.

Cam's Comments:
This makes a lovely topping, but it is a bit of work.
You can add the liquid slowly, or just dump it all at once and keep stirring. It'll work either way.
Ricotta cheese can be used in place of cottage cheese.

WHIPPED POTATO
(For Moussaka topping)

Boil until soft and mash:
4 medium potatoes

Mix in:
1 Tbsp butter
1/3 cup hot milk
½ tsp salt
¼ tsp baking powder
2 beaten egg yolks
¼ cup chopped parsley (optional)

Put on top of Moussaka and brush with beaten egg whites.

Cam's Comments:

I usually use the whipped potato topping. This is easy and fast, but not as elegant as the Bechamel Sauce. I like to double the whipped potatoes recipe and use half as topping and the rest as a vegetable the next day.

This makes a good topping for any vegetable stew to make a meal in one dish.

CREPES CHEZ PHIL

Beat:
2 eggs
¾ cup milk
1 Tbsp olive oil
¼ tsp salt

Add:
½ cup whole wheat flour
1 Tbsp corn meal
1 Tbsp sesame seeds (optional)

Pour about 1/3 cup of batter into a lightly greased or nonstick pan.
Tip the pan to spread the batter into a thin layer.
Cook until edges firm and centre set, then loosen the edges and flip to brown both sides.
Place the filling on the crepe and roll it up.

Suggested fillings:
1. Yogurt, ricotta or cottage cheese.
2. Chopped vegetables (spinach, peas, onion, green pepper, cauliflower, broccoli, mushrooms, asparagus, etc.)
3. Sliced olives, tomato and bean sprouts
4. Salsa

Suggested toppings:
1. Stewed or fresh fruit or canned fruit cocktail
2. Whipped cream, ice cream or yogurt
3. Applesauce
4. White sauce:
   (2 Tbsp butter cooked with 2 Tbsp flour and then 2 cups milk added and heated)
5. Spaghetti or pizza sauce and grated cheese
6. Sprinkle with cinnamon

Cam's Comments:

Make sure your pan is hot enough that a drop of water will skittle around on it.

The whole wheat flour makes these rather substantial so you can use the leftovers sort of like a pita.

It's hard to flip a crepe with a spatula. Try loosening it a bit and then flip it in the air from the pan. It's easier than you might think, and quite a lot of fun.

Roll them up like a big, fat old stogie or leave them flat kind of like a pizza.

ROBUST RISOTTO

Boil for 5 minutes in 2 cups water:
3 garlic cloves, minced
½ cup sweet onion, minced
1 cup fresh parsley, chopped
1 carrot, finely chopped or shredded

Pour off half of the water and save to use as stock.

Add to the pot and cook 25 minutes, adding stock (or additional water if necessary) slowly as the rice absorbs water:
½ cup uncooked, regular brown rice
2 Tbsp olive oil
¾ cup tomato sauce
juice (3 Tbsp) and zest of 1 lemon
1 Tbsp brown sugar
¼ tsp black pepper
½ tsp dried rosemary

Add 1 cup frozen peas and cook an additional 5 minutes.
Serve with grated Parmesan cheese.

Cam's Comments:
Arborio rice makes a more traditional risotto, but brown rice is nourishing and gives it more body.

The peas aren't essential, but they add a nice touch. Asparagus is also colorful and tasty.

TOFU "FRENCH FRY" SNACK

Julienne into ¼ inch strips:
½ of 10 oz package of firm or very firm tofu

Heat 1 Tbsp olive oil in a skillet with:
minced garlic cloves
½ tsp each cayenne pepper, cumin, paprika

Fry the tofu strips until brown and crispy on the outside.

Serve with dip, salsa or relish as finger food.

Cam's Comments:
This makes a good healthy high protein appetizer or snack.
It's better for you than chips and dip.

TOFU LUNCH–ON–A–BUN

Julienne into ¼ inch strips:
½ package (350 gram) extra firm tofu

Brown tofu in a hot frying pan with:
2 Tbsp soy sauce

Add and stir fry:
about 2 inches of thinly sliced ginger root
3 cloves sliced or minced garlic
1 cup mild type onion, coarsely chopped

Serve on a toasted whole wheat or brown hamburger bun spread with mayonnaise or your favourite salad dressing

Cam's Comments:
This is quick, easy and surprisingly tasty.
I usually cut the quantities in half for two people.
If you put it in a pita or wrap it in a tortilla is easier to handle.

TOFU SALAD

Cut:
10 oz very firm tofu into one inch squares in mixing bowl

Mince:
3 green onions
½ green pepper
2 stalks celery

Add:
¼ cup toasted sunflower or sesame seeds

Mix ingredients with salad dressing or mayonnaise.

Cover tightly and chill until ready to serve.

Serve on a bed of lettuce surrounded by tomato wedges, and sprinkle with paprika.

Shave carrot around the edges.

Cam's Comments:
This will make enough for four people. I usually cut quantities in half for all Phil's tofu recipes. But then, he likes tofu.
Seeds are good but not necessary.
This also makes a great sandwich filling.

TOFU SALAD DRESSING

Whip together in a blender:
10 oz box soft tofu
¼ cup lemon juice
1 tsp soy sauce
2 tsp dry mustard
2 Tbsp sesame seeds
¼ tsp salt
2 tsp white sugar

Put in covered bowl and refrigerate (will keep several days)

Cam's Comments:
I would never bother making this. Mayonnaise or salad dressing is so much easier. But if you want to go all out for tofu, this will do it.

VEGETABLE CHILI

Place in large pot:
6 cups of boiling water
1 pkg (450 gram or 2 cups) red kidney beans
2 tsp salt

Turn down heat and simmer covered for 3 hours.

Crumble into chunks and brown with a bit of olive oil:
10 oz package of extra firm tofu

Add to the tofu and saute with olive oil:
1 large onion, chopped into ¾ inch squares
2 cloves garlic, minced
2 small dried chili peppers
1 Tbsp dried mustard
1 tsp cumin
¼ tsp black pepper
¼ tsp cayenne pepper
½ cup mushrooms

Chop into ¾ inch chunks:
1 green pepper
1 cup mushrooms

Slice thinly:
2 carrots
2 stalks celery

Add vegetables and onion to beans.

Add:
1–5 oz can (156 ml) tomato paste
2 Tbsp vinegar
1–20 oz (550 ml) tinned tomato with juice

Cook on low heat for 2 hours (add water as necessary)

Cam's Comments:
Everyone, except Phil of course, buys kidney beans in a can.
The tofu isn't necessary except as a great way to provide protein.
Two teaspoon of chili powder will work instead of dried peppers, but it tends to give me indigestion.
Make mushrooms the same size as the tofu to hide it.

CASBAH VEGGIE–RICE PIE

Cook:
1 cup brown rice in 2 cups water

Add to rice:
1 beaten egg
grated rind and juice of 1 lemon (3 Tbsp)
250 gram (1 cup) of 1% cottage cheese
½ cup light raisins (or ½ tsp powdered cloves)
½ tsp cinnamon

Saute in a large skillet until soft (5 minutes):
1 Tbsp olive oil
1 chopped mild onion
2 garlic cloves, chopped
¼ tsp cayenne pepper

Add to skillet and sweat until soft:
6 cups firmly packed fresh spinach leaves (or 2 pkg frozen)
2 cups carrots, coarsely grated
¼ tsp dried rosemary

In a large baking dish make layers using:
½ the rice mixture
½ cup tomato sauce
all the spinach/vegetable mixture
the rest of the rice mixture
½ cup tomato sauce

Bake at 375 F for about 1¼ hours (until heated through).

Let cool for 5 minutes before serving.

Cam's Comments:
When Phil says "sweat" he means to cover them in a skillet and let them steam. You'd think he could just say that.
Ricotta cheese is good in place of the cottage cheese.

The leaf frozen spinach is nicer than the chopped because it gives more texture to the dish.

For a truly elegant and impressive entree, get some frozen phyllo or puff pastry from the supermarket. Place several layers in the bottom of the dish leaving lots hanging over the edge to be folded over the top after the mixture is layered in.

VEGGIE LASAGNA

Boil in salted water (½ tsp salt):
9 whole wheat Lasagna noodles 10–15 minutes

Saute for 5 minutes in 2 Tbsp olive oil:
1 pkg firm tofu, sliced thinly
¼ tsp powdered cumin
¼ tsp black pepper
¼ tsp cayenne pepper
½ tsp dried oregano
½ onion, chopped or sliced thinly

Add and continue to saute 5 minutes:
1 large carrot, coarsely grated
2 garlic cloves, minced
½ cup mushrooms, sliced thinly

Mix separately:
1 cup (250 gram) of 1% cottage cheese
2 cups tomato sauce (save ¼ cup for the bottom of the oven dish)
3 Tbsp corn meal

Thaw:
1 pkg (300 gram) frozen leaf spinach

Grate:
¼ Mozzarella cheese
1 oz Parmesan cheese

Pour in 14 x 12 inch oven dish a thin layer of:
¼ cup tomato sauce

Place along the bottom of the pan:
3 strips of lasagna noodles

In layers, place:
½ of cottage cheese/sauce mix
All the spinach
3 strips of noodles

All the vegetables/tofu
3 strips of noodles
Remaining ½ cottage cheese/sauce

Sprinkle the cheseses on top.

Cover with foil and bake 40 minutes at 350 degrees
Uncover and bake 10–15 minutes more. You may wish to leave out the cayenne if you are using spicy tomato sauce.

Cam's Comments:
If you have fresh spinach available, use three cups (packed), but then wilt it with boiling water.

LENTIL OAT BURGER

Cook with water:
2 cups lentils

Cook in a skillet until starting to brown (5 min):
1 tsp olive oil
2 onions, finely chopped
2 cloves garlic, finely chopped

Add to skillet and cook additional 2 minutes:
1 cup mushrooms, finely chopped

Combine and mix in a large bowl:
cooked lentils, coarsely mashed
skillet mixture
½ cup oatmeal
¼ cup whole wheat flour
1 tsp dried basil
¼ tsp black pepper
2 tsp dried oregano
add water if necessary to make sticky

Make into 6 patties and cook in a skillet with olive oil until brown (about 4 minutes per side) and serve on a toasted bun with cheese, lettuce, tomato and/or sauce.

This recipe can also be used for a main course Garden Parmigiana by putting large patties in an oiled 8 x 8 inch baking pan, pouring 3 Tbsp of meatless tomato sauce on top of each and covering with grated skim mozzarella cheese. Broil them in the oven for a few minutes until the cheese melts and bubbles.

Cam's Comments:

I prefer the mild Spanish type onion, but Phil likes the stronger cooking onions.

Why does Phil always have to be so nutrition conscious and use whole wheat flour? Plain white flour is fine for me.

Phil uses about 1 teaspoon of oil. I think a bit more is OK. After all, they say that olive oil is good for you.

Half a tsp cumin can replace the oregano and basil.

Don't forget the parsley garnish from the plant on your windowsill.

DIPPING SALSA

Chop coarsely:
12 ripe tomatoes (skinned)
3 green tomatoes
3 medium onion
1 stalk celery
4 green pepper

Mix in:
2 tsp cinnamon
½ tsp nutmeg
½ tsp ground cloves
2 tsp ginger
1 cup light brown sugar
1 tsp salt
1 cup vinegar

Simmer 2 hrs or until of proper consistency for dipping.
May be frozen or stored in sterilized jars.

Cam's Comments:
This makes a fine general purpose dip for Tofu French Fries
or for taco chips.

GREEN TOMATO RELISH (PICKLE)

Chop finely for relish, or chop coarsely for pickle:
10–12 green tomatoes
8 cooking onions (or 4 large mild)
1 bunch celery

Add to vegetables and cook slowly for 1 ½ hours:
3 cups sugar
4 tsp dry mustard
1 tsp cayenne
1 tsp cinnamon
2 tsp powdered ginger

Add:
1 ½ cups vinegar

Cook for additional ½ hour and put into sterilized jars.

Cam's Comments:
As a relish this goes nicely with lentil burgers, hot dogs or hamburgers (Phil would buy veggie burgers, of course).

VEGGIE MINCEMEAT

Combine and bring to a quick boil. Avoid scorching:
5 green tomato (chopped)
6 apples (chopped)
2 cups sugar
2 cups raisins
2 cups currants
1 cup vinegar
4 tsp cinnamon
1 tsp cloves
½ tsp allspice
1 tsp salt
1 tsp powdered ginger
grated peel of 1 orange & 1 lemon

Boil with stirring until the extra liquid is boiled off.
Use as filling for pie or tarts.
May be frozen or stored in sterilized jars.

Cam's Comments:
This mincemeat is so authentic you even get the sensation of suet in your mouth, as if this were a good thing.
This can be put on crackers as an appetizer or snack.

About the Author

Charles (Bill) Shirriff was born and raised in Saskatchewan during the depression years of the 30's. After graduation from the University of Manitoba with a Bachelor of Science in Math, Physics and Chemistry, he went to Swan River to begin a teaching career that was to span thirty–five years and would take him as far north as Cranberry Portage, Flin Flon and Norway House. Most of those years were spent near Winnipeg in the city of Portage la Prairie where he held positions as teacher, counselor, and co–ordinator of programs for Special Needs students and for the Gifted & Talented in the School Division.

A brief foray into the field of Meteorology provided him with the opportunity to work and live in Moosonee on the tip of James Bay.

His love of learning and a penchant for different experiences led him to obtain a B.A. degree from the State of New York and a Master of Science in psychology from the University of North Dakota. Additional courses in a variety of subjects were taken at the University of Toronto, University of British Columbia, University of Connecticut (Storrs) and Stanford University in California.

Email: cwshirriff@zyworld.com
website: www.zyworld.com/cwshirriff

9 781583 485477